BONDED

IN

BLOOD

For Brigitte
in Friendship
Chad R Chandler

CHAD R. CHANDLER

Title ID: 6402912

ISBN-13: 978-1535132749

For my mother, Wendy.

For her strength, her love, and for knowing when to let me daydream.

A special thank you to my beta readers!

Brandi Williams

Amanda Simons

Wendy Hobbs

And to my one and only sister,

Loretta Gerow

For without whom none of this would be possible.

Edited by: http://wesleysauthorpromoservice.weebly.com/

BONDED IN BLOOD

By Chad R. Chandler

PROLOGUE

"Jeral Damaste, the Prince of Petsky, husband of our beloved, Queen Asanna, is dead."

"Dead."

That one word, spoke with more power than the rest, was the only word from the priest's mouth that Kerra had allowed herself to hear. She stood beside her sister: The Queen of Carn, and shed tears in shared sorrow of Jeral Damaste's passing. Though they all wore the customary black attire to his funeral, and all shared faces streaked in fresh tears, it was her sorrow, her pain alone that was the most genuine; the most deserved.

She looked to her sister, far along now with child, a hand, motherly, gentle, placed atop her swollen stomach. She looked next, down; at the tomb, where the child's father would stay forever more. Anger fueled her sorrow. While those around her mourned the Queens loss, and the child who will soon grow without knowing a father's love, Kerra wept in anger for the loss of her friend, the light that lit her soul, and her lover.

A gentle touch at her shoulder, her sister's, one she had to restrain from swatting aside signaled the end of the ceremony. Kerra, lost in an abundance of grief, and anger, that she had heard nothing as the priest had rambled on until the end. She was too numb. Words fluttered over her, no weight to give them meaning. Another touch, slightly more firm as her sister the Queen leaned on her for support as people began to disperse, stopping as they passed to offer brief words of sympathy. The condolences' only angered Kerra more. The people's misplaced grief was not her only source of anger, she was enraged at the deceased Prince himself, for dying, and for the circumstances in which he met his end.

Poison, she thought, watching people pass by. Her eyes accused every one of them. Names flashed through her head, matched them to faces she recognized and filtering through her knowledge of them, their pasts, their standings in the court, who would benefit from her lover's death the most, and the least.

As the day brought about the passing of the father, so the night brought the arrival of the son. The Queen gave birth late into the night. Kerra had tried to hide herself away when murmurs and the commotion started with servants rushing busily through the halls; but they found her eventually. Her duty to her sister found Kerra wandering through the halls toward the Queen's rooms.

"A boy, milady, how wonderful!" a servant, young and pretty, said. Kerra forced a smile, it was all she would offer, and that was without eye contact. Baby or not she would not lower herself to that of a lesser.

Something was wrong, Kerra could see it the moment she stepped inside and met with her sister's eyes. The Queen lay before her, propped up with a dozen pillows behind her back.

She looked exhausted; as one would after child birth. But there was a sickly color to her sister's flesh that for a moment, made Kerra forget that she hated her sister; it did not last long. In her arms, the Queen held a baby, one that though fresh to this world, already had the look of his father.

"Have you chosen a name yet, Asanna?" A simple question, an expected question and yet it took everything she had to force the words past her lips.

"Not as yet." Her sister had begun, and any words that had followed, now, were forgotten, as Kerra looked down at the baby boy in her sister's arms. He was beautiful and she could not help the feeling of love for the child that tore at her heart, and clawed at the shadow of anger within her. The tears had come again, and when the babe met her gaze with his blue eyes, it proved too much for her sorrow to handle, she spun, and fled from the room. She ran.

Kerra ran as best she could, through eyes blurred with tears. She wiped at them as she made her way through the Keeps halls. Yet it all continued to pass her by as a blur. The servants, the nobles, the Keep's guests, all that she ran past she had either bowled over or nearly missed and none gave chase. *Why would they?* She had never been as loved or respected as her sister, nor did her own parents before their passing think that fondly of her. Always second to Asanna, always cast aside, always in her sister's shadow. Time alone is what she now sought. Time to think, and vent her anger; without anyone asking after her with mocking and insincere concern.

It was late when Kerra snuck out the Keep's gates, not even the guards gave much of a start as she raced past. This was nothing new to them. Through the little forest attached to the Keep's western side and down the worn and familiar path, she fled. The path led down a cliff side, out into the beach that bordered the Keep's west wall and stretched into a series of tall hills edged with large jagged rocks. Here she slowed and as always was her habit, she carefully looked behind to insure no one had decided to give chase for once, and when no one showed signs of following, she crept closer to the rocks and the series of caves that they held.

The caves that she had found while avoiding the toils of court life at a very young age. They had always been breathtaking and today was no different. The caves were tucked, hidden, and safe behind the half moon shape of the giant rocks jutting along the beach. Some of the caves flooded with the tide; she had learned which ones to avoid. There had been some with treasures, or at least they had been treasures to a child. Now grown to womanhood she made no mistake in identifying such finds as regular travel equipment. Left behind by others that had long since used these caves as refuge, a safe haven from whatever her young mind could think up.

Kerra's breath was heavy until she closed her eyes and let the sound of the sea fill her. The crashing of the low tide against the rocks was soothing, however, she knew that only one of these caves would be able to quell her mind and ease her aching heart: her cave. Her own safe haven. She opened her eyes and let go of the lace that held her hair back, letting it flow freely in the gentle breeze. It would smell like the ocean by the time she left this place, and it would linger for the next few days, helping as it always did, to make court life tolerable.

Her safe haven was perhaps untrue; Kerra had always shared it with her friend, her secret keeper, the visage etched into the cave's far wall, the one that had drawn her to it as a child. She was educated as a young Princess should be; and was deep in her studies when she came across a word, a name that would change not only her life but also the lives of every human in lands near and far. The name sat under a drawing of a great demon upon a battlefield piled high with the bodies of the Thereon people, a race long since passed from this world. Other words followed, slaver, conqueror, sadistic, fiend. To her however, it meant only friend.

Once inside, with the sea breeze at her back she knelt, and spoke her *friend's* name before the stone etched face upon the wall.

"Azamoth."

It had happened slowly at first, a tickle in the back of her head. The longer she sat talking to the stone carving through the years, the louder and clearer it became. Until one day, the stone face had spoke back.

"My little Kerra, long have I watched you grow. Your presence filled me with hope that one day someone worthy would speak my name." The voice of a demon should have been terrifying, but for Kerra it was as if she had heard her best friend's voice for the first time and yet, felt as though she had always known it. *"What troubles your young mind this day? For as it has, and always will be, I am here child, I will always listen."*

Tears streaked her face, and broken hearted sobs escaped before she had a chance to summon the words that hurt as much to say spoken, as they did within her thoughts.

"He should have been mine; they know nothing of our love." She managed to whisper in a voice laced with anger. "But they married him off to my sister, to unify our two kingdoms. And now he's dead, and my sister has given birth to his child...a child that should have been mine!" She raged letting her temper come full circle. I want them all to pay, my sister, his family, the kingdom, everyone!" she shook with fury but managed to remain kneeling, and she looked up into the cold stone eyes before her. "You were once powerful in life, I have read it, help me now Azamoth I beg of you!"

There was a great silence for many heartbeats and Kerra began to feel as though she had somehow offended her friend with her request and feared he had gone from not only her mind but the cave altogether.

"I will help you sweet Kerra, I can grant you a power beyond reason and wonder," the voice whispered through her mind, chilly as an autumn wind.

"Are you strong enough? For sharing such power with you will intake a heavy price. Are you worthy of such a burden?"

"Anything you ask of me," Kerra almost squealed with girlish excitement, her heart beating its fastest rhythm within her chest.

"When I am powerful enough I will need a kingdom to rule, and a new body in which to rule it with. Dispose of your sister and raise the child as we would, strong and unstoppable and worthy of my essence. Can you do this my chosen?"

Kerra did not wait long to respond and it came from lips parted in a wicked smile.

"Yes...it shall be done. Now please Azamoth, I implore you, grant me the power to wreak my vengeance, and set things as they should be."

A very small black dot formed from the air in front of her eyes and she fought the urge to fall back.

"Embrace the darkness my child and you will be reborn with all the power you seek."

Kerra reached out with a shaky hand, extending one slender finger to touch the black

sphere. It stuck to her finger and quickly began to spread.

CHAPTER 1

Cecil woke with a gasp followed by a startled wild eyed look around.

Sleep had taken revenge on him for the far-too-early journey they had set out on. The sound of hoof beats echoed in his ears. The lazy walk from his steady horse kept him in the saddle as they moved forward. Little in the way of dust from the well-travelled road rose with their pace. Cecil shook himself further awake as the warmth of the near noon sun had lulled his body to relax. He had eaten this morning and yet an uneasiness swelled in the pit of his stomach.

"Cecil?"

Cecil shut his eyes with a wince as he heard his name spoken with a voice not his own. *Here we go.*

"Did you fall asleep?"

"No... Mal I did not," Cecil answered back. A mighty yawn took control then his eyes snapped open in panic, realization of what he had just said, and to whom; his mind scrambled for the proper apology. Cecil shifted in the saddle to better look to his left, the direction the voice had come from and the man it belonged to. He must have looked the fool as he mumbled and stumbled on a few words of apology, before he was met with that man's pearl of laughter. Both their horses' ears perked up at the sudden outburst.

"I swear, Cecil, a day out of the palace and your head has turned as soft and muddled as my great-grandmother's."

"My apologies, Prince Malik, you're right, my heads been somewhere else." Cecil replied, trying to regain some decorum.

"Was it up your horse's hindquarters?" Prince Malik asked while an eyebrow rose in question.

"No it's not up my horse's... Damn' it, Malik I'm trying to be professional here! The king's own council cannot be far from earshot!"

"Alright Cecil, take it easy, the council; has to be more than a mile ahead by now. You would think all the time in the practice yard and master Orson's sword shaped bruises you often sport would have earned you a thicker skin."

"Why are we away back here anyway?" *This wasn't right, 'a mile ahead?'* he thought. *You know who they're going to blame for this!*

"You looked tired so I just let you doze; I let the others go on ahead. I know, don't worry about it I am the Prince after all."

Cecil let his mouth close, his protest now dead on silent lips.

"However," Malik said, taking a glance around and stretching in the saddle, "this looks like a great place for a rest, ride ahead and tell the council to head back. I'll wait for everyone here."

Cecil just stared at the Prince with a vacant look, "by yourself...you're just going to wait here… and what? Hang around? You're sending me to my doom when the council realize I left you here, you do know that right?"

"I have Ce'elevan," Prince Malik sarcastically shot back, and gestured down the other side of his horse.

Cecil could see to who the Prince had indicated through the long legs of the man's horse. "Your dog? I'm supposed to leave the only Prince in the kingdom alone on a road in troubling times and trust your safety to a dog? The council, who I cannot understand, why they let you fall behind without them, Prince or not, will string me up by my neck and leave me to dangle in a tree if I show up without you!"

"Greyhound," Malik responded.

"What?"

"Ce'elevan is a greyhound, a royal canine, he's not a dog, he's not some mutt found in an alley covered in the gods' know what, being fed scraps of what I'm assuming had once been food. He's highly trained, deadly on the hunt, loyal, and bonded with me." Malik finished with a disgusted shake of his head.

I'm sorry." Cecil offered, though he wasn't really sure he was.

"Don't apologize to me, apologize to Ce'elevan, it's him you've insulted."

Cecil scowled at the Prince, who returned the scowl.

Cecil cocked his head and looked at the Greyhound from under the Prince's horse. "Ce'elevan I most respectfully apologize for any sort of insult my words have caused you."

Ce'elevan slowed long enough to meet Cecil's eye and gave a low growl from deep in his chest.

Cecil snapped his head back up; he could see the smile his friend now tried to contain.

"I said I was sorry!"

"I just don't think Ce'elevan likes you, he doesn't think you were sincere." Malik let loose his laughter once again and stopped long enough to wipe tears from his eyes and glance at Cecil before starting all over again.

"Fine, oh that's real nice, always the way with you two, since I became your squire I get nothing but laughed at and am the center of your tricks and jokes. Why couldn't my father find me a nice fletchers house to apprentice in, or a blacksmiths apprentice? I could have done that, or…" Cecil trailed off. He noticed the Prince had stopped laughing and couldn't help but return the smile the Prince offered with a shake of his head. He couldn't stay mad at them, though one day he really did want an explanation as to how the bond between the Prince and the greyhound worked. Some kind of spell or a curse, he couldn't find any books on it or get anyone to tell him, not that anyone seemed to care about this bond, all he had ever heard was that it was old and rarely happened anymore.

"And Perhaps I would like to attend to some Princely business, and I don't need an escort or an audience for such a task, did you ever think of that?" Prince Malik replied in mock disgust. "Now go on, your doom awaits you."

"Fine, as you command!" Cecil threw his hands up in exasperation and spurred his horse on down the road at the Princes earlier orders. "But I won't clean up the mess if you get eaten by some wild animal!" Cecil shouted over his shoulder.

"Oh yes you will!" The Prince hollered.

Cecil knew better than to argue with his stubborn friend, and he was the Prince after all. *Besides, I'm in no hurry to get to our destination anyways.* The carriage that at present housed the four council members must have already entered the forest on the road as it turned west. Cecil had lost sight of them thanks to his nap. He should still have seen the rear guard, a few of the king's soldiers. But perhaps the path had narrowed and they had tightened formation, the trees were thick ahead as the road was almost swallowed up by the forest.

Thoughts of why they were out here and where they were headed, was ever present on his mind. And now that he rode alone the stories he had heard of the warrior Queen who ruled the kingdom of Carn forced a chill down his spine.

No more than one full day ago a messenger from Carn had arrived with a letter that featured the Queen's seal, addressed to the king of its neighboring kingdom of Petsky. From what the Prince had told him, the Queen's newborn son was missing, stolen in the night. *Prince or not, there's no honor in someone willing to harm a child, none at all,* Cecil thought. Blame lay with Petsky. The king sent his fastest messenger back to inform the Queen of Carn that Petsky was at its full disposal in the hunt for those responsible, that he would send his own son who happened to be the best tracker in the land, and his own council as a show of faith, *though sending them seemed more like a punishment than any sort of aid, I hope we can find the boy quickly.*

The king's council was never Cecil's favorite members of the king's court. They where old men, set in their ways, and they had always believed him to be a poor choice as the young Prince Malik's squire. They expressed as much whenever he was in the room, with no tongue held back to spare a young boy's feelings. He had grown, and their view had done little to change, so he avoided them as best he could. Oh he showed the proper amount of respect and manners to their faces, but had wished them all kinds of ill that his mind could think to lash back with. Cecil had not truly wished them harm, just the emotions of a young man who bucked against the wall of stoic traditionalism the older lords of court clung to. *And continue to cling.* When they were gone, he thought, perhaps the next generation of council members would be a little softer, perhaps show him some respect for what he has managed with his life, and the unwavering service he had shown to the Prince and Crown. *Or maybe I complain too much, there might be a reason I'm told that so often.* As he turned his horse around the bend in the trail, he pulled back sharp on the reigns. His eyes filled his mind with the carnage unfolding before him.

The sun did little to penetrate the thick treetops of the forest and yet it mattered little, the fire that raged from the council's carriage lit the area plenty. Cecil could scarcely take it all in. The carriage burned and the soldiers at first, were not to be seen. As he tried to gather his wits his eyes filtered out the chaos, the dark silhouettes that swayed from the high reaching overhang of tree branches took on the limp and lifeless forms of what were once the king's council and their soldier escorts. The smoke now billowing from the carriage sought him out like what often happens at a campfire and no matter where he moved it followed. Cecil could not catch his breath, and coughs began to turn to gasps. His horse turned around before his mind cleared enough to make the decision himself and so it turned to a direr problem. *The Prince! You left him alone you daft bastard*! His horse needed little encouragement to speed away from the fire though Cecil kicked it on as hard as he could.

Cecil approached, a single enemy, dead at his friend's feet, as he could see no others. *Just one man to attack the well-trained Prince*? This just seemed foolish.

"Rear attack, two of them, one fled into the forest, and the council?" Price Malik asked.

"Dead, and the guard, burned and hung in the trees. I didn't stay to find out if who or what did that were still around," Cecil said.

Cecil studied the man the Prince had dispatched. A cloak, the hood still drawn was a mass of thick dark fabric, as was everything else the man had on. *If this have been night already, Mal may not have been so lucky.*

"Ce'elevan," Cecil heard the Prince say, his voice calm, He had just been thinking of the dog as if he his friend had just read his mind. "Took this one down at the ankles" Prince Malik said as the tip of his sword pointed at the man's bloodied and torn leg. "A single sword thrust and he was finished. The other one, the one that fled, received a slash across the chest; I must have cut the straps on the pack at his back as it dropped when he bolted for the woods. That's when I discovered our young friend here." Cecil's breath caught in his throat as Prince Malik turned the contents of the pack he held around for him to see, and now had it gently cradled in his arm. It was the way the Prince held it so protectively that finally allowed Cecil to realize just what, and who his friend held.

"Is that..."

"Our young Prince of Carn? I fear so."

Cecil looked down at the blonde hair and chubby face that peeked out the end of the pack.

"Is he...?" Cecil leaned forward on his horse to see.

"No, he's just asleep. Though I cannot wake..."

The Prince had no chance to finish. The words died on his lips as a Dagger pierced his throat from behind. The man they had thought dead had proven them wrong, and swift, like the ripple of the moons shadow across a night-filled lake that man had struck. Ce'elevan was upon him, biting at anything the dog could lock his jaws around.

"No!" Cecil slid from his horse, drawing his sword on the way as he had been trained to do, all in one swift motion. Prince Malik toppled to his knees as Cecil thrust his blade through the man tangled with the distraction of the greyhound. He quickly dropped his sword and spun to his Prince, his friend, and dropped to his knees beside him. The baby still slept, unhurt, in the pack near by. There was nothing he could have done; the Prince of Petsky was dead.

"Malik."

Cecil closed his friend's eyes and as he stood he held the babes pack by the broken straps, his blade in the other and he shook with fury. Tears stung his eyes as he walked over to the body of the Prince's murderer and stabbed the lifeless body once more, for revenge, as empty as it felt. There was no mistake this time; Ce'elevan had made sure there was nothing left of the man's throat. He would not slither from the shadows of death this time.

Cecil slid his blade back into its sheath at his side without cleaning the blood off first. Then proceeded to tie the straps on the pack together securely and checked on the Prince of Carn once more before he mounted his horse. It was getting dark now and he kicked his horse forward. Ce'elevan, his maw and fur still dripping blood followed, but not before he gave one last look and a whimper in his master's direction.

Cecil knew the dog's loss but they had no time to morn or gather his friend's body. That would come later. Right now he had to get the Prince of Carn back to the safety of Petsky Castle.

After the accusations and threat of war, now the loss of the king's only son; he was unsure just whose troops would be sent first.

The journey home should have taken hardly any time at all, not if he had rode his horse to near exhaustion; however, Cecil did not have that option open to him. It was not the baby in the pack strapped to his chest, for Malik's words rang true as Cecil had attempted to wake the boy as well, to no avail. Nor, the greyhound that ran alongside his horse that stopped him from making the journey quickly. It was however easy to blame the man who sent an arrow, fired from a bow, high in the tree line to his left, which had taken his horse in the throat.

Cecil slid from the saddle as the horse went down with a heavy crash. He stood still long enough to blink once and hope never to try that again before instincts had him flee to cover. Clutching a protective hand to the baby's head Cecil slid over the edge of a small lip in the road to his right and into the heavy underbrush. When he stood, he cast a quick look over his shoulder and then moved as quickly as he could after Ce'elevan, who was already ahead of him, leading him through paths he would never have found on his own.

The greyhound halted and Cecil's eyes had time to focus on the dog a brief moment before two arrows gave off mirrored solid thuds, one embedded in the slim truck of a tree, the other served as a warning jutting out of the overgrowth of the forest floor. Cecil turned his head to look behind and felt panic swell from his stomach to his chest.

The dark cloaks and deep black hunting leathers worn by the two men behind him matched the clothes of his friend's killer. *The one that fled...that dropped the Prince. They must want their prize back.* Cecil thought while he tried to find cover. One had knocked another arrow and the second man rushed toward him closing the distance fast. He knew there was no time to run, he was now, very aware of the familiar touch of leather in his hand, without thought he drew his sword.

A growl at his side drew his eyes from the enemy and in that moment, he watched Ce'elevan blur by him with the unnerving speed of a greyhound. In surprise to all, the dog ran past the man who, with sword drawn, ran at Cecil and chose instead to lunge at the second attacker who had pulled his arm back, prepared to let loose his arrow. He had no chance. Ce'elevan latched onto the man's arm, the arrow flew wide of any target and disappeared into the trees. With a growl, the greyhound pulled the man from his feet. Cecil breathed in, as time seemed to speed up and tensed his body. He spun as the attacker with his sword drawn tried to stab him through with his momentum, hoping to take Cecil by surprise.

Fear let go of his muscles, Limbs trained in long days of practice took control in a move that would have shocked him had he been the one watching this fight. He effortlessly brought his sword up and leaned forward ever so much to slide a hands length of steel through his attacker's side. His good fortune wore off, as his instincts did not expect the now injured man to spin on him without so much as a flinch or a grimace of pain. The man brought with his turn the sharp blade of his raised sword in a quick slash that caught Cecil in the shoulder followed by his chin. The blade came free only when Cecil dropped to his knees; His face could not hide how much pain the strike had caused him. He gritted his teeth, his jaw ached in response. His thoughts were frantic until he looked down with realization that he was not just trying to save his life, but the baby in the pack strapped to his chest. Cecil dropped onto his left side, he landed heavy on his uninjured shoulder and kicked out with all the power he could gather and took the legs of his foe out from under him. He tried to gain his feet and was half way up when Ce'elevan darted past him and ended the fight his way, with sharp canine teeth at a now exposed throat.

17

Cecil, in great pain, looked back the way they had come. Down the path and up the hill, they had slid down. There at the top was one last man, his bow drawn. Before he fired, the man suddenly and sharply looked to his left, and with a look back at Cecil, he lowered the bow to the ground. The sound of carriage wheels was heard from up the road and without another look, the enemy backed away and out of sight. Cecil looked down at Ce'elevan who despite having killed so many men this day still pressed his body against Cecil's leg in support and comfort; the greyhound licked the blood from his face.

"Come on; let's go find some water before we head home."

The Squire and baby Prince, along with the greyhound at their side, left the world of light as the sun set and slid into the comfort and cover of the now darkened forest around them.

CHAPTER 2

King Zhamar Damaste looked up from the papers on his study room desk at the urgent knock upon the door.

"Come in Alex."

The man that entered was clearly a soldier. His squared jaw and solid shoulders gave him almost a brutish image. Though his eyes and soft brown hair had aided in turning confidant women into doe-eyed young girls on several occasions.

"It's done my king." Distaste clung to each word as he closed the door behind him.

"Please don't give me that look, old friend. It had to be done." Zhamar beckoned his friend to the chair on the opposite side of his desk.

"Had to be done? Do you hear yourself, Zham? I've interviewed the boy myself. His story has holes I'll admit, but to accuse him of Malik's murder? He's one boy Zham, how could he have killed the guards, the council, and the Prince?!"

Zhamar watched as Alex shook with anger, and had it been any man other than his oldest friend, he would be dead already.

"What would you have me do Alex? Had Princess Kerra and her escort not shown up half a day ahead of him, claiming she saw Malik fall at Cecil's hands I might have been able to take him at his word. It did not help matters that the boy shows up with the missing Prince of Carn strapped to his chest and my son's dog at his heels telling us of some crazed attack in the woods! By an enemy he could not identify! I have sent men to confirm this and do you know what they have found? My son, just Malik, a dagger through his throat and nothing else, no other bodies, no other tracks, and the council… well, what was left of them…" The king paused to collect troubled thoughts. "I would have liked to have handled this quietly, myself. Malik trusted Cecil, hell I've never known the boy to be anything but loyal. But the Princess…"

Alex walked to the door never having taken the offered chair and nearly yanked it off the hinges. "I don't know what's going on Zham; I hope you know what you're doing. Cecil has been confined and is awaiting trial… as you command my king."

"I'm trying to…" King Zhamar began but it was too late. His friend had slammed the door shut, as he left his angry foot falls could be heard echoing down the hall. "…stop a war." The anger hung in the air; he could feel it. If it had eyes he was convinced they would be glaring red hot and boring straight to his soul. *This could all fall apart, war on my doorstep, and Malik…oh Malik my son, what have I done.* Zhamar felt as if he might burst at the need to morn his son's passing but he forced it back down and gathered his resolve. He stood from his desk and headed toward the council chambers, where the life of one young man might save the lives of his people.

The Kings most senior of council were dead, and he could really have used their guidance this day. What remained of his advisers and councilmen where the younger, more…eager for lack of a better word, eager to show that they understood the laws of Petsky now that those who helped make them were gone. He really did not need a single one of them, the King's command was final and no law yet stood in place to diminish his rule. There were some now among them that would think otherwise and he would have to watch them carefully in the coming months.

King Zhamar took his place upon the head council's chair. The young counsel stood in a row to his right. Six men their hoity looks made his frown darken. Cecil Renland: his son's squire…and friend, stood before a podium in the middle. His look held that of confusion, and yet, trust, Zhamar hated what he must do all the more. He knew to keep the peace; he alone would end the man's life.

"Cecil Renland, you stand before his majesty King Zhamar Damaste, lord over all the lands and people of Petsky on charges of treason and plotting of war between the empire of Carn and your own home, the kingdom of Petsky!" One of the council rattled off from the parchment in his hands. When he was done he rolled it up and handed it up to the King with a bow. In normal circumstances he would have re-read the charges but for now he just held onto it. It weighed a great deal less than his guilt. This brought a chorus of voices from the council members and King Zhamar held up his hand bringing them to silence.

"Should this have been a Petsky only matter, I would differ to the council's wisdom after weighing the facts of such a charge. But seeing as we have the Princess of Carn's word to consider, I feel we should honour a judgment passed from her evidence on the matter as a show of good faith and trust between our Kingdoms." The outburst of displeasure from the council was something new to Zhamar and despite being mad at the situation and not the men before him he felt his temper rising. "She will speak and we will listen!" Zhamar growled at the council silencing them quickly, they were not used to such an outburst from their King. "Princess Kerra, the floor is yours." A weak smile at the woman who stood beside him, the sleeping form of his nephew, the young Prince of Carn cradled in her arms.

How the babe could sleep through this was a miracle to him, his own children had been light sleepers all four daughters and the son he no longer had. As he rubbed his head to ease the pressure he spotted the arrival of a figure near the east entrance and he sighed closing his eyes in frustration. "*Not now Valis, by the gods, this is not the time!*" The youngest Damaste daughter had pushed her way forward to the front of the crowd, her brother's greyhound wormed in beside her and she listened with furrowed brows.

Princess Kerra of Carn began to speak.

"Despite your majesty's claim of messengers sent, we in the court of Carn had received no word of Petsky's response to our call of aid in the matter of the missing Prince. And so my sister, Queen Asanna, commanded that I receive your king's official response in person so as to handle these trying times in the utmost respect and decorum." She finished with a bow to the King as best she could with babe in arm.

"But it would appear as though one man amongst your kingdom, and indeed in your very house, your sons squire...would be the very conspirator we sought."

There was a cascade of rebuttal from the council that Zhamar barley heard, his eyes still focused on Cecil who stood in disbelief of his accusers charges.

"My own scouts witnessed the dark magic's this young man conjured up; the very dark magic that he used to slay his own Prince!" the chamber rang with the angry voices mixed with some of those who supported the Princesses of Carn's accusations. Zhamar would remember those voices and deal with them at a later time.

"Why would you do such a thing I ask of you?" Princess Kerra stepped closer to Cecil who shook, looking confused, and scared.

Zhamar knew better, that was not fear but rage beyond anger.

"Did you do this for money? Did someone pay you? Where you unhappy with a recent decision from the crown perhaps?" Princess Kerra leaned over the podium and glared into his eyes. "There do you see it?" she took a step back, "the anger in his eyes...perhaps he just wanted to hurt a mother by taking her chi..."

"Lies! You tell us lies and sheer nonsense!" Princess Valis Damaste shouted, drawing every eye in the room.

"Like my brother Malik I too have the bond of Talindrall, you know this father, and Ce'elevan was there when his master died! The greyhound tells a much varied tale than the Princess of Carn," Zhamar heard the venom in his youngest daughter's voice, his heart knew the truth of her words.

"If you will allow me to give the dog's testimony we can hear the truth of these matters I..."

"No," the king said firmly.

"No?" Valis asked taking a surprised step back "Father please, Ce'elevan speaks the truth, and we should at least hear his side of this!"

"This, gift...may have been taken more seriously in your grandfather's time child, but I will not pass judgment on a human life based on what a dog thinks." He waved his hand dismissively.

"Father..." Valis said.

Zhamar could see the tears held back, her face working hard to keep anger in place of sorrow.

"You deny the bond? Do you not believe in me? In Malik?" Valis spoke her brother's name in a near whisper as a sob of sadness had broken through her resolve. "This man before you is Malik's friend...we cannot sully his memory..."

The King held up a hand to stop, and even a Princess must obey her king, and so she stood silent, Zhamar did not miss the tears in her eyes and quickly chocked back his own emotions *"For the good of the people I do this."*

"Guards, remove the Princess from the room. Cecil Renland, you will be executed for crimes against the kingdom, the kidnapping of a child, and the death of Prince Malik Damaste." Zhamar stood and quickly left the room, giving no one a second glance and ignoring the outcries of the council.

He could hear the screams of his strong willed daughter as the guards removed her, his son's dog barking at her side.

Cecil was left to stand facing Princess Kerra and if the one could kill the other with only a look, they would have done so in the time it took the guards to return for the soon to be dead man. The King had spoken and the King's word was still law.

One tall slender woman, dressed in a simple yet beautiful blue dress stood at the back of the room as council remained and argued around her. No one had seemed to notice her; the King had glanced with the corner of his eye only once upon her arrival. But none others seemed to care as long as she had stood silent and watched.

Valis had stood outside the audience chamber just staring dumbfounded at the doors that where now barred from her. How could her father have been so quick to judge? Refusal to acknowledge the bond of Talindrall was beyond her mind, a mind that kept going over and over her father's words, and now, Cecil would die despite the truth. Finally, she broke her gaze from the doors and made her way through the castle's halls to her own set of rooms where, once inside, quickly shut the door and slid to the ground leaning her back up against it.

You tried, it's all you could do, Ce'elevan's voice echoed through her skull. For some such as her brother the bond could be heard clearly as if someone where talking right into their ear, with her however the bond worked, but it always sounded hollow, it was far easier the closer the dog was to her and even in the same room it still echoed as if they stood a farmer's field apart.

Valis pulled her knees up close to her chest and began to weep; her hands hid her sorrow but did little to stop the tears that flowed.

"*Why is this happening? Why is Malik dead?*" she spoke between sobs.

"*Malik would want you to be strong.*" the greyhound said through the bond while whining out loud.

"*Malik was always the one there for me, three others sister you would think a stronger bond would be with one of them. When others tried to discourage my interest in things un-lady like Malik would just laugh, take my hand and drag me along.*" A small but sad smile fought its way up from the darkness of her pain. "*If I had wanted to watch him at his sword lessons others would scoff and when Malik had caught wind of it he hauled me by the arm down to the practice yard with him. Soldiers, my father's personal guards all watching as Malik smiled and thrust the handle of a sword into my hands, I can still feel the tightly wrapped leather."*

"I know...he was my master and I..." the voice carried by the bond trailed off and Valis reached out to cup Ce'elevan's head in her hands leaning forward until her forehead rested on his, this greyhound that seemed now her only friend left.

"I miss my brother... he would never have allowed father to ignore the bond." her anger rose. *"Never before have I seen him act so coldly. He knows Cecil as well as me or you, dark magic my Aunt Lillian's fat ass!"* she cursed.

Ce'elevan cocked his head quizzically at her comment, never having met an Aunt Lillian he could not tell if she had spoken in jest.

"Come on" Valis wiped a sleeved arm across her face to be rid of the tears and stood throwing open the door. "We can't let Cecil think he's alone in this, I will find away to get him out." She said aloud. Ce'elevan padded past her, tail wagging.

***

"What have I done?" King Zhamar whispered to himself as his conscience screamed at him, his mind held a firm hold of the excuses that would haunt him this night. Sleep would not come, he knew this yet here he was, lying in bed staring out his bedchambers window, open slightly to allow a cool breeze in. He had hoped that others would understand, that what he did was for the good of the kingdom, but the council screamed for a retrial and even Alex, a friend for so long had only glared at him as he was escorted back to his chambers, refusing to engage in conversation.

With a sigh of frustration, he threw back the covers and began to pace the floor and when his mind gave no answers he settled for resting on the wide window sill, looking up at the stars in the dark night sky. "Please forgive me," he asked any of the Gods that might be listening. His only solace was the arrival of an old friend just before the trial, and as many times before in his life, he would have to rely on that friend to set things right.

***

Valis quickly made her way downstairs leading to the dungeons; the area was not large but did contain several sets of cells which sat empty save for one. It was hard to see in the cold foreboding room, the only light, a lamp upon the table, between the two guards who stood to greet her.

"Princess," they both snapped off chest salutes and bows.

"You may leave me for the time being," she waved her hand dismissively as she stepped past them towards the darkest cell.

"But you can't be in here!" The shorter of the two guards protested. Valis turned and glared at the man, the taller of the two who must have been the senior of the pair bowed his apologies before grabbing the shoulder of his counterpart.

"We can give you a few moments Princess. Nothing more," before shoving the other towards the door and into the hall.

"But the king's orders..." the guard could be heard saying.

"That young man is set to hang in the morning, give them time to say their goodbyes," the older guard finished as he closed the door behind them.

Being a Princess has its moments, she thought, and turned back around.

"Cecil?" she asked into the darkness.

"It's ok Valis; just go back to your room." A sorrow-drenched voice answered back.

"I think the situation is far from ok, now get over here where I can see you at least."

Valis waited until she could see something shift in the shadows, shadows that melted off the young man as he approached as if he were merely shrugging off a dark cloak.

Valis had been Cecil's friend since the day he had arrived at court. The boy may have grown into the strong and muscular man she saw before her but his eyes, blue as the clear morning sky where the same, still. She could still see him chasing after her brother hard at work on Malik's every task, be it cleaning clothes, or to deliver notes to girls her brother fancied. She was glad it was dark on her side of the bars as well, not enough light to see her blush, she was fond of this man even if he had never seen it, and it tore at her heart to see him so downcast now.

Ce'elevan poked his skinny head and neck through the bars and whimpered until Cecil knelt to scratch the dog's neck making sure to get that spot behind his ears that he knew the dog loved.

"What's all this about it being ok? You do know you're in a cell right? About to die and all that?" she tried to make it sound lighter than it did.

"Your father is right," he said not looking up at her.

"Have you lost your mind as well?!" Valis nearly stuttered she was so taken aback at his comment.

"It would probably help."

Valis could find no reply she could only wait for him to realize she had not answered back and look up to find the look of hurt on her face and the silent tear that slid down her cheek and off her chin.

"Princess... Valis, I..."

"We need to find away to get you out of here... If... If father won't listen then we will just have to find another way!" Valis gave a sharp sniff, batted away more tears and began to look around.

"What are you doing now?" Cecil asked leaning his head up against the cold bars that made up his new room.

"Looking for options, do the guards have the keys...or leave them on a peg somewhere like in the stories?" she began searching the walls.

"Listen to me Valis, tomorrow, when the time comes... I want you to take Ce'elevan for a walk, head for the lake and forget about me, just go out and..."

"Shut up, the guards are returning!"

"We have to go now, but will be back as soon as we can figure a way to get you out of the castle and far away, another land where my father won't find us."

"Us...? What do you mean us?" Cecil stammered as the Princess and greyhound reached the door just as it opened and in stepped the guards who bowed their heads respectively.

"Have you had enough time, Princess?" the older one asked taking the lamp from her and handing it to his companion who placed it back on the desk.

"For now, I shall be returning in the morning." She ignored the spluttering of the shorter guard and silently thanked the older one with the hint of a smile she hoped he had caught before she moved to the stairs and he shut the door behind her.

There has to be a way, think Valis you silly girl you grew up in these halls what's a safe way out? She was so focused on trying to find a solution and cursing the palace for lack of secret entrances that she didn't notice the other figure on the stairs until she had barrelled into them only then realizing that Ce'elevan had been trying to warn her through the bond.

She gave a startled, "oomph!" And nearly fell backwards down the steps, a slender hand had shot out to steady her and when Valis looked up to see a woman in a blue dress she burst into tears wrapping her arms around the woman in a tight hug.

"They're going to kill him, Jan!" Valis cried into the soft dress.

"Valis, I..."

"And father won't listen, he's not himself...that witch of a Princess has some sort of spell or a curse upon him and, Jan..." Valis looked up with eyes red from too much crying, "Malik's dead...he's dead, Jan." she buried her face back into the soft blue dress.

"I know," Jan smoothed a hand through the Princess's hair.

Valis looked up confused.

"I arrived in time to bear witness to Cecil's trial." Jan closed her eyes.

"Then you have heard the same as I! Father ignored the bond of Talindrall Jan, you're an Earth Maiden! Can he do that?"

Jan opened her eyes once more followed with a heavy sigh, "Valis I do not control the bond, nor am I such a person as to tell a King what laws he may enforce. Though I differ with his decision, it is his to make."

"But, Jan, Cecil would never have hurt Malik... He was my brother's best friend and he's..."

"Hush now, Valis." Jan ran her fingers once more down the young woman's black hair.

"I have known your father since he, and I where both young and I have always placed my trust in his hands. Now, for the sake of that lifelong trust I believe we will have to extend him that courtesy."

"But, Jan..." Valis sobbed.

Jan held her close and rested her chin on the top of Valis's head, "I have watched you grow into a strong young woman over the years, strong and smart with a good soul, Valis." She kissed her forehead and took her by the arms, "everything will be alright, I'm sure your father knows what he's doing."

This just clouded Valis's eyes with doubt and worry at her friend's words.

"You trust me, right?"

"Of course I do, Jan it's just that..."

"Then trust me and go get some sleep, you will need your rest." She gave her another kiss on the forehead and gently pried herself from the Princess's arms.

Valis turned and watched Jan as she moved a few steps down, turned and looked back up while scratching Ce'elevan under the chin.

"Valis? I've always wondered... Where do the guards empty the dungeons waste?"

Valis blinked in confusion. "It's emptied into the drain at the far end. The guards are always complaining about it, they say the servants spill on purpose but the drain is just too big, it allows the smell to come back up that's why the guards cover it but you can still smell the..."

"Alright, thank you." Jan raised a hand followed with a quite chuckle. "Now off to bed, and don't worry about your friend I'm here to give my blessing for his quick and painless return to the Earth Mother." With that Valis watched her turn walk the rest of the stairs and enter the dungeon.

Valis stood there in disbelief at how Jan could tell her everything was going to be ok and yet still go through with Cecil's departure blessings. It was Ce'elevan's whining that snapped her out of her trance. Valis headed back up stairs and towards her room even more drained and with even more questions that would fight her for sleep this night.

There was a soft knocking upon the door and Zhamar flung himself across the room in a haste to answer it. He was still wide awake, sleep eluded him as if slumber knew what he had done and was punishing him for it, but he hoped that on the other side of the door was his redemption. He stopped and leaned his body against the door, taking a deep breath to steady his nerves and when he was ready he cracked it open just enough for his late night visitor to slip inside.

"Have you found a solution, Jan?" Zhamar asked not bothering to greet his friend properly.

"I may have." She replied quietly, taking a seat on the edge of the king's bed her head hung low, hands folded in her lap.

"Good...good the boy will live then." The king said running a hand through his hair as he stopped the pacing he was not aware he had started.

"Zham, I could only set events in motion. I can't control who steps up to play the next part."

Zham looked at her and all the worry he had just lost came rushing back so fast he nearly became sick where he stood, his stomach knotting up worse than before.

"What are you not telling me?"

"Valis..."

"That damn idiot child! I told her to let it go she should have more faith in her father!" Zhamar shouted before he caught himself and lowered his voice.

"What has she done? Is there no way for you to keep her from getting entangled in all this?"

"I can go with them, keep them safe until they are..." Zhamar started waving his hands and shaking his head in frustration.

"No, I need you to go with the escort in the morning, see to it that the Prince and his Aunt return to Carn safely." He paused as he wracked his mind for another solution but when he could come up with none he looked at one of his oldest friends and continued. "No, Valis and Cecil are on their own, with the escort leaving tomorrow it will buy them time for whatever it is they need to do to get away."

"If war escalates...what about your other daughters? I won't be here to protect any of you, Zham." Deep worry laced through each word.

"I'll send them to their mother's parents they live deep in the summer land, it will be safe enough... Until Petsky falls... If it comes to that." a whimper crept along those last words.

Zhamar felt a hand on his shoulder and when he gave no reaction that hand spun him around gentle and wrapped him in long arms.

"I truly hope it won't come to that Zham...I truly do hope it."

"Valis, she must hate me so much right now, why couldn't she be more like her sisters?" He was savouring the comforting embrace of his friend.

"She will understand when all this is over, for now let her anger at you drive her on."

"She is too much like her brother." His voice broke with the thought of his son.

"She's too much like her father," Jan teased, "but don't worry, she is with good friends who will do their best to keep her safe."

The King of Petsky could not remember how long he had stood clinging to his long time friend that night; however, he remembered the tears on his cheeks and the sun on the back of his neck as the first early morning rays arrived.

CHAPTER 3

Valis arrived in her room to a familiar sight; her nightgown, neatly set atop her bed. She fought with the servants, arguing that unlike her sisters, she could manage to dress herself...it had been a long battle, eventually she had won, not without a few servants storming off in anger and a few in tears. However, they still set the day's attire for her. This was the deal worked out and she still thought it absurd. At this moment, she was far too tired to give it more thought. She changed, leaving her discarded clothes where they fell. Her mind was full of anger and hurt as she crawled into bed.

At first, she was far too alert for sleep and so tossed and turned until finally coming to rest on her side. Her eyes were full of wakefulness, the fire to which Ce'elevan had lain down before, made the shadows upon the walls.

I wish I had a greyhound's ability to sleep at any time. She smirked at the thought. The poor animal had been through much in such a short while. She was not worried about him being here, despite the fact that the dog should have gone to her father upon her brother's passing. *He has his own dogs.* Bitter thoughts towards her father fueled her anger. No one would argue with her if she claimed him as her own, the Goddess help those who try.

Valis lie like this, watching the skinny dog breathe in and out, until her eyes finally became heavy with sleep. The warm blankets and soft pillows combined with the crackling sound of the fire, helped strip her of her worries. She chased away the silly notions of being under an enchanted slumber before they could take hold, however brief the thoughts were.

Once sleep claimed her however, fear had become a constant companion. She ran through the city streets, streets that where dark in the dead of night, and yet the shine from the moon was near blinding as it reflected off the puddles left after what had been a heavy rain. Every sense seemed almost too strong to bear, her footfalls echoed sharp in her ears, she could smell the foul stench of the docks not far off as she ran, and yet she dare not stop for she knew what gave persistent chase, the Princess of Carn, as Valis truthfully thought of her… a witch.

She fled as best she could. However, her legs felt increasingly heavy, and no matter which way she turned, every direction sent her further and further down alleyway after alleyway until what she feared most finally happened... The alleys ended. She now faced the task of confronting her pursuer. Fear held his grip on her shoulders; she could not see anyone but felt the chilly fingers through her shirt and on her flesh.

Moonlight that spilled at the alleys entrance began to wane and dark tendrils of thick black smoke choked the already soft luminance until all was black as pitch. She wanted to close her eyes yet something in her already knew it would spare her little. She continued to stare forward, she could feel the witch getting closer, and she could even hear the breathing of the one who haunted her dreams this night. Backed against the alleys wall she pleaded to every God she had ever heard of for salvation. She begged for a chance to flee, or to become one with the wall behind her, but they did not listen, they never did. In a breath the witch was upon her, she could now feel the woman's darkness climbing up her arms, consuming her as a spider does its meal, when caught up in its web. She felt her heart pounding so hard that she hoped it might burst before she could be swallowed whole.

A pinprick of light dotted the center of the blackness; the sound of a fresh forged blade thrust into cooling water filled her ears. The light became more intense until finally, she had to close her eyes, and despite the painful scream that rattled the stone walls around her she refused to open them until the sound had faded to nothing.

Valis peeked, just a sliver, and winced at the brightness. When she had dared open them further they adjusted, and the light was no more brilliant than any other warm summer day. She was no longer in the ally, no longer in the city for that matter. The smell of fresh air carried a scent of a particular flower she remembered from the first day she could walk and give chase to her older Brother. She was sitting in the summer land where her grandparents lived and where her mother had grown up. A figure stood under a great oak tree she remembered fondly, but she could not make the figure out under the cloak of shade the tree provided.

"I will always keep the darkness away Valis, I promise."

"Malik?" Her voice caught in her throat, choked on emotion of joy and sorrow.

"Valis."

"Malik, I'm here! Wait!" She scrambled to her feet.

"Valis...wake up."

Valis heard the voice again; it was so close to her brothers. No, no she stopped running as the figure by the tree began to fade. It was not her brother's voice, could not be, he was gone.

"Please, Valis, wake up we have to go, now!"

"Ce'elevan?" Was it the bond? She was still connected to the bond even in a dream?

Her eyes shot open and in the shift from asleep to awake she gave a startled shriek, flung herself off the bed, and landed in the pile of discarded clothes she had left so unceremoniously on the floor. She lay there on her back, eyes wide open staring at the ceiling until Ce'elevan, arrived to hover over her. "Ce'elevan, move, you're on my hair, I can't…" From her spot on the floor, the youngest Princess in Petsky had a new view on the situation, and the key ring clenched in the Greyhound's jaw. She smiled. In her mind, a plan began to form.

"Where did you get these?" Finally able to sit up, she took the keys.

"I was dreaming, and when I awoke, they were here, hanging on a hook on the fireplace, beside that sword over there," Ce'elevan gestured with his head.

She already had her nightgown off and her shirt from earlier in the day back on; when she followed the dog's gaze... she sat back down. There leaned up against the fireplace below the hook where Ce'elevan had found the keys, was her father's sword. The sword she had seen dozens of times in his room, but was never allowed even a finger on. Even Malik suffered punishment the only time father caught him with it. "What is that doing here?" She looked back at Ce'elevan forgetting to ask through the bond, a tilt of the head his only response.

Valis Changed and laced up her boots a little tighter then she would have normally liked, she did not want to run the risk of them coming undone at a critical moment. She carefully went over and picked up her father's sword in both hands staring at it in wonder before strapping the scabbard to her side. The darkest cloak her wardrobe offered, completed her outfit. She cursed as she had to shift it over the sword, a feeling she would have to adjust to.

With the sword and the keys was a pack, containing a small coin purse, soldier's rations, and a change of men's clothes. Whoever had set this up knew she would not be returning for a while. *Or ever*, she thought. With the pack over one shoulder, she looked around the room for anything else she thought she might need. When she was satisfied there was not, she opened the door and left the room, Ce'elevan followed her into the hall.

"Are you sure you wish to come with me" The bond to the greyhound was strong with him close at her side. *"We won't be back until we can clear Cecil of his charges."*

Ce'elevan gave her no response and waited for her to shut the door.

She felt a sudden pang of loss when the door clicked shut, her mind gave way to thoughts of her father and sisters. Her sadness had quickly turned to anger at her father's foolishness and she finally settled her mood on steel hardened determination.

They encountered little trouble on their way down to the dungeons. Ce'elevan warned her through the bond whenever he could smell a guard around the corner and they waited for what, to her, seemed a painfully long time before he gave her the all clear and they moved forward. The door to the stairwell leading to the dungeons creaked, and for a moment, she dared not breathe. The guards could arrive from down the hall or from below, should they have been roused by the sound, but when after a few moments no one arrived, she slipped inside. They moved down the stairs as quiet as they could, she cursed the click clack of the greyhounds' toes on the stone stairs.

She stopped at the bottom as her mind threw her another problem: the guards inside. She thought about sending the greyhound in first but she would be in enough trouble after this night and did not need to add the deaths of her own people to the list of future charges.

"Perhaps they will be asleep... Or drunk! Guards often did that right?" The bond echoed in her head, she looked to Ce'elevan for an answer.

"I can hear them breathing, it's deep and steady...It sounds like they are asleep." He answered.

Valis sighed heavily, grimacing as she realized how loud it sounded and found the courage to open the door. Their luck as it was, held, inside the guards where indeed asleep. Deep snoring emitted from both men who, sat slumped over in their seats at the small table. Cups of wine lay spilled and the drink dripped through the cracks in the wood making a puddle below.

Valis moved quickly, over to Cecil's cell. She grasped the key ring and searched for the right one. "Why are there so damn many? There's not even as many cells as there are keys!" She cursed every time the keys jangled and clanged together.

"Valis?" Cecil followed his voice out shadows. Valis could tell he had been crying as his dirt streaked face left clean lines of his sadness. *Best not to mention It,* she thought, and cursed again as she dropped the ring of keys.

"Valis, what are you doing here?" Cecil leaned his head against the bars.

"Getting you out... What happened to the guards?" She replied with keys once more in hand.

"The strangest," silence followed.

She looked up and when Cecil did not elaborate she resumed her efforts on the lock.

"The Earth Maiden, Janian, had come to give me the Earth Mother's blessings before...Well, she poured what I had assumed was wine for the guards, and a cup for myself."

Valis had slowed to cast a curious glance over her shoulder at the table where the guards lie asleep and paused lost in thought.

"Before I could drink from my cup she had placed her hand over the top to stop me and kept it there as we watched the guards drink deep from theirs and soon after, fall asleep, it was potent whatever it was they had drunk. That was over an hour ago and they are still snoring."

"What did Jan say to you after?" Valis asked as she inserted another wrong key.

"Nothing...she just smiled and left. But it was such a smile… as if to say everything would be alright."

"Click."

The lock fell to the ground. "Finally! Really, do all these keys have a purpose? Well don't just stand there looking at me like I've just grown two heads... Let's go!" Valis said.

"Go where? I don't want you to get in..." Cecil began however Valis was already on the move.

She grabbed a lamp from the table as she passed sparing the guards little interest, she had faith knowing Jan had a hand in their slumber; they would wake when the time was right for them to do so.

With Ce'elevan by her side Valis made haste down the dungeons only corridor, the dark cells on either side sat empty, and she could not help but feel as though eyes followed her. *Nonsense.* It was quiet, the only sounds where their own footsteps and the squeak from the hinge on the lamp's slim moon-shaped handle.

"Be careful, don't knock over the lamp," she sent through the link to Ce'elevan.

Kneeling on the floor, the lamp beside her Valis looked up as Cecil approached.

"Help me with this," she gestured towards the large metal cover the guards had placed over the dungeons sewer drain.

Cecil did not move to help. "That's the sewer, Valis... I'm not going down into that. Who knows what's floating in the water, I..."

"It's the only way out," she tried to keep the wobble of emotion out of her words as she looked sadly at the cover. "I can't let you die here, not in a cell, my brother would never have let you..."

"Alright." Cecil agreed.

Valis watched as he knelt down, slid his fingers into the groves along the side, grooves now dulled from years of use. As soon as Valis lifted from her end the stench filled their nostrils. She almost dropped the heavy cover and wondered how she hadn't, and then she remembered whose sister she was, and would do whatever it took to get the job done.

Pinching her nose closed she waved Cecil to go first.

"You know..." He started as he swung his legs over into the hole and looked down. One rust covered ladder led down into blackness. "This is exactly the kind of thing Malik would be sending me into... If I closed my eyes, I'm sure I would hear his voice..."

"Get your ass down that hole, Cecil!" Valis snapped at him, smiling as he smiled. "When you get through there meet me at the far end of the docks, we can head east and circle the lake."

"Wait... what!"

Valis wanted to laugh as she watched her friend nearly topple down the hole.

"You're not coming with me? I have to go through this filth myself?"

"Look," she said, handing him the lamp. "If I'm caught in the halls I'll be fine, it'll be light soon enough and I can say I was taking my dog outside to do his...Well, you know." She finished with a wave towards the sewer earning her a scowl from Cecil. "But if I'm caught with you, well what would I say then? I'm taking my friend here for a walk to stretch his legs before you stretch his neck?"

They both glared at each other until Ce'elevan whimpered and backed away from the hole.

"If I die down here I'm going to find where ever the Earth Mother keeps your brother and I'm going to kick his ass for dying and sticking me with his little sister... I swear!" Cecil grumbled, grabbed the ladder and headed down the first few steps before reaching up and helping Valis move the cover back into position.

"I'll meet you at the docks, I promise." She wasn't sure he had heard her but she could not linger. She looked to the guards, still sleeping, and looked in horror at her hands a breath away from wiping them off on her clothes. They were covered in filth.

"*Let's go get cleaned up, we can spare the little bit of time, it will take him a while to find the way out, should have asked Jan for a map.*"

"*Do **you** know where the sewers empty by the docks?*" Ce'elevan asked.

44

"Come on Ce'elevan, adventure awaits."

They made their way back through the corridor of cells, "*Hold on,*" Valis took the key ring and hung it back on the wall where she had found it. These two would be in enough trouble without losing their keys. "Whatever in the hell they are all for." She mumbled to herself.

CHAPTER 4

"Stop it, Alex," King Zhamar warned.

He had returned to his study after attending an execution that did not occur. He sat behind his desk with a worried head in his hands, exhaustion was taking its toll this day and he did not have to look up to know his friend was grinning from ear to ear.

"Did you see her face, when the guards gave their report?" Alex, so overcome with what happened, almost giggled as he spoke.

"Alex..."

"The prisoner has escaped!" Alex gave a throaty laugh, leaning on the chair in front of him for support.

"When the first guard...what's his name, the short one, when he stood before you and Princess Kerra and said 'we uh...can't find him' I thought she was going to tear the flesh from his bones with that look of hers! Me, I nearly pissed myself Zham!"

"Alex..." the king tried again in vain to grab his friend's attention.

"I don't know how he got out but I'm glad. I hope the boy is halfway between here and the Tendaly lands by now far from this..."

"Alex!" the King shouted, having kept his outrage in check till now.

"I have a dead son, kidnapping allegations, conspiracy of war charges from our neighbors and one pissed off Princess marching back to her warrior Queen of a sister! Do you think you could cut the crap long enough for me to think?" The king finished, slumping back in his seat after nearly coming up and over the desk at the frustration towards his friend.

"Zham, I do know what you're going through, but you and I both know the boy is innocent. The Prince of Carn returns with his Aunt, and this gesture alone should dissuade any talk of war. The Queen has a temper, that's a fact but..."

"Valis is with him," the king said as he rose and walked toward the room's large bay windows, windows that showed him the horrified look upon Alex's face in their polished glass panes.

"That poor lad," Alex tried to make the words sound genuine but the grin was quickly returning to his face.

"I miss the old days when I could have laughed at your humorous view of the world, Alex, I truly do." The king stood quietly staring with a sad smile, down into the courtyard below. A carriage was being readied and the knights he was sending as an escort had begun to gather.

"I have a feeling our old friend has her hands all over this, has she gone with..."

"No, she will be going with you and the young Prince, I can't take any chance of something else going wrong, and I'll worry less knowing you're both there," the king replied as he turned away from the window.

"So, Valis and Cecil are on their own then?" Alex asked with a raised eyebrow.

"We had better get down there and make sure everything's ready," King Zhamar said, brushing his friend's question aside.

"As you command my king," Alex finished, his smile was gone and as they left the room both men wondered if they would ever be free to do so again.

At first glance you would not find the Princess of Carn a visual threat. As, Zhamar and Alex arrived in the courtyard she well could have been mistaken for one of Zhamar's own daughters'. She stood with her back to them; the dress she wore was a royal gold with soft lace in intricate patterns along the sleeves. Her hair, pinned up with a string of pearls that wound their way through. It was her eyes that gave her away. As she turned on the men's approach it was those eyes that showed a darker occupant within that beautiful body and for a moment Alex thought her eyes where glowing red. Though he finally convinced himself that it was simply a reflection, of the blood red pendant, she wore tight around her neck.

"Your knights are slow Zhamar," Princess Kerra sneered, making no attempt to hide the once over she gave Alex.

"I will have to concede defeat on the issue Princess; we certainly lack the military prowess of the great nation of Carn," the king replied. His voice conveyed no hint of sarcasm earning him an angry look from Alex. The Princess turned and declined the offered help into the carriage. The young Prince still tucked in the nook of her arm fast asleep.

"I trust you will carry my message to your sister of our continued friendship and my heartfelt apologies at not being able to return her son at..."

"The Queen will hear all of it Zhamar, rest assured she will know every detail." She snapped, cutting the king off.

Before the King could offer more words Princess Kerra stuck her head through the open carriage window. "If we could dispense with the pleasantries, I would like to get this under way before my nephew awakes and I must spend several hours playing nursemaid."

"I would be willing to send a wet nurse along with you if you like," the King gestured towards the castle.

"No," was her only reply.

***

Cecil's nose had grown accustom to the smells as he sloshed through the mess. The sewage was knee-high and he focused more on moving forward and less on the mystery shapes floating around him.

I may not be able to smell it anymore but the burning in my nostrils does not have my stomach convinced. At least if I'm sick down here nobody would be able to tell. Even that thought almost made him sick and he could taste the bile in the back of his throat as he tried desperately to push those thoughts aside. Instead he focused on his goal of reaching an exit; somewhere that would lead him back to what by now was an early morning sky. He wanted to blame Valis, as he once more reached a junction leading Gods knows where. But he knew she was not the real enemy and tried to be calm, his only compass was the knowledge the water had to go somewhere, and he prayed he could follow it out.

"The real problem here is that you had to go and die... Damn you Malik, why didn't you listen to me? Why did I listen to you? That's a better question," he said as he paused at a junction and stood still to feel which way the water was flowing in the near darkness of the tunnels. He sighed and scolded himself for blaming the dead for his problems. "Show a little more respect, Cecil." Talking to himself was doing little to ease his nerves and every time he heard or thought he heard a rats squeak he had to force himself to keep moving and not tighten up with fright. "Oh if you could see me now, here I am talking to myself, covered in...I don't know what, all because your sister thought this was a good idea!" Cecil gave an uneasy laugh.

***

"Well, look who it is Zham, our little Sister, Jan." Alex nodded his head towards the woman with the scowl on her face as she approached them.

Zhamar hoped Alex would realize the scowl was directed at the carriage and not them.

Jan stood with them and when her eyes slid slowly off the side of the carriage, they softened at the sight of her old friends. Finally, her foul mood gave way to a mischievous grin as she reached out and playfully ruffled Alex's hair.

"Still playing soldier, Alex?" Jan teased as he pulled away quickly trying to pat his hair back into place.

"Is she...?" Jan asked with a raised eyebrow toward Zhamar to which he replied with a nod.

"Princess Kerra," Jan addressed in a loud clear voice. "I am the Earth Maiden, Janian Poledouris...it is my honor to..."

"I have been informed of your statues, and despite my assurances to King Damaste that we shall be quite secured without your services, he insists you join us. I will allow this, but know

50

the kingdom of Carn does not sanction nor acknowledge your cult or its practices," the Princess's voice came from within the carriage, sparing Janian the courtesy of addressing her directly.

"As you wish, Princess, as you wish." Jan said calmly turning and walking with her friends towards the courtyard's entrance.

"The men are nearly ready, I trust you will both have a safe and... swift journey," the King said, looking displeased back at the carriage.

"Zham, there is something not right about all this, I can't sense what's inside that carriage, it's as if all my senses suddenly disappear into a fog when I try." Jan said in a hushed voice.

"We will just have to keep a close eye on everything little sister," Alex teased.

"You two behave as well, I can't spare the men to have the both of you watched." Zham said smiling, "be careful my friends... I wish I was going with you," he finished more soberly.

"Just like the old days?" Alex clapped his Kings' shoulder, laughing at the shocked gasp from the servants walking by.

"Yes, but this time I won't be there to pull your fat from the fire, as they say," the king laughed.

***

Cecil's heart raced and he had to steady himself as the sudden light from the sewers exit spilled down the tunnel as he rounded the corner. He rushed, slogging through the murky and vile smelling water and panicked when he nearly fell several more times. He was both elated and discouraged when he arrived to find the way blocked by a set of iron bars stretching from wall-to-wall.

Cecil grabbed hold with both hands and shook the bars with all the strength he could muster, and when they didn't budge in the slightest he leaned his head against the cold hard metal. "Is this what my life is to become? Locked away in a prison of one make or another?" Whomever he thought might answer remained silent. "This is the worst then is it? I'm sorry Malik, looks like the King's council was right about me, no better than the fetid water washing past my feet, sent to rot..." Cecil's anger eased and shock took hold as he kicked the bottom of the bars with his foot under the water. It had become stuck where one of the bars snapped off with little effort. With renewed urgency he yanked his foot out and kicked at the remaining bars. Two, three, four..."*it would be enough*" his mind raced. He could squeeze through, all he had to do... And then his mood dipped once more. "Is swim through... Of course that's the only way," he cursed but steeled his will to the task. With his mind screaming in anger at his decision Cecil plunged down into the water.

When he reached the docks in the lower, more run down part of the castles water District he did his best to stay out of people's way. The looks and scowls of the odd person he had no choice but to pass, told him that his foul mood was matched by his now foul smell. And when he found Valis and Ce'elevan he was already well versed in the reaction she herself presented to him.

"You stink!" Valis blanched as she held her nose.

The only one so far not to make a fuss was the dog, who seemed under no discomfort by Cecil's arrival.

"I... What's the plan? Where do we go from here?" Cecil managed to bite back the scathing remarks he had for the Princess, the remarks he kept on the tip of his tongue just in case.

"I've been standing here for a long while now, thinking over that very question," Valis replied.

"All-night to think about it, had me crawling through the kingdoms sewers and you're not sure yet?" Cecil almost threw his hands in the air and his mind gave way to thoughts of turning himself in, although he was sure in his condition, they would kill him on sight for his smell alone.

"The way I see it is we have two choices, one, we find another kingdom to hide in until all this blows over and my father comes to his senses."

Cecil gave her a skeptical look.

"Or, we go after the escort."

"Or we go after the escort? Why would we want to head toward the enemy? The Prince is safe; they return to Carn... What would possibly make us want to follow them?" Cecil was shouting by the end of it and he tried to calm himself when he realized, Valis had taken a startled step away from him.

"Malik," she began timidly.

"Malik would want you to stay in the castle with your father... Malik would want me to make sure you where safe. Dammit, Valis this is the exact opposite of what your brother would have wanted!" This time he did throw his hands up as he scolded her bringing a low growl from

Ce'elevan, a warning to watch his tone. Cecil waved his hand dismissively at her and turned his

back to them.

"Please," Valis whispered.

"Please, Cecil I must know why Malik was killed, who wanted to hurt the young Prince

of Carn and I want to help prevent a war on my father's doorstep."

"Alright," Cecil said, not at all convincing himself, yet alone his friend. "Beats another

prison, and I doubt I would have been able to stop you anyways, you are, Malik's sister after all,

just another pain in my..."

"We need to clean you up first," Valis said. Without warning she walked up, and shoved

Cecil into the cold water of the lake.

Cecil managed to come up for air spluttering curses and watched as Valis leaned over the

dock and smiled at him.

"What are you smiling at?"

"Don't forget behind your ears" she teased and much to Cecil's surprise, she tossed a bar

of soap into the water which he quickly grabbed before it had a chance to sink.

As she walked away to leave him to his business, Cecil muttered about being better

treated in a dungeons cell. Ce'elevan watched as he began to scrub with the soap and when a

stray bubble drifted upward and landed on his nose, the dog snuffled and went in search of his

master.

Cecil knew where he would find them. From the carpenter's shop atop the largest hill in the village, just outside the castle grounds one could see the portcullis and the path leading from the castle due south without obstruction. He joined his friends behind the building as they snuck peaks around the corner.

"*Well?*" Valis asked Ce'elevan after casting a quick glance back at Cecil.

"*Much better, you have no idea how easy it would have been to track him,*" the dog's bonded voice responded to her question.

"You know I get the funny feeling you guys are making fun of me when I see his face like that," Cecil grumbled. The open mouth and tongue half out looked as if the dog was either happy or amused and Ce'elevan tilted his head to the side in ignorance.

Cecil was still dripping wet, and would have stormed away if not for the fact the sun was warm and he at least was in no sewer.

CHAPTER 5

Love was there, in her heart, as Princess Kerra looked down into the bassinet where her sleeping nephew lie, but so was hate. And that hatred sat higher up within her chest.

The hate she felt had started out strong in the beginning and had only strengthened its hold upon her heart; a heart that was left torn and shredded to ribbons. The hate had brought her back, binding the wound within its dark embrace.

I will find a way, Kerra, repeated in her head, determined to bring down the mighty kingdom of Carn and with it the catalyst of her decent into darkness, the birthplace of her one true love. *They will all suffer as I have suffered, I will take all they hold dear and make them watch as I desecrate and shatter their wills, one by one if I must.*

The hatred urged her to end the young Prince's life right this second; there would be enough of Petsky's knights around to pin the death on a suspected assassin. One sent along to finish what they had started.

"No," she cooed at her nephew. "No, I made my master a promise. You will serve us greatest when he is once again powerful enough to return, and needs a royal body of his own to rule with once more." she grinned evilly as she imagined the glorious age that would come on that day. "The squire's escape will only anger my dear sister more at learning so, once I spin the tale to my liking of course."

Kerra posed dramatically with her hand on her puffed out chest. "My dear sister, it was all we could do to rescue your son upon finding the kidnappers within the forest. The fools did not have enough sense to hide further from their own lands. We lost many soldiers in the battle. The man who stole your son, a squire, on orders of his Prince, thought to run and hide within the castle walls. He was found and under the falsehood of justice decreed by the King, the young man has escaped. Or... If I might be so bold, set free by the King in an attempt to blind us from his real intentions...war." She grinned, satisfied with the tale.

When I slaughter the escort it will be more than enough to set my dear sister into war. She paused as a thought occurred to her; she truly did lose a good deal of her soldiers in their attack on Prince Malik and the council of Elders. The voice of her master was whispering a delicious solution to replenishing her ranks. There was just one little pest of a problem to take care of first.

***

Jan felt a chill run down her back as she continued glaring at the carriage, as if a single bead of cold lake water had found its way into her shirt.

King Zhamar was serious about sending the royal family safely back to their own kingdom, ten of the kings most trusted knights, all seasoned veterans of countless battles rode with the wagon as they left the castle. Well trained as they were, it was not long before they had set up a perimeter around them, eagle eyes, all of them as they scanned the trees and surrounding areas. A pair of knights had gone on ahead, and Jan knew when they returned, two others would take their place.

And yet safe was as far from the feeling she carried with her since they left. There was dark magic's involved, that much she could sense... Almost taste in the air around the carriage. And for a moment she wished she could share her horse's ignorance on such matters. As they rode on, no other was disturbed by what she knew was there, even if she could not see it with her eyes.

If not for the babe inside the carriage, Jan would have told her friend no, and stayed away from such evils, at least on her own she would have. The King in his wisdom was quite right to send her along however, as an Earth Maiden was rare enough to see at the best of times, and her friend had seen it as an opportunity of luck that she had arrived when she did. And of course it didn't hurt that they had been friends since childhood.

I will go at your request my old friend, and for the sake of the child's safety. Those words just might be her undoing one day, and Jan sighed heavily at the thought. She continued to stare at the back of the carriage, half expecting it to roar to life in flames or the form of some great beast. Jan flinched, startled by the taping on her shoulder from the man who had silently ridden alongside her.

"Try to relax, Janian," Alex chuckled lightly.

This man's voice brought with it fond memories of her adventures when younger.

"Alex by the Goddess, don't sneak up on me!" She scolded playfully swatting his arm. "I'm tempted to turn you into a potted plant, although I suppose you would still find away to be under foot."

"In all the years I've known you Jan, and in all the adventures we have been on, that threat still rings hollow in my ears, so shut up and do it already or come up with something new. I'm thinking Earth Maiden is just a fancy way of saying Gardner," Alex fired back.

Janian only scowled back playfully, waving him off as he rode ahead to join the other knights and his duties. She would share her concerns with him when they stopped for the night. Perhaps he could even put her mind at ease about the foreboding she felt this day.

Time for setting up camp came earlier than she realized as she had been lost in thought, preoccupied with the mysterious energy of the carriage and soon the sunlight lost its battle with the rising moon. They set up camp, with the carriage off to one side. When Janian asked how that could possibly be protected so far from the knight's camps, she was informed, it was on the Princess's orders, a weak excuse of how the smoke from the fires would make the baby ill. Jan had yet to see anyone leave the carriage and that only doubled the gnawing feeling in her stomach that something was not as it should be, and she desperately wanted to know if the child was well.

Alex had welcomed her to his fire, she was grateful he remembered, forbidden to touch or create fire herself, the Earth Maidens seeing it as a destructive tool of man, despite arguments that fire can happen naturally in nature. Such was the way when off on their younger more foolish adventures, with Zham gathering the wood and Alex set to tending the fire, how she missed those days.

"You're going to wear a hole into the back of that carriage, Jan," Alex said gesturing with his finger as he sat taking a mouth full of stew from his bowl.

Jan's own bowl sat at her feet, cold now and untouched, she continued to glance the carriage's way paying her friend no mind.

"Jan," Alex tried again.

"There is something seriously wrong with that carriage, but my senses are clouded. Almost as if there is some invisible barrier around that damn thing keeping me from reading anything inside. It's maddening!" Jan protested.

"Maiden powers not working huh? I don't remember you ever having trouble before; remember that time in Welton, Zham and that barmaid, in the merchant's carriage? Said you could hear, taste and smell all the..."

"Alex!" Jan scolded as she whipped around, her face red hot. "That is not something I wish to re-live thank you so very much."

"Maybe it's just old age catching up with us?" Alex sighed and put his bowl down.

"I beg your pardon, sir knight?" Jan asked in a hurt tone. A sly smile was all Alex would give in return before they both started to laugh.

"Do you think much about the old days, Alex? When you and I and our now great King would head off for parts unknown, seeking tales and adventure?" Jan asked quietly.

"We did that?" Alex smirked as he asked.

"We did that," Jan smiled back.

"Some days... It's the only thing that keeps me going." Alex trailed off lost in thought and forgotten memories. "Things change though, we changed. News of Malik dying brings no tears to our old friend, and yet here we are escorting another's son." Alex's words could not hide the touch of bitterness as he spoke.

Janian shook her head, "he wants to keep the peace, believe me Alex he's hurting inside more then we will ever know. Appearances is what he is keeping up, if he showed any weakness now..." Jan trailed off not wishing to finish the thought.

"Something's not right, that I will agree with you on." Alex half mumbled as he flicked the last bit of stew on his spoon into the fire and moved to his bedroll. "Get some sleep, Janian."

The Earth Maiden offered no response, her gaze once more fixed on the carriage that so vexed her.

"Something's not right with any of this."

CHAPTER 6

"It's just not a very good story."

They had been walking the path Valis had suggested, in hopes that the greyhound would pick up the familiar scents of soldiers, or Janian. Valis kept them as entertained as was possible with stories from her childhood.

"Well I think it's wonderfully romantic, two lovers torn apart, only to fight back against fates equally unpleasant, with only love as both their weapon, and their shield." The Princess countered and finished with an airy sigh.

"Utter nonsense." Cecil grumbled. As they walked, his clothes had finally dried, and although the Princess gave her assurances the smell was gone, Ce'elevan kept his distance. The Princess remained an arm's length away and could only offer a smile accompanied by a shrug of her shoulders.

"Maybe he's just tired of listening to you argue just for the sake of arguing." Valis suggested, and to enforce her point the greyhound paused to look back at them both.

"Besides, I've listened to my father tell me stories of his great adventures when younger, we could think of this as..."

"And that's what you really think this is, don't you, Princess, just an adventure? We are now enemies of the kingdom, me even more so, and not to ignore the fact that I'm sure I'll get charged for kidnapping! They were going to hang me before, imagine what they'll do to me now!"

They stopped; even the greyhound suspended his search to watch the humans argue.

"Let me tell you the truth about your sweet and fancy stories Princess. In the real world, the enemy burns the village, no knight comes to the rescue, and nobody lives happily ever..." Cecil's harsh words died on his lips as they rounded the bend in the road.

The escort they had hoped to catch up too was now the remains of what looked like a fierce battle. A battle entered by many more combatants then the number of men they had first seen as the escort had left the castle.

"Cecil..." Valis stammered as she took in the broken and splintered carriage, the abandoned bedrolls, torn and singed.

"The Prince!" She shouted and ran toward the carriage. Cecil tried in vain to grab her before she dashed past, but missed and cursed as he quickly followed.

"Valis don't!" the ex-squire said cautiously as the young Princess reached out to open the door, which hung askew on its hinges. She let out a small startled shriek as the door came crashing to the ground at her touch. After taking a deep breath she braced herself and took a look inside. She sighed. "It's empty." She told Cecil as he came up beside her.

Small rings of fire burned sporadically around the area. Cecil could see no reason for their continued being as fire needed fuel to burn, and yet these strange circles seemed to require no wood or oil that he could see. Swords of the knights of Petsky lay covered in blood.

"Where are the bodies?" Valis asked. Cecil moved in close.

"Not one single body, weapons and armour, a dented helmet, a blackened sword...but no bodies." She continued.

Ce'elevan began barking, Valis tried to use the bond but his thoughts were too fast for her to cipher and she swore at the dog to slow down through the bond.

Ce'elevan darted back behind the carriage, Valis and Cecil followed cautious in their approach. Their fears eased as they came around; there on the ground, with Ce'elevan pawing at it, sat an ornate wooden chest.

"I don't get it, what's he doing?" Cecil gestured at the dog in confusion. "It's just a chest, probably full of Princess Kerra's wardrobe or something."

"I don't know... Could be supplies," Valis suggested.

Cecil had quickly grabbed a discarded dagger from the ground. "Maybe it's food! As grateful as I am Valis, getting me out of that cell. You neglected to bring much in the way of travel rations, and what we did have you fed most of it to the dog!" Cecil grumbled as he worked on the lock securing the chest with his dagger.

"Alright, move!" Cecil ordered, perhaps too harshly as he pushed a curious Ce'elevan out of his way.

The lock was not a complex one nor of a sturdy design, more of an inconvenience than anything. Cecil's dagger popped it open with little effort. Without thinking or perhaps over-thinking with his stomach instead of his head, he flung open the chest lid and reached inside. It was quickly pulled back out with a start and he leaned wearily back over to peer inside. "It's not food." He said standing, rubbing his hand. "It's another greyhound, can you...you know?" He taped the side of his head then pointed at Ce'elevan who despite being rudely treated was still sitting patiently close by.

Valis rushed forward shoving Cecil away as harshly as the man had the dog not a few moments ago.

"*Why can't I hear anything?*" She asked through the bond to Ce'elevan.

"*The bond is weak, even I cannot hear, only a faint whisper. The box, it smells of magic, be careful.*" Ce'elevan finished with a whine.

Valis rubbed the top of the weak greyhound's head soothingly.

"Water," Valis said, her words breaking through a heavy hearted sob in her throat.

"It looks like its been in there a long time, maybe we should..." The look he received was every bit a royal command and he quickly headed towards the stream they had past not more than ten minutes ago.

CHAPTER 7

Her breath would have been in gasps, and her body screamed for such an action. It would, had Janian not been paralyzed with fear.

"There's no time," the voice that startled her awake spoke in a hash whisper. It was Alex that had woken her. She soon realized his hand was clamped tightly over her mouth.

"Quiet, Jan," Alex hissed. "You have to run, it's not safe here!"

He pulled his hand away, not in consideration for her need of air, but instead, to clutch his head in what looked to be absolute agony.

"I can hear her, in my head... I can't shut her out," Alex groaned.

"Shut who out? Alex what's going on?" Jan asked as she scrambled over placing a concerned hand on her friend's shoulder.

"She's so loud, Jan. Her voice is full of..." Before he could finish Alex stood and roughly pulled Janian to her feet as well.

"Princess Kerra! She's got control of some of the others!"

Jan felt her friend shove her away, a mix of confusion and startled anger lasted only a moment when she realized that Alex had just saved her life. The sword meant for her fell between them and in a flash of steel on steel, in the dark night, Alex had begun the dance of death.

The Earth Maiden stood in shock as her other senses awoke and soon the sounds of a fevered battle were all around her, she spied Petsky knights fighting Carn guards and Petsky knights fighting amongst themselves.

It was Alex, who once again shook her, and she was growing angry with herself for taking so long to react. "You run, Janian!" Alex commanded and he thrust a small bundle into her arms. "I'll hold them off as long as I can resist, Jan, I..."

His unsaid words would haunt her dreams in the coming days, but as several more knights set upon him, reason and survival instinct grabbed control of her mind. Soon she found herself running as fast as she could, faster than she had ever remembered running before and her fear-filled heart fled with her into the woods.

It was not until she could no longer hear the ringing of swords in her ears that she stopped for breath, and it took even longer to remember the bundle in her arms. Un-wrapping the soft cloth as she leaned her back against a tree she stopped breathing altogether. In Janian's arms was the sleeping form of the young Prince of Carn.

Her breath returned in the form of a night-chilled gasp, and her lungs burned as she held her breath once more. The sound of shouts and grunted orders shot through the trees toward her like arrows. As Jan covered the sleeping Prince once more, she realized with her back to the tree that she had tapped into her Earth Maiden abilities, as was evident of the slight blue aura that traced her fingers upon touching the trees rough bark. They had warned her she realized, the trees had carried the sounds of her pursuers to her, and now she had a few moments more than would be normal to get away.

Kerra seethed with rage.

Twice now, she had failed to set her plans in motion. Oh, the battle had gone as planned and the carnage they had left behind would serve its purpose, but the child... Her nephew had been taken. That was very much *not* a part of her plan.

The man that stood before her, shivered in the night. He stood, naked, stripped of his armour, clothes, and sword before being brought to her. If she were not overflowing with so much hatred at this moment, she would have taken him to her bed. For his weather darkened skin, and toned body made her eyes linger in a most un-Princess like fashion.

Using her powers to control the minds of thirty Petsky knights had taxed her greatly, and this one had been the hardest of all to tame. Since leaving the Castle with her escort, she had been casting her spells within the enchanted walls of her carriage, letting the powers she drew upon seep out, slowly wrapping its way around the minds of all outside. The spell had its desired effect on all save two, the accursed Earth Maiden and this knight, Alex. She had control now of course; he had taken down quite a few men of both Petsky and Carn, thus giving her more power to fuel the spell.

"I should kill you where you stand," Kerra said lazily, moving around the man while tracing a finger across his shoulders and back. "But I suspect being unable to help your friend is destroying you from the inside out. You surprised me knight, if I was to suspect anyone of stealing my nephew away from me it would have been that Pagan witch, this... Earth Maiden," she spat at his feet as the last words came out of her mouth.

"Don't fret though, even now I can hear the thoughts of the men I sent after her, and it won't be long till they drag her flayed corpse back to me. I have the power you know, to keep her alive for days... Months, while I let death claw at her. And you my new pet... You will watch it all." Kerra said. She looked almost bored as another thought reached her. "You may wait outside," she finished.

Once the knight had left, Kerra turned to the empty fireplace. Empty for so long that in the moonlight shining through the hole in the roof, the fireplace looked no more that a rubble pit, yet still blackened with soot. She focused for a long time draining the last of her energy to form the summoning spell she needed. The fire that sprang to life was angry and dark red, the flames licked at her face before ebbing slightly.

"Why have you called me here?" A voice, the sound of burning bark growled at her. The face of her master, seen now within the flames, twisted and deformed.

"I have failed master, and now the Earth Maiden has your vessel," she replied meekly.

Silence followed, and Kerra soon thought her master had left her.

"The child should not have left the safety of its home, my Kerra. Go and hunt this...Earth Maiden down. Do not fail me as such again. Your powers serve me first and your heart's vengeance second. Remember this," and with that the flames were gone, and Kerra was now, left to shiver in the dark. However, sadness was not what she felt in letting her master down, she had a second chance and a smile sat upon her lips, and it was hungry for her enemy's despair.

Alex had left the abandoned cabin they had found in the woods after marching away from the escort carnage that his new master had commanded, and stood with the other in-scrolled knights around one communal fire. He did not shiver when not in her presence and his mind, hazy, screamed at him to remember who he was. Through the ever-constant voice filling his mind with dark thoughts he remembered one word, *Janian*, he just wished he could remember what it meant.

***

Adventure was something Jan had always craved, even as a child. When she had grown, those desires fueled the journeys her, and the friends she met along the way, for a great many years. Alex was the first she had met, so long ago now it seemed and it tore at her heart knowing she had fled and left him to his own fate.

The trees seemed to reach out and lower as she ran past them, as if they might hide her during her haste throughout their forest home. The trees, the earth, the water all linked to her gifts as an Earth Maiden. She could separate the silt in a puddle of murky water, or aid a village in choosing the spot for their well by asking the ground at their feet as to which area held the freshest source of water. The animals in a forest might show her hidden paths and safe places to sleep for the night should she but ask, and even the air she breathed, she could always sense the magic carried within the slightest breeze. Now however, it seemed, chased, as she was, that her powers worked without her knowledge or even asking. If she could be a spirit looking in from afar, she could have seen the path that was unfolding for her.

The voices where getting louder and the shouts more confidant as the enemy drew near. Janian was tired, and soon she knew her legs would be fooled no longer by what her mind told them, that they were not tired and that they should continue to place one foot in front of the other with great haste, was a lie her body was beginning to suspect.

With baby pressed close to her breast, Jan bust through the forest as if it expelled her from their protective embrace, and she found herself in a small meadow. The grass was ankle high and softly blew from side to side in the wind that danced around the circle of this tranquil area, void of trees save but one. The tree in the middle of the meadow was an ancient oak, and it looked at once out of place. Yet the tree was rooted comfortably with great massive branches that stretched well above the outer rim of other trees, and high into the sky above. The trunk was at least four men across from chest to chest and a calm wisdom emanated from within as Jan moved closer.

"Shelter, safety, shelter, safety," the great tree spoke within not only Janian's mind, but also deep within her heart, and she knew in that moment what was needed. The words she spoke where of a chant she had learned as a child, within a dream of a dream, when the Earth Mother spoke to her and her alone.

The aura emanating from the tree fell into harmony with the aura the Earth Maiden was now radiant with and without a thought of fear; she stepped within the tree, becoming one with the ancient power of the forest all around her. She began to drift asleep, sheltered from the outside world. She could see within her mind's eye the men that had finally caught up, but it was too late. All they could see was the meadow and the great tree, that to them, was just a tree and split up to continue their hunt. The forest felt no pity for the one who had to report their loss, nor did Janian.

CHAPTER 8

With great reluctance, the abused greyhound allowed Valis to clean it as best she could. The sun would be setting soon and with Ce'elevan's help, Valis managed to get a name from the dog, as it still refused to speak to her through the bond. "Sophal" was her name, and once cleaned up she was a beautiful yet starved greyhound. Soft pale fur and a face full of white, which bespoke her age.

With assurances from Ce'elevan that none here would harm her, Sophal settled into an uneasy sleep beside the fire Cecil had thrown together for them.

"Must you use that? There is plenty of other wood available," Valis scolded, sweeping her hand across the tree line not far off.

"This burns just as well," was Cecil's sullen response as he tossed another broken chunk of wood, gathered from the destroyed carriage.

"Still... Doesn't seem right," Valis half said to herself, so tired that the fight of this argument had left her quickly.

"This is a foolish place to be camping Princess and a fire will give us away just as easily."

Valis hung her head, his words made sense, yet, it was so cold, and they had to keep the sick greyhound warm.

"I... I just mean it would have been wiser to get away from here as quick as possible, the King must have sent men, scouts, out to look for you." Cecil said. His voice was calm now.

Valis, waited for Cecil to find his bedroll before shifting her gaze across the fire. She watched the rise and fall of Sophal's steady breathing. Relief flooded her; the greyhound seemed to be stable for the moment. Food would be a big help in the animal's recovery but she would have to wait for Ce'elevan or Cecil to go hunting as she herself was not very adept at living off the land...Or on the run. Where had this dog come from? And why was she locked away in that chest? She had Cecil drag it some ways off in the opposite direction from their camp, the wood, dark with a slight red sheen, not only smelled of dog offal, but gave her a feeling of anger and spite; she could not understand how.

"Were did you come from?" Valis tested through the bond, only to receive the same silent treatment as before. She shook her head in disappointment. She tried to cast out the questions from her mind long enough to give in to the day's exhaustion. Curling up with her knees to her chest as she had always done even as a child, she fell into a dream-filled slumber.

This was unlike any dream she had before, she felt not herself in the least. The eyes she gazed from where not her own, and the room at which they looked upon was not one she had ever set foot within. Two voices could be heard, one loud and one soft, and as Valis listened she could hear fear in what one of the women was trying to pass off as respect. The room, lit with lamplight, and a cool night breeze came in from the open window, at which the woman with the gentler voiced stood. Valis almost did not recognize the Princess of Carn. Worry was on her face, but it had yet to acquire the look of evil at which she herself had seen etched into this woman's at Cecil's trial. No this was a woman whose path to damnation was only just starting.

Across the room from the Princess Kerra, lay the other women to which the more vocal, more command filled voice had come from. She was pale, a sickness held a sheen of sweat upon her face. However, despite being bed ridden this woman obviously controlled great power, which was the impression Valis got from her, that this woman would not go quietly into the night. Though, something was wrong, terribly wrong. Emotions flooded through her as she watched these two. She could not understand the words, but every gesture, every sound, and the tones to which they spoke, seemed to tell the story all the same. They were fighting, these two women, each passionate about what they had to say but she felt suspicion from Princess Kerra, something told her not to trust this one, the smells she gave off where unpleasant and not from personal hygiene but deeper, from within the soul of this women.

A vase smashed against the wall and the frustration from the woman within the large bed was overpowering and it made Valis flinch back against a wall in fear. She did know this woman! Her temper was legendary. It was not since her uncle had married her that Valis had seen her last, the Queen of Carn. Kerra, the distasteful one as she would call her from now on, spewed a final string of words before barely bowing and quickly slipped from the bedchambers.

Valis wished she could comfort the bed-ridden woman for she looked as though all she wanted to do was cry, and yet the stoic expression that followed made it clear that such an act would not happen. This is when the Queen looked over at Valis and her heart nearly stopped.

"Go with her, find my son, Sophal. I trust no one more than you, not even my own sister." The last word spoken with as much heartbreak as one could muster into a word and yet the tears still would not fall. The words, spoken through the bond, and as Valis left the room, for the door was always kept ajar, she paused in the hall to consider this. With determination, she finally moved on with her task. She followed the scent of the Princess Kerra through the castle and down into a courtyard below. The next moment, Valis was feeling hands at her waist and she

tried to bite at the one who held her. Carried roughly, and shoved into the chest she had asked Cecil to remove from their camp, the very one that Sophal had been found in. As the lid closed, her own eyes opened violently out of sleep, she sat up, now knowing who the dog across the fire was.

Sophal had opened one eye watching her through the dance of flames in the fire that separated them, "*now you know. Go back to sleep.*" The bond drifted the words lazily across the fire and Valis found she had no ability to argue and closed her eyes once again; this time however, no dreams came.

CHAPTER 9

Janian was calm in her slumber. Had she ever been this calm? When she was a child Perhaps? It seemed easy now to remember, each night, tucked into bed, cozy beneath the blankets; her mother sat by her side and read to her until she fell asleep. She had loved her mother's voice and it would drift along with her as she passed into the world of dreams.

"In dreams we find our hopes and joy, what is and what will be, and even what frightens us, scares us to our core, can be found when we close our eyes at night. You must face these nightmares, in the same way as you do the joyful dreams and in this, they will hold no power over you." Her mother would tell her. Therefore, when every night, once in dreamland, it was neither strange nor unusual, to see creatures from the softest rabbits bounding around her bed which now sat in a wide field of green, or to wake sitting atop a mountain to which she had no name for. Or neither was it strange to see shadows in a dark forest, an owl whose head could turn all the way around, staring at her with wide freighting yellow eyes. These she faced as her mother had instructed, and soon, the dreams of shadows and creatures that frightened her gave her no more pause than a deer drinking from the water's edge. This is how a child dreams. It was the woman who began to visit her, the one who at first had spoke not a word. She stood at the foot of her bed and accompanied her on her dreamland journeys, and when Valis gave the woman no more thought, that's when she first spoke.

"Greetings my child," the woman's voice was as peaceful as the wind through a willow tree.

"I am not your child, I'm my mother's child," Janian said with pity, for the woman must be confused, lost even.

75

"Truly," the lovely voice agreed. "But I am mother of your mother, and your mother's mother before her, in fact I am the first mother, and you are all are my children."

This gave Janian time to pause and she set a logical mind to work. "What about the animals?" she had asked with genuine interest, as she now sat up a touch straighter in her bed.

"This is a smart question, and I'm so very proud that you would consider the forest folk, for you see Janian, they hold a special place in my heart. The animals of the world are family as well. My son was the first to create them and with a sacrifice now unheard of, gave his life so that they may live."

"Will you tell me of how this was to be? Do you miss him terribly?" Janian's question sparkled in harmony with her young eyes.

"I do not miss him, for he is not really gone. This is a story for another night, however." The woman smiled at Janian's pouty face. "I will teach you many things if you wish it, how to make the most muddied water drinkable once again. How to listen to the trees and animals of the woods, to heal with only a smile." Mention of the last lesson made Janian giggle; it would be many years later that she would realize the woman had made no jest. "Would you like that Janian?" The woman always used her full name when addressing her and she would never get used to it.

"I would like that, yes please." Janian replied politely nearly jumping out of bed with excitement, her hair fell in her face.

"Then you are chosen, Janian and I will teach you all I can and more." By the time Jan brushed hair from her eyes the women was gone. She slumped back into bed. When she opened her eyes again it was already morning.

These fond memories stayed with her, as she and the Prince sheltered together within the great oak tree. The tree itself must have sensed the presence of the Earth Mother within her dreams, of times long since gone, and it warmed having what must have been its own fond memories flood through it. As Janian's consciousness stirred, she wondered if the baby in her arms was dreaming as well. Soon she would need to find out what spell kept the child locked in peaceful sleep.

Magic, is what Janian's mind tried to recall. Soon, her thoughts became less heavy, and clouded within the protective spell of the tree. She should know how it worked fully; she trained not only with the Earth Mother but also by powerful teachers in their own rite, at the Earth Maiden's sanctuary. Jan's mind slipped back into slumber at the memory and soon she was standing once more upon the tall marble steps that wound an intimidating path to the top where the great hall stood, the dream state of the tree had sent her back again.

"Welcome child," the Prelate had greeted her, "you have arrived as one of our sister maidens discovered your gifts." The Prelate was an older woman, with hair hidden away in a tall black hat that Jan would soon learn was for ceremonies. The Prelate's smile was genuine however and she was the first and only person to whom she would tell of her early training as it slipped from her lips or so she thought, even though it felt quite natural to say.

"The Earth Mother has sent me; she comes to me in my dreams." The young women smiled innocently at the Prelate.

"We shall see," was the response she got, not cold or in anger but with little warmth as well. With that, Jan was led into the hall, and soon, Jan, had been assigned classes, and lodging.

Educated by the best, Jan thought, awaking slightly within the tree once more. Each time it was beginning to get harder to wake. Fear crept past the safety of the tree and shot through Jan's heart. *I should know what to do; I should know how to set us free once the dangers over.* She thought as she fought the urge to sleep once more. However, the answer would not come to her, and the tree offered no explanation. Jan knew they could not be guests within forever; life could not be in balance that way. Soon the great tree would want to be complete again. Moreover, she was starting to get angry that she lacked the knowledge on how to end this spell. The tree had given her the words to enter, but even it seemed to lack the way to let them leave.

She fought against the wave of fatigue that in the end sent her back to her dreams.

She was in class, sitting with other children around her age as they watched the water in the large stone basin that sunk into the middle of the floor, go from being filled with the dirtiest water they she had seen to the purest, clear water. The teacher, an Earth Maiden dedicated and skilled with water bonding was one of her favorites. She had excelled at all her classes, surpassing the other students within days in what should take an Earth Maiden in training, months to master.

She had learned not to mention her training from the Earth Mother in her dreams as the other students already disliked how quickly she advanced before them. Even moving to the classes with the older students only resulted in her being labeled a freak.

The scent of the surrounding forest filled her spirit on the harder days and she had always wished the gentle breezes that carried it would send her thoughts to the Earth Mother. They would tell her that she did not belong here and to come and finish the training she had ended upon her arrival here. They never did however, not that she was aware of, but it gave her an outlet for such thoughts, perhaps this tree had heard her wishes, felt her sorrow and upon meeting years later, took pity on her. It was nice to believe in these things but as Janian grew, she tried to keep her mind in the here and now and not look to the future as often. She knew the happiest days in her life so far, were the ones she had spent adventuring with her friends, after being sent from the school to complete her training. Janian struggled awake once more at the thought of what had happened with Alex, and the sorrow of Zhamar's inability to mourn the loss of his son.

Jan's sense of smell seemed intact within the oak tree and she took in the scent of the trees upon the wind as it passed by around them. She would very much have liked to send a message within the wind's wake, through the trees and to her friends. However, her friends did not have the magic or the understanding to receive such a message anyhow. It would take a bond with the Earth Mother.... Janian's spirit soared as an idea filled her mind, she only wished she could stay awake long enough to put it in motion. She prayed with all her heart and soul that the Earth Mother would listen to her prayers, just this once.

CHAPTER 10

Morning came despite the weary traveler's objections. As the humans scrambled about and bickered with each other, Sophal continued to rest, lying next to a cold fire pit, the flames long since moving on to their next lives, wherever that may be. Sophal had always wondered where the short-lived souls of flame went, when at last their flickering dance ended. For it was her understanding that anything with that much movement, that much passion, had to have a life, however short.

"Please stop that pacing, pup, you're making me nervous."

Ce'elevan's ears perked up and he barred his teeth in warning as he rounded on their newest companion.

"I'm not a pup!" he snapped.

If Sophal had been intimidated by her new counterpart's display, it was not shown in her movements or her voice.

"You have had what? Three maybe four seasons of hunt?" Sophal sounded more mocking than she had intended, but let her words stand.

"Five!" Ce'elevan said as he came near. *"I am head of the hunt... Or at least I was until my master was killed."* The dog hung his head.

"I had assumed the human girl was your master, surely not the boy."

"Valis, my master's sister, shares our gift of the bond. It is my duty to serve her and an honor to protect her. It's what my master would have wanted," Ce'elevan said without a fight.

80

"I'm the Queen of Carn's hound, raised by her own hand and no others. I recognize your loyalty, pup and I honor you for it."

"I'm not a pup. I told you, and besides my new master is royalty as well, a Princess. And she's the kindest and the bravest." Ce'elevan challenged but Sophal did to want to continue the sparing.

"So you share the bond with the girl... You heard all that was shown to her in the night then?" the older dog asked raising an inquiring eyebrow as she looked at her new friend.

"I heard... I'm sorry for the way..."

"Do not fret about the past, pup. I'm going to hunt down the sister of my master and when I find her I'll tear her throat out, and return the young prince home."

Ce'elevan was about to say something when Sophal cut him off, changing the subject once more.

"I will continue with my quest; I hope you will join me. I could use the help. These two however... They will only slow us down." She said staring hard at the two humans.

"I can understand your misgivings about them, especially the way you have been treated, but these two..."

"The boy smells as though he is unsure of every step he takes and the girl reeks of anger and vengeance... She will be blind without training." Sophal cut him off.

"Would you stop interrupting me? You know, for a royal dog, you lack the basics of manners," Ce'elevan scolded.

81

"I... Pup, it's just that..."

"I have told you, I am no pup! And as for the humans, they are quite capable; I have not only seen it but experienced their pain over the last few days. Both are after the same thing you are, the prince of Carn and they have worked damned hard to have made it this far. I will not leave without them.

Sophal sat in silence for a while as Ce'elevan continued to pace.

"'Damn' is such a human word." Sophal thought sourly.

"Why do they keep staring at us like that? It gives me the chills." Cecil shivered as he leered back at the dogs.

Valis paid her friend no attention as she took a final look around, "We should move towards Carn, I guess. Jan, we could really use your help right about..."

"We have to go, now!" came the message, blasted through the bond from Ce'elevan, so strong that Valis clutched at her head and almost doubled over as if she had been punched.

Cecil ran to her side taking her arm in support. "Valis, what's wrong? What's happening?"

"I don't know!" Valis groaned as she tried to steady herself with Cecil's help. "All I can get now is faint words, 'message' and 'hurry' something about the wind, I don't know. The bond had never been so loud before, but it's fading as the dogs gain distance."

Cecil stared in the direction at which the dogs took off and shook his head. "If it's nothing more than chasing rabbits then I say we leave them out there in the woods."

"Cecil," said Valis, her voice near to tears. "I'm scared."

The Squire helped the Princess to her feet and slung her pack over his shoulder opposite his own. "As am I, Princess... as am I."

They ran after the dogs for as long as they could, and they stopped to rest for short breaks along the way. As hard as they tried to catch up, they could not, the greyhounds were just simply too fast for them. However, occasionally one or both of the dogs would send a message to Valis through the bond and the pair would have to change course. Valis could tell if they were getting near or far judging by how close their four-legged friend's voices sounded within her head.

The day had marched forward and they were both tired with sweat dripping into their eyes as they struggled forward. Valis was so tired and yet so focused on the dogs that when Cecil grabbed her arm and yanked her into a deep thicket beside him that she gave a startled cry. Only her friend's eyes, calm but carrying a warning for silence keep her from biting into the fingers on the hand he had closed over her mouth. She followed his eyes as they moved in the direction he had pointed. It took her a moment to focus on what he was indicating but soon, there in the not so distant trees, a shadow moved. *No, not just a shadow, and not just a man,* she thought as Cecil slowly removed his hand from her mouth. Seeing a man in the woods would not normally be such a great cause for concern, the Princess knew that. However, it was much more than that which gave her concern at this discovery, and one particular detail caused her heart to skip a beat, the man wore the armour with an emblem of Petsky. This was a knight from home.

"Could it be a survivor from the escort?" Valis whispered as Cecil pulled her back down.

"Perhaps, or a search party for the kidnapped Princess," Cecil said mockingly.

For once, she was afraid he was right. She had truly hoped her father would not follow that course of action, but he was not the father she knew... not now at least, under these circumstances.

"So, what do we do? Wait for him to move on?" Valis hoped Cecil really did have the answer, but his face looked as panicked as she felt.

"We cannot let him know we are here." When Cecil glanced back at Valis, he could tell she wanted an explanation. "We or at least I am a wanted criminal. If we are going to catch up with that witch of a woman and insure the Prince's safe return to his mother, then we cannot risk this one man bringing the whole city guard down on us. Who knows how many others are with him."

"Knights... magic... don't trust... follow... east," were the words that trickled through the bond and into her mind. Whatever Cecil had said during this time she had not heard. She shook her head in an attempt to gain his attention and listen to her as she tried to get the words out quietly and quickly.

"Cecil, listen, we have to go east, the greyhounds say east. What do we do about him?" she said almost breathless, still tired from the run and for some reason she would have to puzzle out later, drained and tired after each use of the bond. Perhaps distance played a part, she was unsure but let it slide from her mind for now.

Cecil moved forward at a crouch, almost breaking cover before Valis reached for his arm.

"Cecil!" she hissed. "We cannot just kill him; he is still one of my father's knights!"

"Then what would you have me do Princess?" he snapped at her, a little too loud and he ducked back into cover for fear of having drawn the knights attention. They stayed silent until the man had past from view and they both let out a grateful sigh.

"We... We could knock him out, leave him tied up on the side of the road and then perhaps someone, a merchant wagon or something..."

Cecil scowled and drew the sword he acquired at the caravan site.

"You're a silly girl," he scolded. "Now, draw your sword," he hissed, nodding to the ornate sword at her waist.

Valis rushed to stay close to him as Cecil headed for the trees that had soon enveloped their target. They slinked from cover to cover as they pursued him deeper into the woods.

It was not long until they had caught up, as close as they could to the knight of Petsky. Cecil held his breath gripping his sword tight. His eyes saved his life as they caught the sudden glint of armour to his left, as another man moved through the forest. Now, there were two and confidence in his plan wavered. He made to move right and clearly spied a third man, this one dressed in the colors of a soldier of Carn. He cursed, as he had no other choice but to retreat to where he had left Valis a few dozen feet away.

From the shadows of their hiding spot, they watched and shared a confused look as the knight of Petsky greeted the two from Carn and conversed on which path to take.

Valis took hold of Cecil's arm and leaned in close to whisper.

"The dogs are near, they say the scent they have been following led to a glen not far to the east of here, but they say the soldiers are looking for the same thing as we are."

"What's going on? Looking for what?" he whispered back then watched as the soldiers, Petsky and Carn moved off to the east.

"What now?" Valis asked feeling as though her confidence had run away, far away from her mind, making it harder to rationalize their next step.

"For now Princess, you win. We follow," Cecil said through clenched teeth.

CHAPTER 11

"Wait," Valis instructed. They had lost sight of the men they had been following through the heavy woods and not for the first time.

Cecil waited impatiently as once more Valis sent out a call through the bond to the greyhounds that moved ahead of them.

"This way, hurry!" the young woman half hissed, half whispered.

After traveling so far in to the forest Valis knew she shared the same thoughts as her friend, even if he would not admit it. *I hope we actually have lost them.* Their luck so far had not been a helpful companion on this quest, as Cecil blocked her way with his arm and pointed. Perhaps six rows of trees in they could see the glen and within, their enemies.

"What's so special about this place? Why would the dogs lead us here?" Valis asked as the pair moved closer, still using the trees for cover as the men in the glen milled about, and each looking unsure as of what to do.

"Cecil?" Valis asked as she realized he had stopped advancing and was now white as the backside of a deer.

"Do you see that?" he asked in wonderment.

"Yes, I see them; I asked why they would be standing around," Valis replied, annoyed.

Cecil stared at her with such a dumbfounded look that Valis started to get mad at herself for not seeing whatever it was she was supposed to see.

"There!" he hissed, pointing.

Valis followed the line of sight from his outstretched finger. The only thing he could be pointing at was either the back of the enemy's head or the massive oak tree at which they stood in front of.

"OK... It's a tree, I still don't..."

"The Earth Maiden!" Cecil hissed with exasperation.

Valis brushed a loose strand of hair away from her eyes as she looked around, her blood now pumping faster.

"Where? I don't see her!"

"Are you blind? She's there, in the tree." Cecil stammered, "She has the Prince with her."

"What in the name of the Mother are you talking about?" Valis asked but went quite when Cecil tensed, as they had both heard the growl that caused the men before them to draw their weapons.

They watched as the enemy, two knights from Petsky as well as two soldiers of Carn turned to watch the sleek black form of Ce'elevan advance from the tree line, teeth bared and snapping at the air.

Two of the men whipped about as a growl approached from behind them out of the western trees. Sophal had arrived, the same wild look on her face as was on Ce'elevan's.

"Now, while the dogs have them distracted!" Cecil nodded at Valis.

"Cecil, wait I..." Valis faltered, her friend moved into the glen low and steadily approached the two men facing Sophal.

Valis wished she had a bond with Cecil at that moment so she could try to explain why fear was gripping her so tight she couldn't move. Her hand rested on her father's sword, still in its scabbard.

"Now, move, fast!" Ce'elevan's voice crashed through her mind, startling her awake from fears hold on her.

Cecil began to run and closed the distance between him and his prey within the span of one breath and his sword slid in and out again of the first knights back, he swung with all his might at the second who had hoped back, his sword crossed defensively across his chest. The tip of Cecil's sword sliced through the startled man's throat. The look in his eyes showed that he had not been prepared for Cecil's swift aggression.

Valis had run towards the other set of men, but her mind had not been as keen to kill as her friends had. When she approached, her hesitance had given the closest Carn soldier time to bring his sword to bear and parry the woman's first sword strike, sending her arm out wide.

Time seemed to slow. She was on the defensive now, being pushed back. The man was good and she knew her brother's lessons would not be enough to win the fight with this seasoned Knight. One strike, a parry, a second strike and her blade was knocked wide once more. The hilt felt slick in her hand. The Carn soldier stepped in seeing her off balance and Valis felt the heavy blow to her head as the man struck with his fist, spinning her to the ground and losing her sword in the journey.

Time still moved lazily as Valis struggled to her knees. She watched fate as it wove itself around her enemy's blade, now raised high. She knew death would be waiting with impatience. But death was cheated; he would have to be happy with the other exposed souls this day.

The tip of a sword pierced through the man standing ready to end Valis's life. Blood sprayed outward covering Valis's face, the warmth of life quickly cooled and she felt as though her own heat went with it. The sword was drawn out of the Carn soldier's chest through the hole that Cecil had put in his back and when he fell forward his eyes still held the look of surprise that would now haunt Valis till her final last breath.

Time sped back up and at first Valis just watched Cecil panting hard as he stood there, blood soaked and a crazed look to his face. Valis flicked her eyes over to the where the last of their enemies had stood only to witness the man's quick but painful demise at the mercy of the greyhound's jaws. It was a dreadful thing to see. When Cecil tried to help her to her feet she shoved him away, stumbled back and emptied the contents of her stomach and began to cry.

Cecil angrily turned and began thrusting his blade into the body's that lay still before them.

***

Janian, the Earth Maiden had watched from her prison sanctuary. Within the essence of the great oak she had wanted to scream out when the battle began, now all she wished for was the ability to shed tears. It was hard to watch the outcome of Valis's battle, Jan had always liked her best of her friend's children though she had never told the Princess that, Valis had reminded her of herself at that age and she had always tried to watch over her as well as the rest of royal family. It was killing her inside that she could not help. She seethed at her own weakness as she watched a large part of Valis's innocence drain away on that battlefield.

***

"How do I get you out?" Cecil asked as he looked to the old oak tree. Cecil wore a deep scowl upon his troubled face as he walked around the tree. He stood there with hands on hips as he continued to wrap his head around just what it was he was seeing. Thoughts of finding an axe and chopping his way to them came to mind but did not feel right and so did not linger long. Cecil shook his head after he had found himself staring at the tree as if in a trance. It had calmed him and this made him uncomfortable. He wanted to look away and he knew his mind was telling his body to do just that, but before it would obey his commands, his eyes began to notice a faint light etched into the trees bark. Without thinking or at least it had seemed that way, Cecil reached out and followed the now moving ray of light with his finger. The light line twisted and looped its way along the trunk of the mighty oak and Cecil allowed himself to fall into the calm trance as before, tracing his finger left and right, up then down and all around the tree only moments behind the light. When it finally stopped, Cecil was left standing behind the tree. His finger was warm as if he had dipped it in heated honey and when he brought his finger from the tree closer to his face for inspection the trance was lost. His finger was bleeding freely and when he looked to the tree he could see he had followed each intricate pattern and left blood in its place.

Cecil felt a longing to hear the voice filled with song that had been running through his head since he had approached the tree and the sudden quiet was unnerving. He felt as though if he concentrated hard enough he could still faintly hear it but even that was out of reach now.

"Blood magic."

Said a voice from the other side of the tree and Cecil was so confused by what had just happened that he stood as rooted to where he stood as the tree before him, and thus had to wait for the speaker to come around to him.

"Well done Cecil. I never suspected you had the gift within you." Janian spoke once more as she came around the tree.

"Janian... What in the Goddess's name just happened?" With eyes wide he barely controlled his voice.

"Blood magic." She repeated. "Ancient and of the Druid aspect of the Mother," Jan explained as she laid a comforting hand on Cecil's shoulder. She cradled the infant Prince in the other. "Everything needs balance, I had the magic to get in but you had to let me out."

"But, I..." Cecil could not finish the sentence; his mind was just in too many places all asking separate questions so he continued to stand where he was even after Janian had walked off. He had barley heard her mention Valis before she placed the baby in his arms and left. Now all he could do was look up at the ancient oak and beg to hear the song once more.

*****

Janian knelt down beside the Princess of Petsky, placing a hand gently on the young woman's back. "Valis," she said softly. "Everything's all right now."

Valis turned and threw herself into the Earth Maidens arms, just as she had upon seeing her friend back in the castle. Although, this time the tears where rawer and they did not stop for a long time.

"Easy now, it's alright, try not to make yourself sick," Jan said softly.

"I was so scared...We saw the remains of the escort, the carriage... Oh, Jan I feared the worst!" Valis cried all the harder. "Father will never let me come home now for my part in helping Cecil escape, and Cecil... Jan he's not the same, something wrong, what's going on? I wish the Goddess had spared Malik, he would know what to do."

"I know child; I wish he was here as well." Jan's own tears could not be contained now and the two women sat huddled in the middle of the grassy field. The ancient oak loomed over head, it would never again open itself up to magic as it had this day and now it returned to silently watching, as it would till the end of its days.

***

The power granted to Kerra was more than she felt she could contain at times. The power welled up and it felt as though she had been pushing it back for some time now. She knew the magic granted to her was strong but they had underestimated her own strength. She was the daughter of the most powerful of men and she was stronger now than even her sister... She should be Queen; she would be Queen, and rule at her master's side.

The more she used her powers the easier it was becoming to shape and to bend them to her will. After every single spell cast she felt lighter and more at ease with its use, controlling the darkness would even be considered relaxing and she smiled knowing her strength and power now knew no equal within these lands. The guards she had sent after the Earth Maiden had not returned and she could no longer feel the link her dark powers had granted between them.

Kerra had decided not to give chase, instead she would return home to Carn. It would be just as easy from there to continue her plot to pit Petsky and her homeland against each other, the Earth Maiden's abduction of her nephew, the royal Prince, would be enough for her to bring tensions to a head. Still, she would need to insure the Child's safe return. Her master's wish for the child's future would be one she could live with. The boy would not die; just become host to her master.

"The Earth Maiden still remains a threat, the cursed bitch!" Kerra shouted as she paced within the broken down cottage she had made shelter as she had waited for word back from her men.

She stopped and began to focus her dark powers, searching her mind for the visions of what she needed to succeed. Her master's gift to her was vast and her mind cried out at so much information. Spells and creatures long since past fill her mind, information that would have taken a Mage or Druid a lifetime to learn was pounding her senses so hard that she nearly blacked out. With a wave of near ecstasy, the visions became clear and Kerra knew what was needed.

Her hands began to radiate with the misty darkness as she chanted and formed the words she would need. When she could feel the power was enough she brought her hands together with a sharp clap which shook what was left of the cottage with thunder. When the dust settled she stood before a tear in the fabric of her world and she quickly took a few steps back least something from within reached out and took her. Two shadow cloaked figures stepped forth from the tear; they stank of dust and death and floated like wraiths on clouded feet.

"You two are the best at what you do; the darkness has told me this." Kerra greeted them by staring them both into the void of blackness coming from within their hoods. The two Wraiths only looked at each other before nodding their obedience at Kerra.

Kerra grinned, "go forth and seek out the Earth Maiden's head and return to me my nephew, alive, least you anger our master," she finished coldly.

94

"As you command," the voice that came out of the shadow cloaked figure sounded like an old rusty door hinge and without another word they sped off, floating on mist just below their ankles out of the cottage and into the forest beyond. They were as silent as the evening wind.

Kerra felt the light headiness she always got after casting and had to sit down beside the empty fire pit and began to laugh. The guards that remained outside the dilapidated cottage all smiled, happy that their master was happy. All the guards smiled except for one, who continued to scowl all the harder.

CHAPTER 12

Jan sat with Valis nestled up close, one arm wrapped around the young woman's shoulders. The fire she had Cecil make was burning bright and the wood they burned was dry. It cast a warm aura that battled the chill of the night. Valis, for all Jan's reassurances that they were safe now, could hardly stop shaking. So, she gestured for the dogs to sit with her for a while as well. Ce'elevan protectively draped himself across Valis's lap while Sophal made herself comfortable lying at her side.

When Jan was sure that she would be alright she moved to Cecil. He chose the great oak tree to sit under, his back against it, so she joined him. Jan could feel the heat from the ancient oak even before she sat, and more so as she slid along it to the ground.

"It's so quite now," Cecil said. Jan looked at him with a raised eyebrow.

"Oh, yes, after a battle you really notice and appreciate the calm." She sighed.

"After awhile you even begin to fear you'll never have this kind of peace again," Jan replied. She closed her eyes and rested her head against the tree.

"You did well today," Jan said breaking the silence once more. She was glad to be on the outside of the tree but she did miss the warmth that had flown through her and adjusted slightly to try and absorb more of the heat through her back.

"Janian?"

"Hmm?" she responded drowsily.

"What...what *did* I do today? Why was I the only one who could see you and the baby within the heart of the tree?"

Janian had almost forgotten, she had so quickly handed the child off to the squire and, opening her eyes she leaned over to check on the babe. Convinced the child still slept in its enchanted slumber she rested back against the tree and sighed deeply before granting Cecil and answer.

"It has always been the choice of the individual whether or not to follow in the path of the Earth Mother, Maiden or Druid. Somewhere down your family line a choice was made not to pursue the gift and through the years it may very well have been forgotten."

"As far as I know...no one has been an Earth Maiden or a Druid in my family. My father is a glass maker by trade. His father was one, my mother's side it's always been servants." Cecil shook his head in disbelief at Jan's suggestion.

Jan continued to listen as Cecil asked her questions regarding the Druid order, but as he talked she continued to flash back to the scenes of battle that happened just a while ago. The man was unflinching in taking a life and that could be a problem, still these were harrowing times and she did not feel the need to add to the young man's stress.

"They don't usually take on students so old, Cecil," she watched as a shadow darkened his face.

"However, I may know a few Druid orders willing to take you on."

"Thank you Janian," Cecil beamed now, even if a touch of the shadow still remained etched in his face.

He's been through a lot Jan... Show some faith. The Earth Maiden scolded herself as Cecil continued on.

"It's not like I have much else going for me," Cecil said once more downcast.

Janian caught the moment the squire almost shifted his gaze to the now sleeping Princess surrounded by the two greyhounds.

Another problem...for another time. She sighed and smiled with encouragement, but wished the glen would return to silence and for once this day it seemed she had received her wish. When the sun began to re-light the sky for morning a new set of problems where soon to rear up before them.

"Valis calm down!" Cecil begged as his friend angrily paced before them.

"Calm down? I am calm!" Valis shouted, forcing Cecil to shrink back.

"OK, we didn't mean..." Cecil stumbled.

Jan stepped forward.

"We only meant that the choice would ultimately be yours, we won't take offence should you choose to go home. I personally would... now don't look at me like that, you know it's because I care about you that I wish to see you home and safe with your father." Jan tried to cool her with these words but only seemed to have increased the woman's agitation. "I don't want any harm coming to you," she finished with a pleading sigh.

"My brother is dead!" Valis continued to shout. "And I intend to confront his killer. By the Earth Mother I will have answers from that piss poor excuse of a Princess before I squeeze the life from her with my own hands!"

Cecil looked foolish and hung his head.

"I'll cut down any who keep me from her with the steel of my father's blade," Valis slid the sword from its sheath.

Both Jan and Cecil took a step back in caution.

"I... I'm sorry, I didn't mean to..." Valis lowered the tip of her father's sword and stared in horror as the anger ebbed and she realized how far she had let it take her.

"It's settled then," Jan said holding her hands up in front of her to indicate they had moved on.

"Now, what about you two?" Jan asked the greyhounds, both of which were watching Valis intently, Sophal testing scents in the air with her long nose.

"They come with us!" Valis said looking at Jan with distaste. Jan, despite her concern for Valis's outburst let it go with a nod of her head.

"We head for Sanders Villa," Jan said evenly as her eyes watched Valis's hand until she fully restored the sword to its home. Still, she received the look she feared as the young Princesses' head snapped back up with an angry glare.

"Sanders....that's in the opposite direction, Jan!" Valis snapped.

"Valis you need to calm down," Cecil tried to interject which only earned him a scathing look as well.

"Listen," Jan began, "we need to resupply. Not to mention come up with a better plan than rushing head long into a fight we are not prepared for and Sanders Villa is the closest."

"Jan... What about soldiers and knights from the castle? They have to still be looking for us," Cecil asked as his eyes flicked nervously between the women.

"I don't think there would have been too many sent, even if he could, the king needs his forces close to home right now," Jan watched as both her companions gave a visible sigh. Her mind wandered on that topic and she found herself thinking of Alex, the fear in his eyes when last she looked upon him. *Please Alex; make it through this, just like old times.*

Ce'elevan had pressed himself up close to Janian's side and the Earth Maiden reached down to pet his neck. "Even without the bond, you greyhounds can still sense when you're needed," she said with a smile.

"Besides, there should be a Druid sect camped around the founder's stones in the hills behind the Villa, for the blessing of the season. We can ask them for aid." Janian made a point of looking at Cecil when she spoke and she could see both the excitement and the apprehension warring amongst his soft features.

When they finally left the Glen, Cecil let Valis and the dogs take point and he fell into step alongside Janian who seemed to be lost in thought, her brow locked in a permanent frown since they started out several hours ago.

"Jan, can I asked you something?"

100

The Earth Maiden stopped frowning long enough to look at Cecil and smile weakly. "Of course."

Cecil nodded his thanks, "What do you think will happen should the Druids not accept to train me? I mean I'm older than most their students right?" Cecil waited for her nod before continuing. "What I mean to say is...would you train me? Should they say no?"

"Oh Cecil, were it possible it would have been an honor to teach you myself."

"But you can't?" the young man asked with hurt and confusion mixed within his voice.

"Although both the Earth Maidens and the Druids gain their abilities through the earth and thus from the Earth Mother herself, the mother of us all, the Druids are granted a different aspect of that power." Jan began but paused when Cecil looked more confused than ever before.

"Let me try to explain." Jan raised a hand slightly begging for patience.

"Take winter and summer for example, they are both of nature and yet are opposite in effect."

"How so? I mean I understand the difference in the seasons I'm afraid that I'm just not understanding your meaning." Cecil stated as they continued to walk.

Jan gave a smile, "Well, for a start, Fire. Earth Maidens are forbidden to create or wield flames of any sort. Whereas the Druids can almost make it dance at their command. There is always a balance and in this balance lays all things. One is able where upon the other is not, do you understand?"

"But they can touch water, they need it the same as you or I," Cecil continued as he ignored Jan's last question, his mind already working ahead.

"Ah, they can touch it, drink it, yes. But can they use magic with it? No. It's balance Cecil, despite an oath not to, I can still touch fire, but if you have noticed...it's also rather hot." She gave him a wink and Cecil rolled his eyes in playful exacerbation.

"And as far as drinking it, well I can't say that's a good idea, and..."

"Alright!" Cecil protested with a laugh, "I get it. I hope the Druids answer my questions without so much sass," he playfully chided her bringing a hurtful look to Jan's face, who then quickly reached over and tousled his hair.

When Cecil pulled away he tried to smooth his hair back down and the smile quickly left. "Jan...It...It, what did you do, it won't go back down!"

Jan left her young friend spluttering in frustration as she quickened her pace to go catch up with Valis and she was still chuckling when she caught up. The cold look Valis shot her told her she did not approve but Jan stayed at her side despite this.

"That young man has great potential, I can feel it," Jan said pleasantly. "I really do wish I could train him myself."

"You shouldn't tease him," Valis said.

Janian raised an eye brow in question and a sharp smirk soon followed.

"Cecil tends to hold onto things until they eat him up inside." Valis said while glancing back over her shoulder at her now follicle-challenged friend who was now walking with his hands on top of his head to keep his hair down.

"Oh...clever," she finished as she paused for a step before following; the lesson Jan had just shown her had finally sunk in. She had done the same thing, let it all pile up inside, and she had lost her temper.

"I'm not here just to look pretty my dear," Janian laughed.

"You care for him I think, more than you will admit. That's why the idea of him sending you home struck such a chord within you, to bring up so much anger. I've know you all your life Valis and that was the first time I have seen you truly angry."

"Yes, I only wish..." Valis's face suddenly was overcome with the heat of a full-on blush. "No, no, it's not like that! I only meant that I feel responsible largely in part for his exile!" Valis said waving her hands in front of her, eager to erase the confusion.

"You think I shouldn't have sent Ce'elevan with the keys? We should have left Cecil to die?" Jan asked shaking her head in mock confusion.

"No. Of course not! But it was my father that sentenced him!"

"Do not be too harsh on your father, he and I go a very long way back. We have been friends much longer than you have been alive. I'm not convinced your father would really have sent Cecil to the noose." She finished by making sure Valis was looking in her eyes, so she could see the honest truth within them, hear the words issued from her lips.

"More the reason to kill the Princess of Carn." Valis replied, her foul mood finding hold

once more.

They continued to travel in silence. Every once in a while one of the greyhounds would

wander back to report in, then take back off down the trail, or dart into the trees.

CHAPTER 13

"A rabbit, honestly, are you a royal dog?" Sophal chided Ce'elevan as the two padded along a long forgotten game trail, forgotten to all except the rabbit that the younger of the two greyhounds had bolted after.

"They have to eat as well," Ce'elevan snapped as the rabbit in his jaws finished its struggle.

"Yes, well a lot of good it will do them if we can't find our way back, the girls link through the bond is different than the one I share with the Queen." Sophal droned as she scanned the area with keen eyes and a sharp nose.

"Well," Ce'elevan paused, *"If you are truly a royal dog, as you claim, then I don't see how we could possibly be lost."*

"Well played, pup." Sophal tilted her head as she looked up at him, flecks of dirt falling from her nose.

"I am not a pup!" Ce'elevan growled, out of the corner of his mouth. *"Did you not let a human put you in a chest?"*

"You know it's not considered polite to snoop around other people's dreams, my story was meant for the girl, not a pup who has took too long hunting one little rabbit," Sophal replied coldly before once more lowering her nose to the path.

"For the last time, I am not a..."

"Quite!" Sophal hissed through the bond.

They had been traveling parallel to their human companions for most of the journey, scouting ahead but mostly remaining out of sight. However, Sophal had been with them long enough to know their scent, and the stink that assaulted her as the wind shifted was definitely not one of them.

"Hide!" she tried not to shout, even through the bond it was like standing next to each other, the bond working far better between the dogs than it had ever with the humans.

Both greyhounds darted under thicker bush just off the game trail, fallen branches and broken twigs jabbed at them as they got as low as they could. Neither gave a yelp in pain as sharp thistles scratched at their legs and underbellies. Sophal snapped at the air tasting the same foul odor to confirm its presence, she was a warrior queens hunting dog and she knew the scent of danger.

With sudden fear both dogs looked on at the rabbit Ce'elevan had dropped in the middle of the path and Sophal had to nip at him as he made to break cover to retrieve it.

"Leave it!" she hissed.

"Why don't we just run? There is nothing in this wood that can keep up with us."

"Because I want to know what it is I smell, if it's a bigger threat then we can handle then we need to get back and warn..." before she could finish both the dogs trained their eyes out onto the other side of the trail, two shadows blurred through the trees, too fast for any human eyes to have seen.

"What was that?" Ce'elevan asked in a shaky voice.

"Hush!"

At first nothing more occurred but before they could move the shadows returned, and once they had stopped they took on their more human forms. One of the shadows knelt, legs still floating in dark mist and leaned over to hover above the abandoned rabbit on the path. Neither dog caught the motion of the shadow when it had shifted its gaze in their direction and it was this that without a doubt saved them as they remained motionless in the underbrush.

The second shadow hissed like rain off hot rocks at its companion and just as quickly both had blurred out of sight once more.

"What were those things? I have never hunted such a creature." Ce'elevan asked more to himself then to Sophal but she answered him nonetheless.

"Evil, pup... that was pure evil." there was another scent in the air, one she was familiar with and she knew who opened the veil those creatures called home.

"Let's go, fast as we can now, we have to get back to the others!"

Before they left Ce'elevan stopped to grasp the rabbit once more clutching it in his teeth. The look Sophal had given him could have turned a kitten away from its milk.

"What?" Ce'elevan asked with his head tilted, *"why waste it?"*

CHAPTER 14

They arrived at the Villa three days later. Travel had been long and tiring but Jan tried to keep their spirits up with tales of her past adventures. Valis was particularly interested as most of them involved a side of her father she had never known existed.

"We can resupply here, move on to the druids for further aid and then..." Jan stopped as they passed the Villas entrance. There was not much to see, it was the dead of night by the time they had arrived and the lack of a greeting or even a warning had unnerved her, *"no guards, not even a sleepy watchman,"* she thought.

"Jan... how are we supposed to pay for supplies? Valis and I have no coin on us to speak of, unless we sell our swords... or the dogs," Cecil smirked, until the look Valis shot him melted it off his face.

"Leave that to me. "Jan said as she continued to scan the area. "I doubt the King would have sent anyone this far out yet and so we can rely on Valis's status as one of the kingdoms Princesses, send her signed invoices to the King." Jan raised her hands before the protest she knew Valis was about to unleash had a chance to flare, "we will be long gone from here by the time the King gets the bill." This seemed to placate the Princess for now; at least she had stopped turning an angry red.

"Then we should get some horses as well," Cecil grumbled as he stretched, hands on his lower back.

"Let's not push our luck, all the same leave the talking to me when we are in the shops..." Jan replied but something was still bothering her and she let the words hang in the air as she once more wondered what was wrong.

"No guards at the entrance. Streets are empty of people... not even a street lamp lit." "There's no light at all," Jan spoke aloud.

"That's not normal?" Valis asked.

"Where are the dogs?" The sudden panic in her eyes made Valis take a startled step back before answering.

"I'll...I'll ask, give me a moment."

"Jan... did you just see that?" Cecil asked, pointing to a small house amongst others of its size that lined the Villas Street.

Jan turned and followed the man's line of sight and at first had seen nothing.

"We don't have a moment, Valis." Jan said as a hiss. "Run!" she shouted as she twisted around and shoved her younger friends out before her, spurring them to make haste.

"We can fight! We won't leave you here!" Valis said defiantly as she tried to turn and follow Jan back into the dark streets, but when the Earth Maiden looked at her with eyes full of command she froze in her spot, only moving when Cecil came back to grab her arm.

Jan could see the panic in the young woman's eyes; she said nothing as the pair quickly moved back out the way they had arrived.

Jan stood before the two shadows, formed now as the bodies of men as they cautiously approached, she held her head high.

"Your release from the darkness is forbidden," they continued to press forward. "By the Earth Mother's grace I command you to return from whence you came," her command made them pause or at least the mention of the Earth Mother did. Shadow was a part of everything and these creatures should have heeded her command. The use of such magic to bring these creatures out however had been forbidden for more than four hundred years. The punishment for such a breach was death, and the job fell to the nearest Earth Maiden, should such a need arise.

"Our master grows in power as we speak, soon not even the Earth Mother will be able to stop our saturation into her darkness," spoke the one in a voice soft as wind.

"Soon, people will have no choice but to walk amongst the shadow filled streets as we will blacken and consume the sun..."

"The moon..." the first shadow continued.

"And even the stars!" the second finished, reaching above his head to mimic the gesture of covering the light of the stars. And for a moment Jan though she had seen a few blink off into nothingness.

"Even the blackest of pitch cannot hold back the smallest of the Earth Mother's light, not forever." As Jan spoke; she slowly drew her hand out of one of the pouches at her side hoping she had chosen the correct one among the many around it.

She could smell them now, which was an odd thing to able to do with a shadow, yet the stink of them was strong and she nearly gagged. A few more breaths and they would be close enough to strike her, she did not waver in her stance and if she could read whatever minds these creatures had she imagined they would be calling her a fool. But Jan was no fool, and she knew it was hope she clutched tightly.

Valis yanked her arm from Cecil's grip long enough to fling herself against a tree as they headed into the forest and into cover.

"We can't stop now; Valis, we have to get further away!" Cecil pleaded as he reached for her arm once more.

"We cannot just leave her there to die! I won't!" Valis yelled between big gulps of air.

"If Jan can't handle whatever those things were then what chance do you think we have?" Cecil angrily flung his arm out pointing back down the path.

"I made a promise Cecil, a promise to myself that..." her words ended in a groan of pain as Valis grabbed her head and dropped to her knees.

"Valis!" Cecil hissed as he knelt and wrapped a protective arm around her shoulders

"It's the dogs! Both of them are yelling at me through the bond. They won't slow down, hard to make out. Shadows... forest... they are not far, the river! They are coming to us along the river's edge!"

Cecil had his doubts that even with the aid of the two greyhounds that they stood much of a chance against something supernatural. He got Valis to her feet and they walked as fast as they could move until Valis said she was alright to run. So they set back off through the trees as fast as they could with only the light of the moon whipping by above the tree tops to guide them.

***

"Hope is grown within the heart of those confronted with unyielding despair, when the only way out of a situation is to fight back against that which would keep hope from blooming."

Janian remembered in a moment her lessons as a young student, learning as much about the earth around her as she could. She loved learning the names of every plant and the varied, multi-coloured birds and animals. It was the herb lore, plants and flowers that had always piqued her interest. Which to pick that would sooth a tooth ache, how many aloe roots would make enough paste to fill a wound. Now, as she faced her foe in the darkness she gripped hope in her fist, her favorite flower of all: the star burst.

Janian's mind flashed to the first time she had encountered the flower, only one and yet its power was great enough that she had spent a week blind for refusing to look away. Everyone had gathered for the star burst's bloom. Her botany instructor had tended to only the single flower that sat in her class room in what everyone had thought was an empty pot. Until the time for the lesson on using the Earth Maiden's power, a power to help plants reach maturity at a quicker pace. Everyone was given seeds to a less exotic plant including Jan herself.

"Let the mothers power flow through you, fill the seed with life and watch it grow," her teacher had instructed and at first nothing had happened. Until one girl let out a gasp, her seed had split and from the center a small sprout had greeted the early morning sun.

Jan tried to concentrate on the tiny seed; it sat in the crease of her palm, along the life line as instructed. However, as much as she tried to feel her powers and urge them into the still seed, she was the last to complete the task. Jan had been just as confused as the rest of the student Earth Maidens for she was gifted and excelled at all her instructions save for this one simple task. For the first time since she had arrived, Janian felt frustrated and she focused all the harder, searching for the Earth Mother's voice inside her head to guide her along the task.

But she heard nothing.

Fear began to grip her, had she done something wrong? Had the Earth Mother abandoned her for her assumption that she was something special? And then as the panic peaked she heard it, not the voice of the Earth Mother but another, a softer voice. Although, as she focused on the sound she realized that it was not as such...it was music, soft and warm and she could sense its origin. She carefully placed the seed in her hand into her teachers and closed her palm over top as she moved, in a daze towards the music's source.

The earth colored pot that sat upon a simple wooden table beside the teacher. Her own pot with the star burst seed inside that now sang to Jan as clearly as if another living person were standing beside her.

Jan barley heard the drone of her teacher's voice as it shouted at her to leave that seed alone. Not ready was she and soon the music drowned out the sounds of her fellow students. Who were scrambling in panic to turn and shield their eyes, for the tiny seed shot out of the dirt as a drowning man would gasp for air. The moment it did the flower bloomed in all its glorious light, yellows and intense white was all Jan had witnessed before she felt hands grip her shoulders and pin her to the ground. The others where panicked and her teacher was screaming for the healer. They thought she would be blind for good but the Earth Mother's healer worked hard. She could still see the effect of the flowers bloom when she closed her eyes for months to come; it was very hard to sleep.

And now, as she did then, Jan felt the power rise up within her, listened for the song of the star burst and let the power course down through to her fingertips she flicked her hand out toward the two shadow assassins.

They stood there, the summoned creatures, more shadow than darkness, confidant and unflinching as the woman before them, their enemy, their prey, threw a handful of seeds at them. They looked first to the ground and then back up just in time to catch a small glimpse of their prey sprinting away before the seeds sprouted at their feet. White hot light blinded them instantly their rusty voices screeching out in pain. They clawed at their shadowed skin as it burned and wisps of darkness where singed away in the light of the star-bursts full bloom.

"Cecil, wait!" Valis pleaded as her tired breath choked the words. "We have to slow down. I can't keep up this pace with the child on my back." She patted the pack on her back with the sleep-spelled young Prince within.

"Ok, we catch our breaths and wait for Jan..." the words no sooner out of his mouth when Janian came silently dashing through the trees behind them.

"We have to keep moving; the Star-bursts' won't last long, not against magic that old!" Jan finished as she helped Valis out of the pack and slung it over her own shoulders.

"How did you get away? Or catch up to us so fast...or even...?" Cecil sputtered his eyes wide.

"What won't last, Jan? What, in the name of the Goddess were those things?" Valis asked as she followed behind the Earth Maiden.

"They looked like shadows that moved on their own," Cecil said behind them as he jogged to catch up, casting a nervous glance over his shoulder back the way they came.

"Where are the dogs?" Janian asked ignoring their questions.

"Ce'elevan says they are along the river heading toward us," Valis offered.

"Tell them to stay put we will come to them."

The small band continued to head upwards through the most clear-cut paths they could find, the sound of the rushing water was struggling to reach them through the trees when Jan called them to a halt, holding up her hand for silence. They all heard it, the wailing sound of the shadow assassins and both Cecil and Valis looked to Jan for answers.

"They still give chase, we *must* hurry!" Jan shouted.

When they finally breached the tree line they found themselves assaulted by the roar of the river's water. It raged westward before cascading downward in a grand waterfall. The moon was bright in the sky here in the clearing but Jan knew it would not be near enough light to protect them.

The shadow's wails died down and were replaced with the hiss of mist. They all moved back towards the water's edge Jan warning them not to get to close. The water raged hard here and there would be no escaping that undertow.

"There, in the trees!" Cecil blurted out as he pointed to the tree line, "and again, there!"

Both the assassins had moved to the edge of the forest, sliding in and out of the shadows as if testing the safety of the open river bank. When they discovered the light off the moon was not enough to hurt them, they swept out, rushing their prey.

"Close your eyes!" Jan shouted.

With both Cecil and Valis's eyes shut tight Jan stepped forward and the shadow men slowed.

"No more tricks witch," the one on her left hissed.

"Accept your fate, you don't have the power to destroy us," the one on the right warned.

"You underestimate the light and grace of the Earth Mother," Jan spat at them at the same time throwing the last handful of her star-burst seeds behind her into the waters of the river. So much of her power did she feed into them that Jan dropped to her knees drained and from there she prayed the moon would reflect the water well enough for her plan to work.

The assassins moved in for the kill a moment too late as a mighty shaft of light silently shot out of the water, bathing them all in its light. The last of her seeds had forced the shadow men to retreat back behind the tree line. But the blast of light had not lasted long and it moved quickly away as the river washed the seeds down.

It had bought them little time, one last effort to destroy them, and she had failed. With the seeds gone she had no other way of fighting the darkness of these dark magic born creatures. Jan wished her friends would keep their eyes closed and not see their death approach.

The hiss of the creatures as they neared was met suddenly with the angry growls of two greyhounds that had now darted protectively between them.

The shadows made their move, ignoring the dogs they rushed in. Wisps of shadow still smoldered off their bodies from the damage off the light burst, but as before the light of the moon had no apparent effect.

"Protect the child!" Jan shouted and if the dogs understood her, they listened now. The shadows split their attack, one glided after Jan who quickly thrust the pack with the sleeping babe into Cecil's arms and told him to run as fast as he could. "I will hold them off..." Jan never finished as she was forced to dodge back away from her attacker.

The greyhounds followed after Cecil barking and snapping at the legs and heels of the shadow that pursed them, the shadows dissipated between each snap of angry jaws.

Jan did the only thing she could think to do and called the power of the Earth maiden to her once more. She was so tired that she nearly fell to the ground. The powers answered her call after all and she used it to gather a torrid of water from the river that shot out so fast she had at first thought she failed. But as she looked back at the shadow it had begun to smoke from where it worked to manipulate around the water as it crashed through its body. The wound was short lived as the hole closed over in shadow once more. The assassin reached out and grabbed a tight hold on Jan's wrists. Thick dark veins began running up her arms and Jan gasped in shock and sudden pain.

Cecil had his own problems as the assassin pursued him despite the dogs attacking its heels and legs. Sophal leaped for the creature's throat but passed through its body like a drunk through a smoky tavern.

Cecil clutched the baby in its pack close to his chest. His body tensed, reading the body language of the assassin, he knew it would be over soon. He had one last deep breath before his feelings gave way to truth and the shadow lunged forward, arms outstretched, mist swirled around Ce'elevan. The greyhound went silent, shivering as he came out the other side.

Jan had turned her attention briefly to catch site of Cecil and her heart nearly stopped. She tried to shout out but the pain was too great and she hated herself for not being able to do something. She cried out for the Earth Mother's guidance.

Her answer was delivered in the tip of a sword.

Valis had swung her father's sword, the tip just nicking the assassin's throat. It was enough of a shock for both defender and assailant. The darkness drained from Jan's arms and wrists and its hands broke free their grasp upon the Earth Maiden.

Valis, was quicker to recover and delivered an overhand strike down upon the creature's hand as it pulled away from Janian. The blade in the Princesses' hands shimmered with blue fire and the shadow assassin reeled back wailing in the pained hiss they had heard earlier. The severed limb evaporated and the arm did not grow back. The creature panicked and tried to retreat but Valis managed to jab her sword into the back of its shadow-blurred leg and the creature stumbled.

Jan, sucking in air tried to gain enough of her breath back to shout out to Cecil but it was too late, the man stumbled, not realizing how close to the river he had been forced. When the assassin rushed him Cecil lost his footing. The edge of the embankment crumbling under his heel and baby, squire and assassin tumbled into the fast-moving rapids of the river.

"No!" was all she had mustered, her throat still closed with pain and fear and she flung herself down reaching over the edge and dipping her arm elbow deep into the cold water.

Valis had turned to Jan at her outcry and spun to look for Cecil; she forgot about her sword and forgot about the enemy. Her mind filled only with the mental image Sophal was sending her of what had just happened to her friend and she dropped to her knees screaming and cursing, her anger returned and she knew where she could direct it. When she turned around coming up on one knee she yelled again for the enemy had fled back into the protective shadows of the dark forest.

"Earth Mother, hear my prayers, guide my hand through your rivers water, and let your power flow through me," Jan begged, and she felt the sudden rush of power flow through her arm from shoulder to fingertip. The cold water drained her strength fast but in its place, she gained a sight beyond sight and her vision blurred showing her the path under the river's surface. Quickly did her watery sight lock onto what did not belong, there...being speed toward the water's edge, Jan had enough time to see Cecil, the baby, and the shadow which now clung to Cecil's back, latched on as tight as a normal human shadow, as they all slipped out over the waterfall.

Jan had thought them lost at that moment but she could not bring herself to lose the power flowing within her and bonded with the river. She found the strength to turn her hand; palm upwards as she focused on what she hoped was not too late. Her water sight rushed forward so fast she gasped but it had done its job. Jan pushed the Earth Mother's power through and along the bottom of the river and when it reached the base of the falls she jerked her hand up and through the water sight, watched as great geysers burst upward to catch her falling friend. As soon as Cecil was lowered softly into the waters at the waterfall's base, Jan took one last breath heard Valis's worried voice and slipped into darkness.

CHAPTER 15

Kerra's link to her shadow assassins was broken and she cursed in panic as she fell to the floor, her neck seared with pain and she clutched at her wrist in confusion, watching as a trail of fire burned itself in a thin line around her wrist, all feeling lost in the hand below. She badly wanted to call out for her master but remembered how cross he had become at the last time she summoned him. No, she would figure out what happened on her own. She worried about whether her hand would dangle useless with no feeling for the rest of her life.

Leaning heavily on her one good hand she slowly, body shaking, returned to her feet. As she looked at her lifeless hand she once more thought to call her master and used a flicker of her power to re-light the now empty fire place.

Before the words formed in her mind she cast the spell aside, instead a wicked grin had joined the shadow upon her face and her eyes flicked over to the cottage's still standing door.

"I should have done this prior to sending the assassins," Kerra said aloud as a figure opened the door and stepped inside.

"Close the door, Alex." She directed the man who had come at her bidding through the hold she had over his mind.

Alex said nothing but merely obeyed the arbitrary orders, he said less than the other men still under her control. His face remained as calm and unreadable as a slick river stone.

"You will tell me everything I need to know, knight of Petsky."

"Yes," he answered.

"You will tell me about the Earth Maiden, the one you helped aid in the theft of my nephew," Kerra stated as she turned her back on him.

Alex's face showed emotion for the first time in many hours and only then in the slight narrowing of his eyes as he looked over at his new master.

"I can sense the struggle within you to resist me. This is unwise knight, I could just as easily strip the answers from your mind if I should wish it," Kerra said as a hiss as she whipped back around to face him.

"What is the Earth Maiden's name?" she asked sweetly.

"Janian Poledouris."

Kerra raised her eyebrows in surprise; the knight had let the answer out without hesitance. Perhaps he was not as strong as she had first thought. Then it struck her as the name sank in, she had been told it once before but had paid it little mind. Perhaps she was the fool, as the man who stood before her already knew she had the woman's name and so there for gave it freely. *Clever* she frowned.

"You know of this woman? She is a member of the court?" Kerra began anew.

"Yes, I know of her, no she is not an official member of Petsky's court." Again Alex spoke the truth, the exact words his new master wanted to hear, nothing more and he waited as she circled around him studying him, judging him.

"What is your relationship to the Earth Maiden," began the new line of questions.

When no response came, Kerra came around to look Alex in the eyes, "I asked you a question knight, did you not hear me?"

"Friend," Alex said meeting her gaze.

"You are just friends? Or... lovers?" she moved in close flicking her tongue out to lick Alex's top lip.

When the knight made no response to the question she took a step back, her face swayed from lust to anger within a breath.

"You will tell me." Kerra asked, her impatience growing.

"You will tell me now or I will rip the answer from your mind!" she shouted in Alex's face.

Kerra took a step back in her fury and unleashed her power, flailing through the knight's mind. A small trickle of blood fled from Alex's right nostril and yet his face remained expressionless. The Princess Kerra of Carn, Sorceress of the dark magic's grinned from ear to ear.

***

A memory is what brought Janian from the darkness and once more into the light. She was young, not long out of her training with the Maidens. Zhamar was with her, as was his friend and personal guard, Alex. The three of them had ridden out at the rumours of adventurers disappearing near the lake of Narin. Something had spooked her horse and she had fallen heavily to the ground. The sun was in her eyes, she remembered that annoyed her most of all. And she also remembered the silhouette of a man, in the sun's light, angry at his interference shone bright around him as he bent toward her, hand out stretched and suddenly, Alex's face had appeared, smiling down at her. She reached out and knew he had said something but could not remember the words and just as her hand touched his she awoke.

A deep breath was her first task, her side hurt from where she had fell against the water's edge and there was a young woman helping her to her feet.

"Valis," she said finding her voice. Her head throbbed from the overuse of the Earth Mother's gift, but the memory of recent events flooded back and she grabbed a firmer hold of the princess of Petsky's arms, so much that Valis winced in pain.

"Where is Cecil? Where is the baby?!" Janian let go as she turned and was planning on running to the waterfall's edge but her legs were not strong enough and she fell to her knees. Tears welled in her eyes at the uncertainty of her charge's respective fates, she had done all she could, but had it been enough? She was muttering this out loud when Valis rushed once more to her side.

"They are fine Jan, you saved them!" Valis reassured the weeping Earth Maiden as she knelt beside her.

"I had only just turned to see the Assassin, the one I wounded with father's sword as it fled back into the forest and when I turned you where already unconscious on the ground. I went to you first, pulling you from the dangers of the water's edge and at the same time trying to understand what Ce'elevan was shouting at me through the bond. They are safe Jan, Cecil and the baby Prince survived the fall, thanks to you. The dogs are escorting them back up here to us through the forest path below as we speak."

Janian slumped back to the ground as she tried to steady her emotions, falling back on her training with the maidens to breathe in the good calm air and slowly breathe out the turbulent.

"I remember Alex talking about your powers to father when I was younger, I'm sorry I missed it," Valis winced as Janian's expression became clouded.

"I...I'm sure he's ok Jan, if any of the knights... I'm sure he is."

Janian nodded slowly and her reply was calm.

"He is, for now. But I can feel him slipping from me; he will have to find his own way back."

***

The night had continued on its sojourn regardless of the affairs of neither man nor beast and it had become very late by the time the greyhounds had guided Cecil back up the forest path to where Jan and Valis waited.

"What is that?" both Cecil and Ce'elevan asked, one out loud and the other through the bond.

Valis knew both questions where directed at her and she did give up a chuckle with the shrug of her shoulders for she knew they were commenting on the weak and struggling fire Janian had made her create. Despite her protests that she had no real skill at such things she still went out and gathered the wood for the fire. Despite Janian's oath to never create or touch fire, she had still adventured long enough to instruct her young friend in its creation.

Or so she had thought.

"What would you know of making a proper fire?" Valis shot back at Ce'elevan.

"Yes, do tell us pup as I don't recall fire being an issue of ours," Sophal added, lying down beside the weak flames.

"I have seen it done many... look I am not a..." Ce'elevan snapped irritably but stopped short as everyone turned at once the moment Sophal had yawned. All eyes watched as the greyhound snapped her mouth shut, the fire went out.

"Cecil, would you be so kind?" Janian asked politely.

Valis could only shake her head in apology when Cecil walked by rolling his eyes at his friend.

Once Cecil had returned it was not long before the fire was high and bright, fuelled properly and dancing its protective dance that kept the shadows at bay. Janian had talked with Cecil about the type of magic she had used as she sat with the young Prince, wrapped tight and warm on her lap.

"How long do you think the Prince will sleep?" Valis asked the greyhounds.

"Spelled by Princess Kerra? Well, you saw what she had done to me with that chest. I imagine it will take powers that are equal, to break it." It was Sophal who had answered as Ce'elevan had drifted off to sleep beside her and she gently stroked his black coat, she noted the silver flecks on random strands of hair shinning with the light of the fire.

She had figured Janian if anyone would have that power. And yet, the Earth Maiden had made no attempt to wake the babe. Valis trusted her; no other had been more like a mother to her since the passing of her own. She shook those thoughts from her mind, she did trust her, she reaffirmed. And that meant if Janian had the power to awaken the Prince then she would have. Her mind stayed focused on the topic of power however and her thoughts strayed to the sword that rested beside her. Since its fiery display against the shadow assassin she felt both safer and yet, terrified to have it near her.

CHAPTER 16

King Zhamar Damaste had wandered the halls of his castle without escort. He had been scolded, he mused, scolded by his own Captain of the guard. Rather, his replacement while Alex was away on escort.

"With all that's transpired my king, we cannot be too cautious, from what I was told it was Malik's own squire who..." the older man, Tyson was his name stopped short of finishing his sentence. The look in the king's eyes flashed anger and for a moment the man was worried as he had indeed caught sight of the quick fist the king had made at his side.

"By your leave, king Damaste." The captain bowed his head.

To the man's credit, he had stayed until Zhamar had disappeared down the corridor.

The king knew where he was headed but he had yet to figure out why. With everything that's been happening the last few days he did not understand why he would be standing outside one room in particular. He leaned his head against the solid door, one hand resting on the warm metal handle.

It was not sadness at the events that transpired so far, not the death of his only son, nor the quest of his head strong youngest daughter that had brought him back to this room. Guilt had led him here; it was what kept the king's hand gripped ever tight, until the handle bit painfully into his fingers.

The door clicked open. Zhamar walked on reluctant feet into the cold, dark room. No fire had been lit in the fireplace for well over a year and he had ordered the room remain untouched by servants; which over time had collected a thick layer of dust. The covers on the bed had been folded, the windows shuttered and locked. The room was as dead as his younger brother.

"God I miss you, Jeral." The memory he fought everyday had free reign in this room and the last memory he had of his brother was the argument they had. "It's fitting, the last time we talked was in this room, and now it seems this is the only room in which I can hear your voice." Zhamar gazed into the darkness towards the chair by the cold fire; it was easy to imagine his brother sat there now, listening.

"I will never for the life of me understand why you had to have married a Carnian, Jeral. Your sister in-law just paid us a... less than warm visit," a small chuckle escaped his lips as he thought of the lunacy of being related to that women. Even if bonded by marriage and not blood. And just as quick his mood soured for his brother had only been gone twelve months when the messenger arrived with news of his death. Poisoned he had been told. Two short days after they heard the news of the baby Prince, his nephew had been born happy and healthy.

"I would have gone to welcome him into this world, Jeral... I would have. But tensions were just as bad then as they are now, a few months have done little to allow things to calm. He was beautiful, has his father's hair. I would have told you the color of his eyes but your son slept through the whole ordeal."

"I should tell you," Zham said as he rose from the bed and ran a hand along the shuttered window. "Malik was killed. A betrayal was the verdict but were that you here, I would not of hesitated to dismiss those charges. The truth would have led to open war and I may have lost a daughter for the sake of continued peace with Carn."

The king shook his head wearily and sat in the chair opposite of where he imagined his brother would be sitting.

He had so much more to say, but the words choked before they could be uttered. Tears welled up in Zhamar's eyes and he leaned forward placing his head in his hands; hands that now shook as badly as the rest of him. The dam keeping his sorrow back had finally broken and he let the pain rush out.

The hard sobs of a broken man continued until the moment the King felt a firm hand on his shoulder. Startled, he looked up quickly wiping away the blurred vision... and saw nothing. The room remained as cold as when he had entered. Zhamar closed his eyes and leaned back in his chair and despite the tears that continued to flow, he allowed himself the smallest of smiles.

CHAPTER 17

"They can cast no magic," Jan explained. "Not while on the hill."

They had journeyed further east, following close along the river's path. Trying to forget that their lives had been in so much danger over the last little while had not been easy and as it where, Valis was now scouting ahead with Ce'elevan while Sophal fell behind to watch the rear. This left Janian and Cecil plenty of time to talk.

"Then I don't understand how they are supposed to talk to the Earth Mother," Cecil said with puzzlement, a common occurrence since they had left the waterfall far behind.

Jan smiled. It was a smile of understanding and a smile of forgiveness of the young man's ignorance. She too had been unaware that there was more to this world than what she believed, or had seen... or as a child had been told.

"Long before there was magic, there was the Earth Mother. Cecil, the Mother is everywhere, in everything. And they honour her as such by going one month without casting any magic."

"So they just... what? Sit around and count blades of grass?" Cecil grinned.

"Don't be ridiculous," Jan chided and when the smile left her friends face she allowed one of her own.

"They count the clouds," Jan pointed upwards at the clouds above.

Both Earth Maiden and ex-squire laughed until Valis had stopped and turned, holding her position until the others had caught up, falling into step alongside them.

"What's wrong with you two? Do you want to let every one of my father's soldiers know where we are? What about the shadow assassins?" For some it was near impossible to forget the events so far.

"Are you going to jump at everything now?" Cecil asked with annoyance.

"Your blade and Jan's magic are more than enough to keep them away now. They should know better, especially with that sword, you said it caused the shadow great pain to be cut by it. What kind of a fool sticks around with that kind of danger after it?" Cecil had to quickly say. The look on Valis's face had spoke volumes against his flippant answer, he shifted his gaze to his feet as they walked on now in silence.

It was the rain that escorted them in, the path they were set upon wound its way upwards around the biggest hill in the area. The rain came down soaking them to the bone, the trail offering no chance of shelter.

"All life comes from water, Cecil," Janian spoke at his side.

"There is far too much mind-reading going on in this group of ours," Cecil snapped, slicking his hair back and out of his face.

"No mind reading, I can see it in your face," Jan nodded paying no attention to her friend's rudeness.

The other aspect of the heavy downpour was that it brought with it, the sound of chanting. They had to yell to be heard in the rain and yet the sound of the chant filtered right through and around each drop of rain as it reached their ears.

The greyhounds now followed much closer, gone was their desire to scout ahead and leave their friends open to attack as had happened before. They both looked just as miserable in the wet weather as the humans, but kept their thoughts to themselves.

"There is something else in the air, can you smell it?" Ce'elevan asked his fellow canine companion.

"I can, pup. I don't like it... the Carnian people have little need for druids and Earth Maidens and they trust them even less." Sophal replied with a quick look over at Janian as to make her point.

"It should no longer be possible for you to doubt the Earth Maiden. She has proven herself a loyal friend and..."

"And *I recognize that pup, I do... but these druids, they have yet to earn such trust,"* Sophal interrupted.

"Fair enough then," Ce'elevan agreed.

He did not speak again for sometime after, he as well as the others continued to trek up the monstrous hill, all focused now on just keeping their footing in the path turned to slick mud.

Despite Janian's insistence that they could cast no magic while on the hill, it certainly looked as though it was present. A single pillar of light reached from the ground into the heavens above. Around this pillar knelt men, with heads bowed and lips uttering the words to the chant held within the rain.

Despite the rain on their journey upward there was not a single drop venturing from the clouds above. It was as if here, in the circle, the power which seemed to be brought to life through the collected voices kept the weather at bay upon the hill. Thunder could be heard crackling of in the distance and the dogs pressed into the legs of those closest to them for support. No one moved as the ritual continued, soaked through they could do nothing but stand and shiver and wait.

Janian was the first to move, not far, just a few paces so she stood in front of her friends. They watched as she bowed her head and at that moment the chanting ended and the pillar of light dropped from above to form a thick mist at their feet and all eyes, as well as excited murmurs, focused on her.

To the north of the circle stood a stone dais that was moments ago hidden behind the pillar of light. Atop the dais stood a man, hunched over leaning heavily on a cane and yet this man seemed to carry a sense of great strength that all could feel clear across the hill top. The man raised one robbed hand and uttered a sentence. The men around the circle had stopped their almost frantic muttering the moment the man had finished, and he now slowly but steadily climbed down the stone steps and began his journey towards them. Jan held out a hand to indicate they should remain behind and the Earth Maiden made her way across the hill through the now waist-high fog to meet him. The others continued to stand and watch and their eyes flicked between watching their friend and eyeing the fog as it enveloped the men who had remained kneeling. Not all stayed down, some stood and quietly moved off while a few others remained and watched the new comers with much interest.

"Today my brothers, we are blessed with a rare gift, the presence of an Earth Maiden!" the old man announced loud and in a clear voice. They walked now with Janian holding his arm and when the voices filled of whispers and chatter had risen once more and not all of it was friendly. The old man freed his arm from Janian's and griped his staff tightly in both hands before striking it into the ground at his feet. The hill shook as if in anger at the strike and all fell silent once more. "Here is a place of honour and respect, sacred to all who serve the Mother! And here before us now is one of the Mother's daughters, and you will show your respect!"

The heads that hung in shame were many and not another sound was heard from the gathered men as Janian once more took hold of the old man's arm and finished escorting him over to her friends.

"You have embarrassed them my old friend, it was not necessary I assure you," Jan spoke softly.

"Nonsense, you are as welcome here as the rest of us dear child," the old man snapped.

"Truly, but that was magic just now, with your staff... as I see the fog is scattering now. It is forbidden to cast while upon the hill." Jan, despite trying to keep her voice calm had not sounded as reassuring as it could have to the others.

"You think you are the only one the Earth Mother speaks to?" he said raising an old grey eyebrow.

"The mother commanded it?" This gave Jan a moment to pause and the others could not tell what her expression meant. Disappointment mixed with excitement? Was there a hint of anger, or jealousy? The Earth Maiden appeared to shrug it off in the next moment.

"So be it old friend." She sighed and signaled for her friends to come closer.

"Never too old to learn something new my dear, believe me," the old man cackled as he patted her arm.

"And as such I believe I have found a sheep away from its herd," Janian said as she gestured over at Cecil.

The old man studied Cecil with his dark eyes, leaning on his staff.

"Gifted?"

"In my opinion... very much so, though it pains me to be unable to train him myself," Jan offered Cecil a weak smile.

"No, no I suppose you can't at that." The old man studied Cecil further making the young man squirm and itch but before he could say anything the old man had gestured to another fellow who hovered nearby.

"Take the young woman and the dogs, see that they are dried and fed, extend our full hospitality," the man gently placed a hand on Valis's shoulder, her eyes looking to Jan for the ok. And when Jan nodded her head that it would be, she sent a message though the bond to the greyhounds lest they get the wrong idea of the man's intentions. "Janian my dear we will talk in the lodge; I trust you are here for far more important reasons than a wayward sheep. However..." the old man spoke over his shoulder as they began to walk. "Bring the boy."

"Built long ago" the old Druid explained as they entered.

Cecil stood beside Jan while the old man stoked the fire in the center of the room. The ashes, angry at having finally settled down within heat of the lower burning flames. Finally, when the Druid was satisfied with his fire he seemed to remember he was not along and bade them sit. Janian shot Cecil a warning glance as he grumbled about the point of a cabin with no floor.

"We are closer to the Earth Mother, through the earth itself." the Druid spoke, though it was not a real acknowledgment of whether the old man had heard him or not or perhaps was just stating facts.

"If you would not mind sister," the Druid gestured to a small bench to which sat an old blackened kettle, the sides dented and the handle broken.

Janian rose without complaint and upon seeing the kettle had water in it already she set about using the herbs and tea leaves in the pouches beside the bench, kept in the smallest chest Cecil had ever seen.

"The kettle looked as bad when first I laid eyes upon it as well," the Druid spoke looking across the fire.

"Is everyone I meet outside the castle going to be a mind reader?" Cecil said to Janian who only smiled.

"I'm no mind reader boy; I do see things that want to remain hidden... from time to time. And I'll thank you not to mock our kettle if you please, it was a gift from a grateful town we passed through to which we offered our aid in poultices and fresh herbs," the old man finished with a tinge of hurt in his voice.

Cecil's face reddened with shame.

"My deepest apologies, I did not mean to..."

"I'm also very much lying, boy. It's a kettle. We found it on the road, must have fallen off the back of a wagon, kicked by a horse more than likely," the old man said with a hearty chuckle and even Jan could not hold back the bust of laughter that had escaped her lips. She quickly clamped a hand over her mouth; Cecil could still see her grin.

"Is he always this gullible? I'm not so sure he would make it as a Druid if he were to believe everything he hears." The old man asked Jan as she handed him a mug of tea.

Janian handed Cecil his, the cup was extremely hot.

"Rasan, we have more important things to discuss, such as the baby and a possible war breaking out." Janian spoke firmly to signal the end of the chastising.

"You two know each other... it makes a little more sense now," Cecil said dryly. He took a tentative sip of his tea and waited for an explanation. The tea was bitter and tasted a lot like he imagined a sock would taste should it have been steeped in cow's urine for a week. He nearly choked as it made its way down his throat. The room quickly started to spin and he dropped the cup, spilling the remainder of the noxious liquid. He tried to stand but fell back to one hand, the other grasping his throat. The room was going dark and all he could make out was the dirt beneath him and Jan, who had instinctively started toward him but suddenly froze. She would not meet his eyes and his panic quickened as he struggled for breath and for aid. He tried to stay focused on Jan but she seemed frozen now, her eyes where intently focused not on him but at whatever was behind him. Cecil would not get the chance to find out as the darkness closed in and he struggled to breathe his last breath.

CHAPTER 18

"Folly!" scoffed the Druid known as, Dray.

Cecil's body had been moved from the High Druid's small cabin and placed within the much larger hall the druids used as a barracks while they stayed upon the Earth Mother's hill. The hall was long and curved part way around the hill; the original builders were long since forgotten although the druids each time they passed through repaired what they could in the time they had. The hall was warm with several hearths glowing brightly, the flames well maintained even without the aid of magic. The hall was built without windows and this did not seem to improve the atmosphere among the gathered druids.

The High Druid cursed this lack of engineering as he rubbed the beard that should have stopped itching decades ago and held up his other hand for silence.

The druids had learned their lesson earlier out among the chant stones when the High Druid had shown them that he was still very capable of using his powers where they could not and so not as to incur his wrath once again they settled and the room was thrust into silence.

"What is folly, Dray is not that I say we help this young man," The High Druid gestured to Cecil's still form, "what would be folly is to stand aside and do nothing in regards to the evil festering within him."

There were murmurs and arguments now, the hall was so large that it echoed every word once spoken only adding to the overall noise.

"This man is not one of us, Rasan. Cast him out least the evil spread to our numbers!"

The High Druid shared a quick look with Janian but the Earth Maiden remained silent.

"You forget yourself, Dray. This is no man's club, of hunting and whoring, we belong to the Earth Mother. It is by her will that our order had once hunted down such dark magic's and thus, with this sudden appearance of the void creature wrapped around this man's life essence that our duty is brought forth once more."

The room returned to stillness and they waited as Dryden being the apparent elected speaker for the druids assembled, talked in whispers among them.

"This cannot be allowed to spread. Should the void shadow take hold there is no telling what destruction it could wreak, no telling how many lives would be lost." Janian finally spoke, she did not address the men, she had spoken for herself really, and she needed to hear the words out loud.

"No one here will aid you in this; none here want to put their souls on the line. We are little more than priests." Dray gestured behind himself.

"We will discuss at length your need to speak for the others, as no one has asked you to do so Dray. Perhaps a return to novice, until your compassion finds its way back to the Earth Mothers good graces will do you good," the words had been scathing and Dray stormed from the hall, anger hot in his eyes. But he was right, he could see the others did not agree with the man who chose to speak for them but neither did they seem to agree with *his* planned course of action. This was a problem for another day and he had to push the thoughts from his mind that all the chanting and praying they had been doing was for not. How far had their faith fallen, this was the first he had perceived any such lack of devotion. He would have to remedy this as soon as the Earth Mother was willing.

"One problem at a time," Rasan muttered to himself, looking down at Cecil.

"We will need someone to go into the void and aid Cecil in his struggle," Janian spoke now to the gathered druids, she as well had sensed that something was off with these men. It had been a very long time since anything this dark and as sinister as the void shadow had been discovered or seen. She could understand any man's reluctance. She herself wondered if they had the power anymore to destroy such a creature. Those who hunted such had died out long ago.

No man moved nor raised a hand to offer their aid and the High Druid's brows knitted together as one giant grey mass, looking quite caterpillar like.

"I will go."

More shocked voices rose and mutters of disagreement clashed with the few who approved.

"Silence!" Rasan shouted his patience almost at a loss with his brethren.

"I Valis Damaste, Princess of Petsky will enter the void, the Earth Mother willing."

Janian could not help but smile, she knew this young woman, had watched her grow, knew the amount of bravery she had and reminded her so much of Valis's father that her own heart ached at not being able to accompany her. She nodded her approval despite this, as Valis stepped forward and met her friend's nod with one of her own.

"I can send only one in, Valis. I am unsure how far the Earth Mother's influence will travel in the void. Also I won't be able to bring you back, that lies with the druids...and Cecil," Janian warned.

"Balance, Princess of Petsky. It is what rules all life. The druids, the Earth Maidens, even the Mother of us all must adhere to this order. But this young man shares a body and the balance

140

between light and dark has been tipped...it will not be easy to find out in which direction. And harder still to bring it back." Rasan spoke as he led her by the hand to where he wanted Valis to sit.

"We all have darkness within us," she spoke, and placed a calm hand upon Cecil's chest as Jan indicated.

"You travel with remarkably bright company my old friend," Rasan smiled at Janian as she sat opposite her friend, placing her hand over the top of Valis's.

"And the most foolish. Just be thankful your father is not here, young lady." Both women shared a mischievous grin.

The High Druid smiled and took his place seated at Cecil's head. He reached out and took both free hands of the women on either side of him.

"Lucky indeed, he would only insist that he make the journey himself," Janian winked at Valis who smiled before closing her eyes as Rasan began his chanting.

When finished, both he and Janian opened their eyes. Valis's remained closed, her breathing deep and steady, asleep where she sat. The High Druid nodded at Janian's questioning eyes and he gestured silently. Janian followed and where the old man had indicated nearly made her laugh out loud and that laugh quickly filled her heart bringing her eyes near to tears. Draped across Cecil's legs slept Ce'elevan, his breathing matching the calm rhythm of the now three void walkers.

"Looks like she has her guide, this is good, very good." Rasan whispered.

The druids who had not departed soon quietly began to chant their prayers to the Earth Mother and Rasan, High Druid wondered if not all was yet lost.

CHAPTER 19

Valis was starting to rather dislike trees.

She could remember volunteering to enter the void, the dark place where shadows lived between the realms of light and dark. She did not however remember volunteering to trudge through another forest.

She was tense, the trees surrounding her were far from normal. Green was not a color she would see during her journey this day. In its place where warped and crooked trunks, grey as cooled ash and yet they still produced leaves upon their snake-like limbs, leaves that had gone brown and shriveled from lack of life.

She had been walking for some time, or to what she imagined was some time. She had no way to really measure. Stars littered the sky where she could see through the canopy of death but lacked a moon and without one she could not tell how long she had been walking. Her feet on the other hand, tired and sore, should have given her more aid in this. But she was still new to adventures and such, all they did was further her already souring mood. *If Malik were here he would know what to do.* She thought of her brother as often as she could, not wishing to mask her sorrow of his death with a blanket of forgetfulness. Partly out of fear she may lose the picture of his smiling face she held in her mind, or worse... forget altogether.

Valis wished she had put on a warmer jacket before heading out on this adventure; she still wore the travel clothes from several days ago. "Damn you Cecil, where are you? The sooner we get out of here the quicker I can take a bath!" She grumbled. Thoughts of a cold river stream despite sending a shiver down her back still seemed a more inviting prospect than wandering lost in a dead forest.

"Valis," a voice said through the darkness.

She whipped around looking for the voice. There, at the end of a dark long trail, something moved and it was quickly approaching, easily matching the pace at which her heart had suddenly leapt.

"Valis, I'm here to help..."

"Ce'elevan?" Valis hissed forgetting to use the bond in surprise at seeing the greyhound.

"What are you doing here? Jan said she could only send one into the void," she knelt down and wrapped her arms around the dog's neck.

"The *bond, the moment they began to send you I could feel the tug of magic. I closed my eyes and awoke here. I have been looking for you for some time."*

"I'm glad you're here," she said standing back up. *"This place has such an evil feel to it."* She looked around, trying to see into every dark nook for hidden danger.

"I cannot sense Cecil, no scent, no trail markings. If he is in this forest I should know it. We do not share the bond that you and I do, but I can always tell when he is near." Ce'elevan said with a mixture of confidence and a distracted sadness.

Whatever the greyhound's mind had wandered too would remain a mystery to her, Valis thought. The bond did not go so deep.

Being the only two creatures in a forest full of dead trees made the companions cautious and this caution slowed them down. Valis kept glancing to her side making sure Ce'elevan still walked with her and she had a feeling the greyhound was close for the reason. She wondered what kind of scents her friend was picking up as they continued on and the stark contrast between the world of the living and this place quickly changed her mind.

Not one bird chirped, not one squirrel scampered across branches stretched tree to tree and the wind was just as dead as the leaves. The stillness of the forest was unsettling and the silence near maddening.

"What do you know of the void, Ce'elevan?" even her voice sent through the bond sounded cold and alone as though they shared a conversation in a large empty cave.

The dog had stopped briefly at her question and it was several moments before he gave an answer, his nose sniffed at the ground then the air then to the side and back again. When he snuffled in agitation from the dirt that clung more like soot to his nose is when his attention returned to his friend.

"Not much, Malik never talked about such things, despite the bond I am still just a dog... it's not like we can write stuff down to remember or pass along to our pups."

"No, I... you're right of course, sometimes I manage to forget how much work the bond does to allow communication. I still think greyhounds in general to be a far superior breed, Ce'elevan," she hoped that he had not taken offense and she now wondered just how much of what she said the bond could truly translate to his canine mind.

"Thank you, I think so as well."

Valis smiled, shaking her head thinking how much of the humour she heard in his voice was the dog or the bond, and it couldn't be adding emotions just for a better link to her mind... could it?

Lost in thought, Valis nearly tripped over Ce'elevan who was now still as a corpse.

"What is it? Did you find Cecil's scent?"

"No, much worse, it's the smell of evil." Ce'elevan said.

They continued to walk with caution; Valis strained to catch the slightest sound and looked down in utter puzzlement. When Ce'elevan realized she had stopped he turned his head tilted in question.

"Valis?"

"No sound at all," she said, not looking up. She continued to stare at her feet and suddenly took a tiny hop forward. Not satisfied with her test she jumped straight up and down over and over.

"There is no sound at all Ce'elevan, none!"

"Even the forest knows to make no sound in my presence," the voice came from the trees all around them, a throaty, rust-filled voice.

"Show yourself, demon!" Valis shouted and drew her sword in one fluid motion. This surprised not only herself but the shadow assassin as well as it hissed in response to the sword's freedom.

So, you fear my father's blade as much as your friend did, Valis thought to herself, and took solace that the blade had made it into the void as well.

"Where is Cecil?" confidence creeping slowly back into her voice allowed the words to come out steady and clear.

"He is here... he is mine!"

Valis whipped her head to the side catching just a glimpse of their tormentor as a shadow darted from one tree to the next, growing ever closer.

"Your kind may have been born of the void, but you will also die here, tell me where he is!" Valis had raised her sword now, her stance preparing her for battle.

"*Valis...*" a cautionary message from Ce'elevan caught her attention and she lowered her sword enough to quickly glance over at the greyhound.

"*Run!*" Ce'elevan's shout echoed in her skull and she would have winced had time allowed it. The forest had grown darker and the smell of burning wood became prevalent to her senses and then she saw the fire as it was hurtling down towards her.

Without the dog's warning she doubted she would have seen the ball of fire before it had consumed her. As it were her boots and one leg had not escaped the flames in their hunger and she rolled through the dirt mixed with black and grey ash that made up the forest floor. She had put it out but she could still feel the heat on her skin. She would be burned she knew that much, but there was no time for a real inspection of her injuries.

Valis rose to her feet sword in one hand and her head in the other. Her head still ringing from Ce'elevan's shout through the bond. The pain had little time to ebb and she winced further as Ce'elevan shouted again.

"*Run!*" was the simple command and her feet seemed to get the message before her head had registered, as she found herself already dashing as best she could in the direction the greyhound ran.

Another fiery blast slammed into the ground behind her and she could feel the force of the impact give her a small shove forward causing her to stumble. Even with the heat at her back she managed to keep her footing and another blast shattered the group of frail dead trees to her left. She sucked in a breath tasting the ash being kicked into the air and ran hard. Following directions from her canine guide as they weaved in and out through the forest's twisted landscape was a challenge. She had lost Ce'elevan several times, but thankfully the bond allowed her to quickly adjust her direction. There was no way she could keep up with the animal; it was the fastest canine in the western kingdoms and the world for all she knew. The dog was not her only goal, she raced against the backdrop of destruction that tore at the environment around her managing to stay one step ahead of each blast and even then she felt as they had wanted her from this forest and with each blast it felt more like great unseen hands were shoving her away.

Soon the fires had stopped and for awhile she ran on despite this. She should have never slowed she realized with a look of pure mortification as the ground began to split before her in a web of thin jagged cracks spread around her on the dark earth at her feet. She took one step back; it was all she could have managed before the ground opened up and the fires leapt up in front of her. Black flames streaked with red roared up before her and she nearly fell back on her rear end throwing one hand out to quickly catch the ground. She twisted away from the wall of fire stumbling off to the side and around avoiding another attempt to end her life via the flames in the void. She heard it all now, the roar of the fires and Ce'elevan shouting directions to her the bond so loud her head had gone numb from the pain.

And another voice... a voice she knew, a voice she was here to find.

The fire was following her it seemed, streaking along the ground giving chase and soon it began to flank her on both sides, speeding along faster than she could run. The fiery cracks spit and hissed as they went. The moment they made their way to the front they joined, cutting her off. Valis had very little time to stop at the breakneck speed she was moving to avoid the wall of fire that shot up in front of her. She looked on in horror as the flames burned a ring of fire around her.

What would Malik do? She pondered as the circle began to fill with smoke.

Think! She scolded herself, trying to focus her thoughts as she began to cough.

"What would Malik..." and then she had it, whether the choice she made would have mimicked her brother's actions or not she had made her choice. She took one last ragged breath as deep as she could make it and when she opened her eyes they burned with the reflective essence of the flames around her. With steeled determination she forced herself to her feet and in the same motion began to run. She could feel the heat lick her skin and she almost thought of stopping but her body kept moving ignoring the pain. The flames hungrily grabbed at her clothing as she leapt through the flames.

Valis came out of the air a few feet from the ground and stumbled as her feet made contact, tumbling forward into a wall. She opened her eyes through a wave of pain, and gingerly touched a hand to her side, despite the possibility of having cracked a rib or worse; the sight she took in was enough to dull the pain. She had come out of the fire into an alley, the buildings on both sides where made of brick and dulled with time. Leaning against the wall she steadied her feet wondering where she had ended up. *Was this still the void?*

"Valis, this way."

Valis raised her head through the pain and looked towards the alley's entrance. She had followed her instinct for there was no sound for her ears to follow. The voice had come through the bond and there standing just outside the entrance was Ce'elevan. His head turned to look at her at the same moment.

"I have Cecil's scent, he's in the city" she nodded sharply to indicate he should lead on.

What city? She thought. Again she wondered if the fire had brought her from the void back to the real world. As she left the alley she had for a brief moment believed that it had. The city was home, her home. Or at least the city that had grown up around the palace she had been raised in. Although the sights were familiar she immediately sensed something was wrong, maybe the mind had natural defenses against the void to separate truth from fiction; she wasn't sure. But aside from the buildings there was a great deal not right about this place. Once more she noticed a severe lack of sound. No other people walked the streets, no mutts begging for scraps no birds flying over head and even the clouds sparse as they were made no movement as if they had arrived to discover the same as she and simply paused in confusion.

She was still in the void she had settled her thoughts on. With that realization her heart fell a little, despite being on the run from her father's own soldiers and knights she still missed her home. *"It would have been nice to be home, if only for a little while,"* she thought.

"I know. Come... this way!" Ce'elevan answered, poking his head from around the corner of a building, a butcher's shop a few blocks down.

She had believed her thoughts of homesickness were hers alone, but she must have opened the bond. She would have to watch that. A girl needs some semblance of privacy. With her side in agony she left her alleyway refuge and headed after the greyhound.

150

"Alone."

That was the first thing that crossed Cecil's mind when he awoke. Not 'where I am', not 'am I even alive'. It was the feeling of being alone. His friends were no where to be seen. And he somehow knew that calling out to them would be a futile waste of time. His memory was intact and he knew this was not the hill full of druids and old cabins that he should be with. Then he remembered the old man and his tea. It had tasted like death and so now Cecil's mind allowed the smallest of thoughts on whether he may be dead or not. He had awakened next to a fountain propped up against it as a puppet sits on a shelf. His back ached and he wondered how long he had been in this uncomfortable position. Looking over his shoulder he could tell the fountain had not been used in some time and just his luck there was no water within its large bowl. He did however recognize it. He stood stretching cautiously and looked around with a start, twirling his body as he went. He was home, the streets and buildings of Petsky all around him.

The joy he felt was short-lived when his stomach sank with the thought of city guards. Or his face being on wanted posters on tavern walls. But there was nothing, nobody, he was alone.

Cecil turned back to the fountain at the sound of water. In horror he realized he had been very wrong and how his mind turned on him. For he now wished that feeling of being alone would return.

"Finally awake, you are very welcome by the way; it was I who sat you up."

Cecil followed not the sound of water but the hiss of words that came from the creature perched atop the statue in the middle of the fountain.

"Assassin!" Cecil spit in disgust.

"You remember me human, I'm flattered. Although I do have a name," the creature remained atop the statue tapping his chin with a long clawed blackened finger. "Although I suppose Assassin will do just fine."

"I care not for what you are called! You will die and that's all I need to know!" Cecil challenged the creature, reaching for his sword. When he froze; he had no sword.

The creature laughed loudly above Cecil's head while he tried to think quickly.

"How did you survive the fall? For I trust you are indeed that creature and not the one that sports the mark of my friend's sword." Cecil asked hoping to keep him talking until he could find a weapon, although quick glances around resulted in only frustration at the lack there of.

The shadow assassin hissed angrily at the mention of the sword but quickly smiled as he caught the quick darting movements of his prey's eyes.

"You have only yourself to blame, you see, you saved me. Your hatred is strong and your anger draws me in like a bee to a blueberry patch." The creature chuckled in its rust filled voice.

"Fair enough," Cecil said trying to find calm within his turbulent mind.

"I have only one question further; will you indulge me long enough to ask it?"

"That's your question? To ask another question? You humans are such ignorant fools," the assassin mocked from atop the statue.

The voice really did grate on his nerves but Cecil held his growing temper.

"I can see that you are very clever, but no. My question is simple: how do I kill you? I would like to finish the job."

In the time it took Cecil to blink and for the small smile he had allowed to play in the corner of his mouth, the assassin had vanished. The statue sat in the middle of the fountain no longer there to serve the creature as a perch. The silence brought back the fear in Cecil's stomach and he visually explored the area. "How do you find a creature of shadow in the shadows?" He cursed out loud to himself.

Memories and emotions flooded his mind now as he cautiously walked through the empty city streets. Familiar shops and paths came easy to his mind. He had been sent, as the Prince's squire, more times than he could count down from the palace to fetch this supply or that new jacket. He had even let Cecil fetch his swords when the requisitions were filled. *How many swords a young Prince needs was beyond him.* Cecil smiled at the thought. He knew Malik could have easily sent a servant or even a guard to collect items from the city but he had a feeling Malik knew how much he enjoyed the escape from palace life.

He had money, well... Malik's money, and for a while, these outings had made him feel almost his own man. He was alone, no supervision, no nobles looking down their noses at him and no servants' casting him cold stares for even though he was a servant himself. As a Squire he was slightly above their own standing within the court and that netted him little in the way of friends. Not that he had time for friends as it were; Malik had kept him pretty busy. The thoughts of the past were quickly souring his mood now. The feelings of loss, and guilt at leaving his friend, still held a firm hold on his emotions.

Cecil stopped in front of a blacksmith shop. He knew the place well and yet the sign read simply "DEATH" and he frowned for this was not right in the least. The shadow assassin's laughter echoed through the empty streets and Cecil turned searching with angry eyes for the laughter's source.

"This is just the voids version of Petsky city then? Or a twisted copy of the one I hold in my heart!" Cecil shouted.

"Perhaps," said the rusty voice, "maybe it is *my* version!"

Cecil jumped back, turning as the voice had come from the shadow on the shop's wall next to where he was just standing. Slowly the assassin's body formed coming halfway out of the wall.

"Where are we then? How real is the void?... a straight answer then!" Cecil snapped, his heart pumping almost painfully in his chest.

"Some call it the void or the darkness in a man's heart. Call it what you will you are in my home; I am born of it." The voice grated.

"Then why am I here? I have no darkness..."

Cecil paused as the assassin laughed loudly.

"This is only the first step in a far greater life for you boy. A far darker life." The assassin made a grand gesture with his arms, "all of my kind start with one of yours, one, just like you."

Cecil was no coward but he had to get away, the shadows words had stirred something deep within him that he did not want to understand or even admit. He bolted off down the street, the shadow's laughter following close behind. He cast a quick frightful look back over his shoulder and panicked trying to run faster but nearly stumbling as the shadow assassin rose out of his very own shadow and out of every darkened foot step over and over.

The Assassin surged forward and Cecil felt the force of the push that sent him careening into and through a heavy shop door. He was, for a moment, unsure whether the sound he heard was the door or his shoulder breaking.

"Where did you think you could flee to? You can't hide, soon you will seek me out, and soon you will beg to call me your master!" the assassin taunted from the doorway while Cecil lay upon the shops floor trying to regain his senses.

"Get up Cecil it's only a shadow."

A second voice filled his ears and yet it was a voice that had no right to be there, could not be there. Cecil's eyes where heavy and he struggled to even lift his head.

"You there, shadow creature," the voice said offhandedly. "Go on, away with you now. This man has work to do," the voice was light hearted and casual with the situation, and Cecil had never thought to hear again the man who sounded so close. Why could he not focus, why was his body so numb. Pain could still be felt throbbing from his shoulder where he had hit it against the door followed by the floor.

"Malik?" Cecil managed to croak in a whisper.

"He's mine now! You have no power here, you are nothing!" The Assassin hissed venom heavy in each word. "A ghost, of a memory I shall rip from his mind!"

"And yet," the voice of Malik spoke, followed by the sound of steel drawn from its home. "I can still draw my sword and I imagine its edge is still keen and if not...well I will have to swing a litter harder." Cecil heard the man who could not be; take a step forward on a floor that creaked. His vision still a blur, his head hurt the more he tried to clear it.

"He's mine! I brought him here... he's mine!" the shadow assassin sounded almost as whiny as a petulant child whose toy was taken away to learn a lesson in manners from a parent.

Silence filled the room and the pressure in Cecil's head was beginning to ebb.

"It's gone for now, Cecil, I don't know for how long."

"Malik?" Cecil tried to speak again strength returning to his voice. "How... please don't..."

"Get up off the floor; it's time you got back to work," Malik's voice sounded slightly more distant as Cecil's senses began to un-fog.

"What work? As your Squire, Malik?"

"What? No... Haven't you been paying attention? I'm dead."

The voice was Malik's there was no doubt in Cecil's mind now. As he managed to get to his knees, swaying with dizziness, he could see the outline of the man he once knew standing in the doorway to the shop. An odd light with a pitch black border framed his Prince and master.

"With me gone you have to keep my sister safe. The time will come when you have to be her champion."

His friend's words were as confusing as this day had been. He tried to shake his head until the room spun out of control and he nearly emptied his stomach.

"Oh and, Cecil, be nicer to my dog."

Cecil would have laughed if he wasn't startled to find a furry body pressed into his side. His vision cleared in a sharp intake of breath and his body drained of its odd paralysis leaving him kneeling on the floor. The shadow assassin gone, the ghost of his friend or whatever he had been was no where to be seen and Ce'elevan at his side. He reached a hand up to scratch the dog behind the ears and felt the familiar press of the dog's head against his palm when he tried to stop too soon. "I think this is the first time I'm glad you really can't read my mind... it's a bit of a mess today."

CHAPTER 20

"Home."

Kerra the Princess of Carn lacked the feeling of joy one is supposed to feel upon returning home from a long journey. It's true that she felt queasiness in her stomach as she approached the palace gates, but it was not the same as the feeling of longing and or anticipation. No, this was more a feeling of loathing, dread and a sense of immense weariness. She longed to be away from here the moment she had returned.

The guards had recognized her at once and despite giving the men that followed her in a look of distrust, she had been escorted straight through the courtyard. Leaving her men outside, the remainder of her Carn escort lead the men in Petsky uniforms off in the other direction. She entered the palace through a side entrance. She excused herself from the palace guard escort amidst the sputtering of the men and when she fixed them with a harsh stare they bowed their heads and she continued forward on her own, heading straight for her sister's rooms.

She could not help the self satisfied grin as she approached the large double doors. Normally that damn dog with its constant stare that would follow her around the room, would be not far from her sister. At least that was one nuisance, however small, that was now out of her way.

"You have not come back with my son."

The Queen of Carn, pale and propped up with lavish pillows spoke coldly from her grand bed.

"Sister," Kerra began, bowing deeply. She had rehearsed what she would say the entire trip back home and yet she still felt panic clutch at her heart. Her sister had always intimidated her, she shared the power of authority their father had commanded and Kerra had always felt weak in their presence. Only with time and her master's words did she begin to fuel her confidence with anger and when she straightened she met her sister eye-to-eye.

I fear that Petsky truly is the mastermind behind..."

"I have received a message from Petsky's king, a messenger sent the night before you and my son left under guarded escort." The queen stated flatly.

Kerra's eyes slid off her sister and met the floor, *clever* she thought of the king's move.

"And yet you return without my son!" the Queen had yelled aggravating a cough that had been building for some time. When Kerra made to approach in aid, the Queen waved her back.

"Explain Kerra...where is my son."

"Petsky guards, the ones assigned to be my escort turned on us in the night." She replied softly causing the Queen to lean forward to better hear.

"The kidnapper was captured, tried and sentenced, the man who..."

"Forgive me sister, but I was there when that 'man' was sentenced and in that very room I believe the true mastermind. The leader who coerced others to join her in this most horrid crime, was present and formed a new plan. One that saw most of my men killed and my dear nephew ripped from my arms with a sword to my throat."

"And how do you know this woman works on behalf of Petsky? Kerra I cannot start a war over the actions of a rebel or someone with a grudge against their King."

Kerra watched her sister's face, years ago she would have had no trouble convincing her to take up arms... this child had made her weak both physical and of mind.

"It is well known that the King and this woman are long time friends. One of the Petsky knights was more than willing to confirm the plot to me," she hesitated at these words. She had to be careful. She could bring Alex before the Queen and force him to say whatever she wished but she wanted to keep him for herself and her sister would surely send his head back to Petsky as an answer to the question of war. "Most untimely, he did not survive the interrogation my Queen," she finished with a bow of her head in apology, hoping that answer would suffice.

"No matter, if your words ring true and I have no need to doubt them... do I? Then I will bring our forces crashing down on the kingdom of Petsky and they will fall harder than any nation before them. However, I must have my son returned."

Kerra cursed inside her head, her sister was changed indeed and this would take more time to find a way to make her act.

"What of this lady, the king's friend? Tell me about her, can we hunt her down, what are you doing about finding her?"

"She is an Earth Maiden... one of the king's closest..."

"A witch!" the queen cursed. "Never to be trusted, it's a wonder their cult was not cleansed from our land long before our father's time." The Queen's anger had spurred her into another fit of coughing.

Kerra almost felt a tinge of worry for her sister, it was a small feeling and she brushed it aside as quickly as it had arrived. *She took everything from me... if my master did not need the child I could have inspired the war already. This is taking too long.*

"Sadly other nations do not share our opinion, they near worship these women and their pagan ways. I have everything under control my sister, she will be brought to justice by your mercy and my beloved nephew seen safely back to your arms."

"I'm dying, Kerra." The Queen spoke weakly; it was quite out of character for a woman who had at one time, been so strong. The Queen was the best with a sword in all the land and just as fierce on a horse in battle. And now due to a sickness their best doctors could not hold back any longer she was going to die.

"Sister, hush now. Have faith that a cure will be found soon." Kerra soothed hoping she sounded sincere enough to still appear as a sister who cared, should.

"I must rest now, sister, find my son. Kill the witch anyway you see fit, take as many men as you need but make sure she dies." The Queen closed her eyes and her chest rose and fell in a steady matter, her breathing sounding rough however and it pained her to take each breath.

Kerra did not wait for any other response, she simply bowed despite no one watching and left the room as fast as her failed fury would allow. She had failed to start the war once again. This time she will insure the Earth Maiden's death... this time she would spare no man, one in particular would serve this purpose.

Shaken at the events so far, the surprise arrival of Ce'elevan and the hands that now helped him to his feet. Cecil had just about enough surprises for the day, or night. He had no idea if the daylight outside was real or not.

"Oh it's you, I should have known," Cecil sighed." "Is it too much to ask that you at least **try** to stay out of trouble, Valis?" he said with a little more edge to his voice than was needed or intended.

The young woman took several steps back and the look on her face was a mixture of hurt and anger.

"Oh it's you? Oh it's you?!" Valis stomped a foot hard on the ground, the noise echoing through the empty shop and even Ce'elevan took a step back behind Cecil in worry she may lash out at him next.

Cecil hung his head. It wasn't her fault they were here and he knew that and despite the shame he felt at his words he could not bring himself to say he was sorry. He would not need to however, as Valis was not him. And she was far more forgiving it seems and in this she startled him by quickly closing the gap between then and wrapping her arms around him tightly in a bear hug.

"Thank the Goddess you are alright," she spoke calmly, her face buried in his shoulder.

"We are here to help, Jan and the druids sent us in to bring you out," she explained taking a step back but still holding him at arm's length.

"I made your brother a promise to keep you safe, how am I to do that if you follow me into the bloody void," Cecil asked with a smirk. He truly was glad to see his friends even if the situation grated on his nerves.

"Well now that we have you we can leave so..." Valis looked at him her words trailing off.

Cecil raised his eyebrows in annoyance "so...?"

"Which way do we go? How do we get out?" She said with genuine interest.

"How in the hell should I know?!"

The pair separated both throwing their hands up in exasperation with the other.

"I thought you..." Valis started as she rounded on her friend.

"I was pulled in by a bloody Veil Demon!" Cecil shouted back.

"Ok... ok wait," he said as Valis started shaking her head and pacing back and forth.

"The demon said the veil was his home, we know he's still out there. I doubt even your brother could chase it off indefinitely... now all we need is a way to..." Cecil's words trailed off as he looked down at the dog that was now pressing up against his leg. As if the greyhound feared the human would fall over and was propping him up. "Some days I fear Malik was right and I do have my head up a horse's ass, or rather my own at the lack of a horse."

Valis was looking at him now in half curiosity and half disgust at the picture her friends' words painted in her mind.

"Can Ce'elevan track the assassin?"

Valis did not even have to send the question through the bond as Ce'elevan barked and dashed through the open door into the street spun and pranced around barked once more and took off down the street.

Cecil gestured towards the door and Valis nodded accepting his courtesy. Soon both humans where running after a greyhound they had no chance of catching.

Now we become the hunters for a change? Cecil thought as they ran after the dog. His thoughts lingered on the Assassin's words that soon he would seek him out and would call him master. He tried to clear his mind of these thoughts but they seemed intent on sticking with him.

CHAPTER 21

For a shadow assassin fresh from the void the journey back to its master should have been swift as it glided over land, faster than any horse. Injured however and away from its natural home for so long it had taken much longer, and had only just arrived a full day after Kerra herself. It was still able to use its powers though they came slowly to the creature and it took a few moments for it to gather what was needed to pass through the door it sensed its master dwelled within.

When it finally faded in and out, arriving within the room, it watched its master. The woman did not carry herself as though she had mastered the darker arts; yet, it knew from the hold over itself that she wielded the power with an odd sense of calm. She was not alone, standing before the fire unclothed was one of the men the assassin had seen before. As it and its brother had left the ram-shackled cabin in the woods his master had summoned them from.

***

Kerra had waited too long for this one's return and she spared it only the quickest of glances as it came through the door. She focused instead on the man before her and pressed herself up against his naked form leaning her head on his chest.

She had not lost the link to the shadow that stood silent before the door after all. She knew it suffered still as its pain was linked to her and her own hand was still quit numb, though she had regained a slight ability to bend her fingers. The seared line of flesh that spiralled around her hand still remained as a visual reminder of the hazards bringing these shadows from the void poised to have on her body. It surprised her that she had not lost more of herself with the sudden break in the link with this one's counterpart. But she was still alive so she gave it little further thought.

"I have spent the day in deep consul with my master," she spoke to the both of her servants.

The Earth Maiden has been foreseen as the only current threat to our great lord's return. And the power he has given me will be enough to destroy any man or women, King or Maiden, even a Queen. And what he asks of me, commands of me to summon, requires a sacrifice. I find myself reluctant to put this order forward." She spoke in even tones as she stroked Alex's bare chest, looking up at his eyes. He was compliant now. Kerra barley had to use the control link she had over his mind at all. He had even seemed eager to join her in her bed. She had replaced her anger at the situation with the pleasure she gained from his embrace. Even if it wasn't real she could almost pretend she was in love, could almost forget everything as she basked in the feel of having a man to bed, to hold, to wake up to once more. Almost.

She still found herself waking in the night, screaming at the memories her dreams allowed to surface. Memories she tried so hard to bury. She sighed and pulled herself away from Alex to address the shadow that melded with the others along the wall as if they were reaching out to a familiar friend.

"You have done poorly. You and your brother assassin were to bring my nephew back as well as the head of the witch." The flinch from Alex was caught from the corner of her eye and it made what she had to do all that much easier.

She looked to the wound that seared down the shadow's arm and then to her own, barely flexing a numb hand. He had to have faith in her master, faith this new spell would not destroy her should it fail, and then she scolded herself for doubting his plan and his power. She let the power welling up inside her move through her veins, a feeling of ice and fire. So much was required this time that she felt it would rip from her body. She reached out with one hand drawing the shadow assassin to her. The shadowed shape of a man burst into a thick dark cloud at her touch. There was no scream, no pleading from the void creature it had returned into the spell force for which she had called it from in the beginning. She could feel it meld with her powers from within. No, the screaming and pleading came from Alex as she reached out her other arm and placed her palm flat against his chest and began the incantations her master had granted her knowledge of this very evening.

Tears had welled up at the corner of Kerra's eyes and a woman's cry could be heard over the roar of magic filling the room. She scowled in confusion for the emotions had come unbidden and so she continued to push forward ignoring, oblivious to the sounds of her own despair.

CHAPTER 22

The trio had walked far as they followed Ce'elevan's nose, until they reached the city limits. Once they stepped outside those walls the world melted away from them, a thick smoke, grey, a fog, had taken over until it was all they could see. Cecil reached for Valis' hand and she in turn grabbed hold of Ce'elevan, the dog pressing up close to her leg. The air grew heavy and humid. Soon it felt as though they had walked through a thunder shower they were so drenched. After a few moments, as they waited to see if the fog would lift or should take them somewhere else, they began to walk. Still holding onto each other they inched and shuffled forward. Caution was what slowed them mixed with the fear of what they could not see, and what could be waiting within.

They moved as one and soon the sounds of birds and rushing water could be heard all around them. Without even realizing it they had come through the fog, and looking behind them showed nothing more than forest and an old cart path. No sign of the city. Before them a small mountain path began its winding trail upwards, a mountain they could not even begin to see the top of. As they craned their necks upward it disappeared amongst clouds thick as a sheep's coat.

Valis turned to her friend, curiosity etched into her brow. "Who gets to decide what appears when the whole... you know, landscape change thing happens, the void, or us?" She exclaimed gesturing back toward the mountain.

"I wish I had the answers for you, any answers actually." Cecil shrugged and stepped up to the path stopping to gaze up the slim long trail that disappeared around the first bend.

"The only thing I really know of the void was spoken by my father when I was a child. Even then I covered my ears wishing I was somewhere else. I wish I was somewhere else now," he finished to himself in a hush as he took the first few steps along the path.

Ce'elevan barked once and darted past Cecil and stopped just before the road turned the corner further up.

"Ce'elevan has the scent, come on, Valis!"

"I know that, but don't you think...!" she tried to say as Cecil started up the path at a jog.

"Let's go, before we lose sight of him!" Cecil shouted back.

Valis only rolled her eyes as she chased after her friends.

The greyhound popped his face out from around the corner and waited for them to catch up, dancing around as if he were on fire. They all felt the cold whisper of wind on cheeks and shivers lanced through them all.

***

The elder man who stood before the King was smiling gently his head half bowed. The slump in his back spoke of a body tired of being upright and yet in the man's eyes the King could still see the spark of life shining brightly.

The king wondered why this man had not been a member of the counsel and at the same time was grateful. For if he had been then it was possible he would have shared the other's fate. The road to Carn had cost him his senior council... and his son. These thoughts he pushed away until he could allow them to run their proper course. He would have to make it official and appoint this man as a council member when time permitted. The old man made a lot of valid points but Zham was only just hearing the words being spoken as his mind had wondered.

"I would strongly advise against it my King," the man's bony arms came into view as his sleeves slid down his arms, arms that waved about frantically as he spoke.

"The messenger I sent ahead of my sister-in-law's carriage safely delivered a message to the Queen only to come across the remains of said carriage on his return home." The King said. His face frozen in a frown he had worn for hours.

"That to me would be even more reason not to send your daughters to their grandparents in the Summer-land's, the road..." the old man spoke, pleading.

"And what of the guards?" the King said ignoring once more the words of the old man. "The knights that were with them? My own Captain is among the missing and I have never met the man or beast that could force Alex into defeat, or retreat." The king stared out the window behind his study room desk.

This was not entirely true; he knew Alex was the best at his job but he was not unbeatable. Many times before on many adventures Zham himself had to rescue his oldest friend from one peril or another. No, Alex was not unbeatable but damn near close. The king slammed his fist into the desk losing his control on his temper if only for a moment.

"No" he said calming himself and running his other hand, the one not currently throbbing in pain, over his face. He had not shaven in several days and the hairs were starting to itch, he never did like beards. He remembered his father saying the older he got the less it would itch but so far he had been very wrong. Only Zham didn't have the time or patience to shave or sit still long enough to have anyone do it for him and so he would suffer through, using it as a distraction.

"Has there been no news on my wayward daughter?"

"No, we have two dozen guards out searching in every direction for signs of her passing, however I suggest we do not give up hope, from what I hear she is quite a capable..."

"Send what messengers you can find to call them back," the king said, shaking his head with no remorse at once again interrupting his at this time, only council member.

"We may need them here, every able fighter. Except for the ones escorting my daughters to the Summer-land" Zham said raising his eyes to cut off the protest he could see forming on the old man's lips.

The king could see the horror in his eyes now as the old man realized fully what his King was suggesting and yes he was abandoning the search for Valis. He was never really good at expressing his emotions at the best of times. And as worried as he truly was about his youngest child he knew that out of all of them she was the one he had to worry the least about. She was with a streetwise Squire and a talking dog, *how much trouble could she get into?* At the thought he almost laughed before catching himself. He did not need this man thinking he was a cold heartless monster any more than he probably did already.

"You may go now," he waved his hand dismissively leaving no room for error in his desire to be alone. Though he could not remember ever being so rude and he sighed heavily as he waited for the old man to shuffle out and close the door. The longer he was forced to sit and do nothing while his daughter and friends remained out from under his protective eye, the worse his mood was getting.

As he sat waiting he supposed his mood had been worsening as far back as when Malik had been born. It was the same year his father had passed away from old age as they said. He knew it was more likely from the stress he now felt himself. Zham never wanted the throne; the only benefit he had held firmly onto was that a life in court had allowed him to be there to watch four children grow up, even if some of them were still growing.

Zham chuckled at the thought of Valis always right on Malik's heels since the day she could walk. It was no wonder Malik had taken to teaching his sister the art of the sword. It gave him an opportunity that most brothers would never have, a chance to hit his sister and not get into trouble.

His mood quickly soured at the thoughts of family and friends and he stood from his desk moving across the room to open the doors leading to the balcony beyond. The night was dark and the rain that fell was heavy and loud, only the Earth Mother could have possibly heard him yell and curse his frustrations out into the storm. The weather mimicked and mocked him with every shout he issued the sky opened up with its own shouts of thunder and the lightning that flashed was as hot as Zham's temper.

***

"Can you hear that?" Valis asked as she paused a moment upon the path.

Cecil a little further ahead had stopped to look back at Valis and tried to keep his frustration at the interruption from his voice, "no, what did you hear?"

"Sounded like someone screaming... it was… I just felt like I was scolded, like when I was younger." She looked up at Cecil. "It was the same as when a child knows its really gone too far this time, that kind of feeling."

More hours drifted by and Valis had suggested they make camp for the night. The sky had gained a pinkish hue and they suspected it a sign the day was ending here in the void. It was hard to really know. Cecil had pushed them hard and they had followed, despite his constant reassurance that they were close; it had still taken them the entire day so far. No one was convinced they were anywhere near the peak. The greyhound's ability to follow the shadows scent was rendered useless as the path only led them in one direction as they traveled thus far. The forest they had arrived from was lost to sight as was most below them as they had passed high enough to be above the cloud line. "I wonder if these clouds are clouds at all, or the same strange mist we encountered whenever there was a shift in the void."

"Keep moving," a tired Cecil replied. He glanced back and noticed his friend's sluggish pace and offered a frown.

"Cecil we are going to lose the light any moment and we need to stop and find shelter," Cecil thought the words sounded ridiculous as she said them.

Cecil halted and sighed, hands on hips as he slowly turned around to face his friend.

"I bet Ce'elevan can do it," he said nodding to the dog, which, who, in response, lay down on top of his feet bringing Cecil's frown into a scowl.

"Well where do you think we are going to find shelter on a mountain pass as thin as this?" Cecil chided.

"We passed nothing on the way up, and we sure can't go that way," he finished peering over the edge.

"No, no we have to keep going," Cecil tried to keep the desperation from his voice but he had been in the void for too long and he was quickly starting to have thoughts of never being able to leave.

"We have to keep going," he said, quietly repeated, then snapped his eyes back up to Valis before rushing to the mountain wall. "We can keep our bearing in the dark if we just trail our hands across the rock like this," he placed his fingers on the jagged wall and began to walk away. Valis ran to him as he pulled his hand away when he gave a sharp yelp of pain. "It's alright, I just nicked it," he said pulling his hand away and sticking the bleeding finger in his mouth.

Valis looked back at the wall were Cecil had ran his fingers and could see that he cut it early on, perhaps at the start and had trailed blood across the mountain wall. She panicked at the sound of moving stone and cast a frightened look to Cecil who was already looking above in the same shared panic. And yet no rocks fell. This did not stop their hearts from beating so hard it hurt. A portion of the wall, around half the size of a bear's cave slid inward. They watched in caution as it continued further and further back until all they could see was darkness within.

"I think… Jan will find it interesting that blood magic works here in the void." Cecil said as he studied his cut finger in shock.

"That was far too simple of a solution," Valis said bringing Cecil out of his amazement. He joined her, both peering into the dark of the cave.

"Ask Ce'elevan if he can smell anything from within," he said not taking his eyes from the entrance.

Before Valis could even establish the link between women and dog Ce'elevan slipped passed them quickly disappearing into the cave of darkness.

"It's safe, he says." Valis said to Cecil who was instead looking back up the path and with a sigh he nodded and headed inside to find the dog.

Valis snagged his hand as he passed her and using the bond with Ce'elevan they slowly crept through the darkness, meeting the greyhound at the back of the cave. It was hard to tell the size of the cave and with no light they dared not do any exploring. Buy raising one's hands they had discovered the cave to only be a few feet higher than their heads when they stood. Which both the humans were grateful for and Ce'elevan yawned as Valis and Cecil excitedly made this discovery. For Cecil the urge to continue up the mountain pass was soon set aside as they lay down next to Ce'elevan. Valis was asleep no sooner than her head hit her makeshift pillow of her balled up jacket. One of them had to stay awake to keep watch and he wished he had asked Valis if Ce'elevan was going to take first watch. As he had now laid down he felt his eyes grow heavy.

The sound of thunder shook Cecil from an already uneasy sleep. The lightning that flashed along with it was enough to illuminate the cave they had huddled together within. The Princess, Valis was somehow fast asleep still with one hand draped over the greyhound, Ce'elevan. They looked almost peaceful as he watched them in between the constant flashes of light from the storm raging outside.

Turning his head as he sat, hoping for the urge to lie back down to arrive soon, he watched the storm rage on. The rain was spilling gently just within the cave's entrance and fortunately they were deep enough in to avoid lying on wet ground. As much as he wished for sleep, Cecil would have preferred not trying to within the void. It was unlike any slumber he had before, it felt too real. The sounds all around him could still be heard even though he knew his mind was within dream and his body at rest. And although normally the sound of a greyhound snoring would have flared his temper, this night he welcomed it as a stark reminder of something that felt normal and real. He smiled to himself as he should have been used to the sound by now. In the real world all these dogs did was sleep, aside from when Malik would leave the Castle for the hunt. His mind was wandering nicely, the feeling of a tired foggy mind was returning and he thought of what greyhounds dreamed about, especially ones with the Bond, did he share Valis's dreams? He tried once more to close his eyes but something was too bright to keep them closed, *which was silly* he thought as one normally closed one's eyes with too much light in them.

The lightning flashed and after his eyes adjusted he could make out the faint blue outline of another entrance not far off to the side within the cave. His heart began to race and his mind tried to drudge up a memory of there being another entrance and he scowled hard when no memory came. If there had been another entrance all alone then Ce'elevan would have told them about it, or at least Valis and she had said nothing to him in this regard. With a sleep clouded head, he thought for a moment that he was so tired that this must be the entrance they had come in. Although a quick glance over his shoulder showed him the answer, confirmed by the sound of rain splashing upon the cusp of the entrance.

He should wake his friends; he thought and was preparing to do just that when he heard the low soft sounds of chanting. It was enough to gain his curiosity as it sounded so familiar, the same hum and droning rhythm as the druids chanting when they had arrived upon the hill. He stood and carefully began walking towards the soft blue lit entrance, thoughts of waking his

friends forgotten behind him.

***

Cecil was not alone in hearing the sounds of chants. Dreaming in the void was not like

dreaming in the real world. The sounds of soft chanting were enough for Valis to awake just in

the moment her friend walked through the blue lit entrance through sleep blurred eyes. She

stumbled to her feet and chased after him. Ce'elevan popped to his feet at her disturbance and

had only just stopped his pursuit as Valis noisily and painfully smacked into an unseen barrier of

force keeping her from pursuing Cecil any further.

Valis cursed in pain as she clutched her face, of which had taken most of the impact with

the unseen barrier. Blood was streaming from her nose and she pinched the bridge to try and

slow it.

"Are you alright?" Ce'elevan's concern came through the bond.

"No!" she replied rather sharply not really intending it for the greyhound. *"What in the*

name of the Earth mother just happened?"

"Cecil seems to have gone through another entrance and you just..."

"I know what just happened!" she shot back with irritation. *"I want to know why it*

happened, where in the Veil is that man going?"

She placed a hand, the one not holding her nose, tentatively against the barrier and gave a

little push. It was as solid as if the stone were still there. Only she could see through it, and in the room beyond she could see Cecil standing in the middle as still as a planted fence post. She shouted and pounded on the invisible barrier and to her horror she knew he did not hear her.

***

Cecil stood now within a circular chamber filled with wonderfully large crystals. They ran around the room jagged, large and tall. The blue light was emanating from the centre of each and spread like blood in water. His eyes were drawn to the largest, which sat in the centre of the room. Its large smooth surface shone as clear as glass. Cecil was thinking of approaching, his hand now outstretched to touch its smooth surface when he recoiled in horror. He took a step back as the mirror crystal filled with darkness quickly becoming an ominous dark portal.

The soft blue light of the other crystals did not fade but neither did they penetrate the darkness that had consumed the central crystal. Cecil's blood ran cold just as a voice echoed within and from all around.

"Did you think me a fool?" with those words the slight chanting Cecil had followed in here had stopped and now the dark head and torso melted outwards from the center of the dark crystal. The shadow assassin had arrived. "That I would not follow with your friends nearby?" its tone was taunting and the tone rust filled.

"Follow us? We have been the ones hunting you!" Cecil challenged back, balking against the fear that was ever present within him.

The rust filled voice of the assassin laughed deeply as he watched Cecil go for a sword he did not carry.

"This is my world you rotting sack of flesh and bones!"

The room was dimming and each crystal was going dark in turn and from each stepped the forms of shadow men. They did not talk or taunt as the one in the mirror, but they carried there menace with them none the less and Cecil's blood turned to ice. His face held what grim determination he had left and he fought the weakness seeping into his limbs as he watched the shadows surround him.

***

Valis on the other side of the barrier had continued to pound on the invisible force that kept her from her friend, she still had her father's sword and she knew the shadows feared it. The frustration at not being able to offer the one bit of salvation she could offer was killing her from within and the sorrow clutched her heart firmly, squeezing tears from her eyes as she was forced to watch, helpless.

"Princess, please calm...Valis stop!"

The words of fear and concern from Ce'elevan through the bond, the touch on her mind, was enough to break her off her trance. And it was not until that moment when she looked at her hands, knuckles split and the hint of bone showing, did she realize how much pain she was really in. She had been pounding and shouting at the barrier so hard and for so long, that she had pounded her hands to a sore pulp.

"There must be a way in!" she shouted frantically.

Ce'elevan whined and danced from side to side. Helpless to aid in advise and helpless to aid in battle.

***

The furrowed brow of the high Druid kept his eyes closed, one hand resting on Cecil's almost still chest.

"His time is coming to an end. I don't sense the strength in him to make it through this." He opened his eyes and looked into Janian Poledouris's calm blue eyes.

"Cecil," Jan whispered leaning in close to his ear. They had moved him and the others to the stone tables outside on the earth mother's ritual hill. All druids now stood in a circle around them chanting their prayers softly. It was all they could offer as magic was still forbidden on the hill and Janian lamented the fact that she had not been given permission from the Earth Mother as the High Druid had to use her powers. And so she held Cecil's hand, never letting go and whispered words of hope and faith.

The high druid, her friend for many long years had however held nothing back, taking full advantage of the Earth Mother's blessing to use his gift. He had lit the area with spell fire which hovered above the heads of his circled brethren in a protective flaming circle. And despite the intermittent rain that tried to interject its presence as if feeling left out, the flames only hissed turning each droplet away. The fires burned until they were commanded not to and so they raged on dancing slowly in sync with the soft chanting below.

"Cecil you must be strong, you must fight back against the darkness, fight with more than steel and more than words for they are empty there, hollow." She looked back up at her old friend who nodded his approval.

"It's up to him now. To find the light or accept the darkness." The High Druid spoke hauntingly and closed his eyes to join the others in chanted prayer. The flames above them stood up and took notice at the inclusion of his voice.

***

Cecil felt the first hand upon his shoulder and screamed out in horrific pain, his blood turning to fire and racing through his arm, numbing his fingers.

The room around him slid away into darkness and his mind snapped him back to the day his Prince... his friend, had died. He was back in the same clearing he had left him when he was sent to fetch the council that had traveled on ahead.

"You killed him; you should have stayed with him!"

He stood and turned at the sound of the familiar voice and there beside Malik's horse stood the prince's youngest sister Valis.

"He died because of you!" she screamed. "He died for you!"

"No... He commanded and I obeyed!" Cecil hardly believed the words himself as they passed his lips for he truly did feel, deep down within himself that Prince Malik's fate was his doing. If he had not ridden and left his friend alone then perhaps he could have... his thoughts trailed off as unbidden the memory of something Malik had always been known to say had drifted in to take over his thoughts.

"Fight with more than steel and more than words."

He understood them, and they seemed to counter the hold over the guilt and he stood up tall with confidence and looked the accusing incarnation of Valis in the eyes. "He commanded and I obeyed." This time the words sung true in his heart, despite his sorrow for his friend's passing, it was not his fault. It was enough of a realization to cause another of the shadow men to reach out and clutch his other shoulder. Which brought the same soul rendering pain that made him weep openly as it coursed its way through his body. More pain than he had ever felt ran like a river down his legs and he choke from the shock forgetting how to breathe.

The floor rushed up to meet him and the room shifted once more. This time it was Ce'elevan who stood before him. The greyhound's jaws were slick with blood and beside him the man who had taken their master's life.

"You should have been here sooner!" the dog's mouth moved, opening and closing with a wet bloody snap.

Cecil staggered back a few steps at hearing the dog speak in a chilling human voice. Unlike with Valis, Cecil did not feel he should have to defend himself to this creature. It was anger that filled him this time. Anger seeped in around the edges of fear and pain and Cecil stared down the animal that had taken his chance to avenge Malik. He was left with a desire for vengeance he had no one to take out on and it had festered within him. "*Be nicer to my dog*" was what the apparition in the shop had told him. With that memory he was suddenly seeing clearer.

He should be seeing the loyalty Ce'elevan had showed and he should have realized the greyhound was suffering inside as much as he was for this one kill was not enough to call justice done. They had work yet still. The image of the princess of Carn burned red hot in his mind and he could have sworn he had seen the greyhound smile in agreement as Cecil's hatred shifted to the proper target. He desperately wished he had a sword.

The scene melted away and he was left with his anger and his pain huddled over on himself in a tight ball of misery upon the crystal chamber's floor. The shadow figures had covered him with their dark bodies. Anger, hurt, and dark emotion filled his mind. He cracked open his eyes and watched as his hands began to absorb the blackness; his body was being over saturated with their dark essence.

The shadow assassin remained half out of the mirror cackling madly the entire time. It had never known so much joy as it watched and waited for the creation of its new brother, its newest damned follower.

The fire Cecil felt from within was consuming him, burning him from the inside out. He remembered through the horrors ravaging his body the words Janian had spoken about balance. And that she as an Earth Maiden could not wield the fire. Somewhere deep down he heard his own thoughts give him the answer. The earth maidens could not wield it; Janian could not train his power for his was of the Druid aspect of the earth mother. But he could wield the fire. The simple thought gave Cecil the smallest of hope and from that hope a light was born from within the flames.

From the other side of the barrier Valis and Ce'elevan watched in horror as the darkness enveloped their friend. Valis had screamed until she was sure she had ruined her voice permanently for now it was even difficult to swallow making the act of crying so much more painful. She didn't care about the pain at this moment, only that they had come so far to help and had failed in every way possible to help their friend return home from the darkness. she banged her raw, bruised, and swollen hand against the barrier one last time before slumping

down in front of it, resting her head painfully against it. She stared at the dark form that used to

be her friend, she could see the shadow assassin's head thrown back in laughter. She hoped when

their time came they would make it quick. She did not want a lingering death. When the demon's

head came back down from its delighted laughter she noted the change in its face and demeanor.

There was anger in those eyes now, mixed with shock and revulsion.

The last of Cecil's body had been consumed from within by the fire. But the spark he had

created had begun to fuse with the fire. Soon it was spreading faster than anything known to

man. His blood cooled and the fire raged back through his veins as a fierce blue white light up

through his chest, his arms, neck and finally his eyes. The new fire filled with brilliant blue

luminance burst from his mouth and eyes, the darkness that had covered him was burned away in

moments and Cecil found the strength to get his body to his feet.

"You fool... you have no power here this is the void and..." the shadow assassin wailed as

he cringed away from the shining eyes of Cecil reborn in the blue fire.

"No" Cecil said, reaching out and wrapping both hands around the creature's neck he

yanked it from the crystal, that returned to its brilliance the moment the assassin was ripped free.

"You said it yourself, for every one of you there has to first be one of me. We are not in

the void of your home we are in the void created by my own hatred and self loathing. You are

simply a curse living off of me. Within me!" This time the flames began their journey not

through Cecil's body but outwards. They extended to his outstretched arms traveling in long

snake-like spires, until reaching his hands where they leaped like a coiled serpent. They struck

the shadow assassin in the face where it quickly began to absorb the light. Soon it was hissing away into a smoldering handful of blue ashes that blew around the room as brilliant little flecks of light. When it settled on the smooth surface of the floor it burned away into little tiffs of cured smoke.

The barrier holding Valis back now popped like a bubble. She fell forward, quickly scrambling to her feet to rush in. In a flash she flung herself around Cecil, crying and thankful he was alright.

"Hey now what's this?" he said gently pulling her away enough to look her in the eyes. He wiped away the tears and smiled as more took their place "I'm alright now it's ok"

"How did you defeat the shadows Cecil? There was so much I thought I had lost you as well" she sobbed into his chest as he gently stroked her hair.

"There has to be balance, the fear guilt and anger were my own to control and deal with. The shadow was one further problem throwing my body off balance and creating a void for which it could work its dark powers. I can see how most would be overcome by this. Lucky for me I have you and Ce'elevan and Jan who I'm sure had a hand in my soul's liberation.

"And the Earth Mother?" Valis added.

"I have no doubt she was with us the entire time." He brought her back into a gentle embrace laying his chin on her shoulder.

"Ce'elevan says he's glad you made it through" Valis said as she pulled away and dried her eyes on her sleeve, before promptly slapping Cecil across the face, hard. "Don't you ever let something like this happen again! It's not fit for a princess to go chasing after lost souls!" She yelled, waiting for the stunned look on his face to settle. As the shock soon melted from his face she reached out and grabbed his shirt. Before he knew what was happening she had pulled his

lips to hers. If Cecil felt he was in trouble before, the feelings just doubled.

CHAPTER 23

"We're packed father. The carriages are ready."

"Sanossa," the king spoke softly as he held out his arms for his oldest daughter. She was mad at being sent away. He could see it in the way she hesitated before stepping up to be enveloped in his hug. He squeezed her just that little bit tighter and growled like a bear that always made her laugh. Even now that she had long since left childhood far behind he could tell how angry she was at the situation.

"This is all Valis' fault." she pouted, laying her head on her father's shoulder.

"How so? Why would you say such a thing? Are you not stricken with worry for your wayward sister?" he gently pushed her to arm's length.

"Of course I am father; I love my little sister though I think she much would have preferred it to be born a boy." She said with soft eyes that clearly showed the love she felt. "But if she had not run off with the traitor... then none of this would have happened and we would not be having this conversation or being sent from our home!"

The king looked taken aback. He could not tell them of his suspicions of the validity of the boy's crimes. He personally doubted very much that he was filled with enough malice to kill the Prince and plot against his king. No he had looked into that young man's eyes and there was only a loyal servant of the kingdom staring back at him. It brought sick to his throat.

"Sanossa, this whole situation is so twisted that I really have no idea what to expect next. What I do know is that no one loved your brother as much as Valis. Now can you honestly tell me that she would run off with his killer?"

"No... I suppose not, more likely to have run him through." She nodded her approval at her father's take on the situation. "Still, there are rumors abound father, they say Carn's warrior queen seeks our bloody downfall for not killing the traitor, whether you feel he is guilty or not."

Sanossa looked and reminded Zham so much of her mother that he sometimes slipped and called her by her mother's name. He had worked hard at avoiding that as it only served to make them all uncomfortable. She did have a striking resemblance though; the first child usually does. The same love of court and gossip, the same tone in her voice, and even her hair was worn in the same fashion, the color matching her eyes.

"Have faith, I will not let a war happen. I've helped end one before and I can quell this before it gets any worse" he said taking her arm in his and escorting her to the chamber doors.

"Yes, but father..." she protested.

"My Sanossa, my daughter and light of my eyes. I am sending you and your sister to your grandparents in the summer land not out of worry but out of precaution. You will be safe there and in a few weeks I'll send for you to come home, maybe even come get you myself." He explained gently cutting off any other attempts to stall him or his decision.

"Where is safer than here with you?" She asked.

"Sanossa... I…"

"You don't plan on going to Carn do you father? That's madness! Promise me you won't go!" she protested at seeing his plan laid out in his eyes.

The king's face was stern despite his aching heart and he remained silent.

"So be it. I hope I have a home to comeback to... and a father." She ignored the look he gave her as if he were ready to say more. Under guard escort she stormed off. The king was left standing with his mouth agape, his frustration and worry gaining strength.

CHAPTER 24

When Valis opened her eyes, spasms of cold shivering assaulted her as she looked around in confusion. The druid's hall. Her fogged mind began to piece together from the brief time she had spent within the building. Thick robes of fur where draped over her shoulders and Jan's voice filtered through the final chaos of her scattered brain.

"Easy, Valis your back now," Janian spoke, rubbing the shivering Princess's arms. Janian spared a quick look to her side, where the druids were doing the same for both Cecil and Ce'elevan. Although the sleek form of the greyhound seemed perfectly at ease with the journey from the void to the land of the living.

"...I... Cecil is he?" Valis tried to say, her words slow to come.

"He's fine, as is Ce'elevan. You're all fine now. Oh Valis, I'm so proud of you!" Jan's face was smiling and yet tears ran down her cheeks.

"Do you understand why the shadow assassin was able to pull you into the void boy?" the Druid master asked. His first words a question not of concern but of caution. "I would hate to think you had gone through all this to have learned nothing from this trial of the soul."

Despite the shivering the void had left him with, Cecil appeared calm. He looked up at the old man and smiled calmly. "I do. I will never allow such a thing to happen again."

The Druid master paused for a moment on the answer given. Before nodding his approval and gesturing for the druids holding bowls of hot food to bring them forward.

Valis wrinkled her nose at her offered bowl.

"You have to eat; it's a Druid restoration broth... I know how it smells and believe me... it's going to taste worse. But you have to get it down, we are short on time and you three have been gone for quite awhile. You will need your strength back and quickly." Janian explained gesturing to the bowl and as Valis touched the spoon to her lips and frowned at the shake of her hand.

"How long have we been gone?" she asked, coughing as the first little bit of broth trickled down her throat.

"Three days..."

"Three days! But we were gone no more than a few hours!" Valis said nearly spilling the broth as she knocked the druid's hand that held it and he scowled at the sudden outburst.

Even Cecil with his new found calmness frowned slightly at hearing this.

"The time flows much slower in the void...I thought you knew this." Janian said a little surprised "they do teach you about the void in your lessons do they not?"

"No... They do not" Valis grumbled as she turned her nose up at the offered spoonful of broth.

"I'm going to have to have a word about that with your father," Jan said mostly to herself, looking at the ground, lost in another world.

"It will have to wait," Cecil said. His bowl empty and strength already steadying his limbs enough for him to stand.

"We have to stop the Princess of Carn before she has a chance to let loose anymore of her conjured minions."

"You must rest before you..."

"I have rested enough!" Cecil cut the old Druid short.

"The Princess of Carn has made it clear *she* won't rest. Not until there is war with Petsky and *we* are all dead." Cecil did not stay for a reaction; he made his way to the lodge's entrance. He did not look back as he pushed open the door with a creak and stepped out into the light of a new day.

***

Ce'elevan was beside him, the greyhound having slipped out alongside him unnoticed until he had closed the door. The greyhound stayed with him as Cecil made his way to the edge of a small cluster of trees that passed as a forest so high up on the hill. Someone had set fallen logs in a half circle in a small clearing within. As Cecil sat down he could see that it had been used frequently as a camp site. By the druids or other wayward travelers, he was sure.

With Ce'elevan lying at his feet, Cecil could clearly see the stone dais through the trees where they had first seen the High Druid. He felt an odd attachment to that stone; it was big enough to be used as a table.

"Can you feel it?"

Cecil turned at the sound of the familiar voice. It was a voice that had just broken his moment of silence and solitude. Though, he did not mind.

Janian had followed him out into the clearing within the small patch of woods after insuring that Valis was eating enough of the broth to recover properly. She placed a gentle hand on the young man's shoulder.

"May I join you?" she asked gesturing to the log seat next to him.

"Please," He smiled and gestured to the seat as well.

Ce'elevan's ears twitched but showed no other signs of stirring at her arrival.

"Can I feel it?" Cecil said in response to Jan's original question. "Yes, even more now than ever since coming out of the void. It's beautiful."

"This hill is possibly the only place you will feel the Earth Mother's heart beat so loudly," Jan said closing her eyes.

"She truly is in everything," Cecil said closing his own and letting the steady drumming noise fill his ears. It had escorted him back from the void at the moment of Valis's kiss and it made him smile widely now to hear it still.

"Yes, everything. Her essence gave life to a world that at the time was black and decaying. This was her gift to the world when she had chosen to stay, giving up her life with the other gods."

"Except fire." Cecil stated as he pondered her words.

"Truly," she said, eagerly enjoying the lesson.

"Fire was already present in this world, a creation of another god. It had no malice in its original creation but the Earth Mother in her wisdom, deemed that it would hold too much risk of abusing its power should she breathe life into it. And yet how could she not? For this would be cruel to give even the rocks a spark of their own even though it is just a small one. So she met it half way. She would grant the fire a spark of its own but under the strictest of rules and guidelines. Fires life span would only last as long as it was given fuel to live off of, and then must relinquish its flame."

Cecil hung on every word, however he could see a hint of disappointment in Janian's eyes, and he did not press her for more. Resigned to simply sit and wait for her to continue in her own time.

"Cecil, when I was a young child the Earth Mother came to me in my dreams. She began to teach me the ways of the Earth Maidens far before I arrived at the school. She did not teach me anything in the lore of fire and neither did the Maiden instructors. I have often wondered about the relationship between the fire and our Mother. The story I told you I learned from a tavern balled," she finished sheepishly.

Now he understood the hint of jealousy he could see in her when in the presence of the High Druid. She really did wish to teach him, but could not instruct him in something she had never been given lessons in.

"I wish we could ask her," Cecil said with a smile.

"Perhaps you will have that chance, when you return for training. When this is all settled, the High Druid can fill in the gaps for you," Jan said with a smile.

He knew how hard it was for her to admit she didn't have the answers for him. It did not diminish her in his eyes and he hoped she understood this.

They sat in the silence for as long as they dared, finally Jan stood and told him to join her and the others inside when he was ready.

He had questions filling up his mind about the Earth Maiden School and the lessons that went on there, but they would have to wait. He reached down and scratched Ce'elevan between the ears and rubbed his neck. Which was welcomed as the greyhound pressed his head firmly into Cecil's hand.

"Let's go, we have work to do."

They had assembled in the little cabin the high Druid used for himself. They sat upon the ground around the fire pit in the center of the cabin. Cecil kept a close eye on the old man and had made a point of dumping his tea into the fire which brought a smile to Jan's face and a raised eyebrow from her old friend.

Thanks to the restorative effects of the druid's broth both Cecil and Valis looked as well as they had before entering the void, although Valis still had a slight shiver. All effects had fled their bodies from their extended three day stay in the void.

Valis sat idly scratching Ce'elevan's ears and running her hand down the smooth black fur of his neck and back. The greyhound lay with his eyes closed seemingly in a blissful sleep.

Cecil joked about how he thought the only thing that slept longer than greyhounds was spoiled Princesses. No one laughed of course.

"From here," Janian began, "it would take us two weeks to reach the boarders of Carn. And there is no way we would have a chance of catching up to Princess Kerra, she may already have returned."

"What about by boat? The sea wraps around one side of Carn," Valis suggested.

"That would only shave a few days of travel off our journey. There is also the trouble of finding a vessel to go anywhere near Carn's boarders. We have nothing for trade, and we lack the coin to buy our way onto a merchant's ship." Janian answered her question so quickly that Valis felt a little hurt for her idea to be so briskly set aside, and it showed on her face as they continued.

Cecil offered Valis a weak smile before looking over at Jan. "You have a plan already in mind; I assume is what you are trying to tell us, Jan?"

"I do as a matter of fact, although my old and most respected friend here disagrees with this course of action." She smiled sweetly at the high Druid who wore a severe scowl upon his already wrinkled brow.

"Janian..." he began. A raised finger poised to accompany a disparaging remark.

"How safe is this plan of yours?" Valis chimed in, a hint of sarcasm melded with her sweet tone.

"When I was last there, it was devoid of any danger."

"Janian this is..." the High Druid tried once more.

"It's settled then. We take Jan's shortcut." Cecil spoke and then prepared to stand.

"Just like that? You didn't even ask her where?" The old man said hotly.

"Just like that, we follow Janian. So far, she has not led us astray." Valis said as she begun to rise.

They were all interrupted when the infant Prince of Carn made a noise in his enchanted slumber.

"Is there nothing you know of to wake the babe?" Janian asked pleadingly to the High Druid, drawing his gaze.

"No!" he said rather crossly having given up on his earlier protests for the moment to study the still form of the child. He watched as they all did the tiny chest rise and fall, aside from the sound just now this was the only action they had seen the babe perform. "Dark magic is not what we spend sleepless nights studying and don't think for a moment that a baby passing gas is an excuse to change the topic!"

"When I was there last, I encountered no trouble."

"I don't want you seeking the serpent's pass. Janian, it's not safe. Even the Earth Mother is rumored not to be able to see what's inside."

"Foolishness, she is in everything, there is nothing that can hide from her gaze." Janian's argument sounded solid but even she at times had called upon the Earth Mother's blessings to give her sight beyond sight and been met with a wall of nothingness. Her mind flashed back to the carriage the Princess of Carn had traveled in and the frustration she felt at not being able to read the energies inside.

"Besides, the pass was built for just such an occasion."

"That does not excuse the fact that it is hidden within a city occupied by soldiers of your enemies." The old man was red faced now as he argued with the stone faced Earth Maiden.

"It will be fine I assure you. Now if you don't mind we should really be on our way as we have a long journey ahead of us." Janian did not wait for any further argument from her old friend and allowed Valis to secure the Prince in his backpack, onto her shoulders, and led the way from the building not giving it a second glance.

Valis raised her eyebrows in question at Cecil and he responded with a shrug and shake of his head as he followed Janian out.

If Janian had hoped that by leaving the cabin and walking away from the High Druid would end the conversation she was wrong.

"Restwick is still under Carn control, Janian!" the old man said keeping pace despite his age.

Cecil's face registered with understanding. Restwick was the only major city east of both Petsky and Carn. Only from what he remembered; Restwick was in the opposite direction from where they needed to go.

"Restwick, are you insane? There's nothing there but muggers and drunken sailors!" Valis protested as they continued to walk the path leading to where they had first arrived.

"You see, even your young friend here has more sense! I'm sure if the dogs could talk they would say the same!" the old man gestured to the two greyhounds following on either side of Janian. If either one had issues with the plan they didn't speak up. Not that they understood what was being said anyways, and Valis did not appear to be in the mood to check.

"Every idea has the potential to be a bad one or a good one my old friend," Janian said, turning and offering a wide smile as he shook his head at her.

"I truly hope you prove me wrong sister, I truly do."

Several monks had gathered to see them off and they offered both Valis and Cecil light travel packs with enough rations to see them to their destination.

"You better be sure about this short cut Jan, there is enough food for maybe four days and we lack the money to resupply in a busy port town," Cecil said, in a low voice as he stood beside her. A smile was all she seemed to be willing to give anyone as an answer and he simply nodded his head in acceptance.

"Wouldn't horses be faster than walking?" Valis grumbled as she fought with a twisted strap on her pack.

"And pay for them with what? I suppose we could sell one of the dogs," Cecil said with no hint of humor in his voice. Until the look Valis was giving was too much and he revealed his jest in an open smile and mischievous laugh. Both dogs growled up at him having been let in on the comment and Cecil stopped smiling. "I was only kidding!"

"Perhaps if I..."

"No." Janian answered Valis firmly. "I know what you were going to say. Right now it's for the best that your father does not know where you are. If Princess Kerra were to even suspect he knew your location then she would have reason to threaten him. And what would happen if she sent some monster after him without his sword? Without... No, as long as there are still soldiers out looking for you, then the safer you and your family will be."

Valis looked as though she very much would like to argue, but her features eventually relaxed as the Earth Maiden's logic sunk in.

"Listen to Janian, even if I do not agree with the plan to use the serpent's pass, I trust that she will see you safely through." The old man said, addressing the younger members of the party. He reached out and grabbed Cecil, pulling him aside, giving Jan a nod that he would send the young man after them in a moment. Jan nodded in return and started down the path.

"Listen to what she says and what she does. She may not be able to teach you all you need to know, but she can begin the basics for you. When this is over and she has no more need of you, then come and find us. I will begin your training in the druidic arts. The Earth Mother willing, you will not retain Janian's sass mouth." The High Druid smirked, and nodded that Cecil should hurry to catch up with the others.

The High Druid watched them disappear over the crest of the hills path downward. If he could have he would never have let them go, especially the boy. He no longer sensed the shadow that had seeped into his soul but there was still something else, something he could not see. That worried him as he turned back to the druids and his own problems. He shuffled along, as if the encounter and strain of the last few days had finally caught up to him.

CHAPTER 25

"It looks like a regular city, Jan." Valis said, as they stood on a ridge overlooking a valley that winded downward and off to the east in where laid a port city.

"We are a little far yet for you to see the truth of Restwick, it really is no place for a Princess." Cecil spoke as he tried to fight back a yawn.

Both Valis and Janian exchanged worried looks.

They had traveled at a decent pace, heading toward the coast from their time upon the Earth Mother's ritual hill and the druids that had seen them off. All had been at ease, until night fell on the first day. They had set camp as light as it was, jackets and packs as pillows. Ce'elevan relayed through the bond to Valis that the greyhounds would keep watch during the night.

It was peaceful and warm, a light rain had come and gone leaving the ground spotted with wet drops but remaining dry for the most part. As Janian and Valis slept without difficulty, Cecil could not close his eyes. He had tried to sleep, his mind just as drained of energy as the rest of his body was. But it had soon become apparent that he was not as well as the High Druid had declared him to be. Each time he shut his eyes the void kept rushing back, and with it so too did the shadows.

For the next three nights it was the same. They would travel until they could go no further and while the others slept to regain their strength, Cecil continued to suffer. Janian had been the first to notice as the young man tried to ignore the problem, as young men often do. But the darkness under the eyes and souring mood quickly drew the other's attention.

"Last night seems to have had little effect, though you did sleep for a few hours," Janian commented as she watched Cecil closely.

"I know. I welcomed your idea to sooth me with the Earth Mother's gift Jan, believe me I did. But it only seemed to trap me there." Cecil gave a tired shake of his head.

"Was it the same as before... just the shadows?" Valis asked placing a hand gently on his shoulder and quickly removed it at the irritated look her friend had shot her.

"Yes! I'm sorry," Cecil's face softened and if possible looked even more tired at the effort to carry on even this little bit of conversation.

"There was no shadow assassin?" Jan finished the line of questioning.

"No. Still no sign of it, not even a whispered voice." Cecil's words were sluggish with the effort.

They all startled as two animals came with abound up the path towards them, and they sighed with relief at the pair of greyhounds who approached.

"Ce'elevan says they have already scouted the path and it's clear all the way to the bottom. The road below intersects with the highway and so we will see people there." Valis reported on their behalf.

"Thank you, we are on our way." Jan smiled at the dogs trusting Valis to let them know what she said.

With a nod of Valis's head, the greyhounds bounded back off down the path. Ce'elevan cast a quick look back at Cecil as he followed after Sophal.

"You worry too much about him, he's not even your master" Sophal said as they fell into a lazy pace.

"And I wish sometimes that the bond did not allow this kind of communication between us. Canine speak with you would be just fine," Ce'elevan snapped back.

A low growl accompanied the baring of teeth from Sophal as she rounded on the younger greyhound.

"Was that dog enough for you? You forget that the bond is a gift."

Ce'elevan stopped and gave a growl of his own *"A gift between us and our masters!"*

"Did you say our masters? The boy is not your master and the girl can barely hear us through the bond at the best of times. The bond between my Master and I is far greater than a pup like you, will ever be able to grasp!" Sophal snarled back.

"That's enough!" A shout came through the bond. The others had caught up as the dogs stood still to argue and the look on Valis's face said that she had heard most of the argument and was not impressed.

"You both disappoint me greatly. Ce'elevan take rear guard, Sophal takes the lead," she commanded.

"I do not take orders from you, only my master, girl! You can't..." Sophal said loudly holding her ground.

"I am the only one of royal blood in this party and until we get you home, that makes me your master, now, move!" Valis had reached the dogs and pulled them apart by the back of their collars, pushing Ce'elevan behind her and Sophal off to the front.

Both dogs obeyed. The assertiveness seemed to have been needed.

"You still think we are more than just dogs?" Ce'elevan asked Valis as she looked down crossly at him.

"I do Ce'elevan and you should have more faith in yourselves. You will patch things up with Sophal before we reach Carn as I will not have you both at each other's throats, am I understood? As weak as I am with the bond?" Valis finished.

There was no further argument from Ce'elevan and he allowed the other to walk on ahead of him as he hung back to take up his post as rear guard.

Janian cast Valis a look with one raised eyebrow to ask if everything was under control and Valis answered with a curt nod. Cecil walked on behind them nearly oblivious to what was going on around him, far too tired to care.

***

One foot in front of the other, it thought. The creature's mind was sluggish, as if waking from a week long slumber. However, it still managed to put one foot in front of the other.

Its skin itched as it walked. The sun beating down had hurt its eyes until finally, day gave way to night and the itch was replaced with shakes from the cool twilight air. What remained of its clothes had been torn to shreds and hung as lifeless as the creature's arms. Its breathing was interrupted from its steady draw every so often and that's when the pain increased.

The creature had a direction, though why it was headed that way was lost to it. A feeling, deep down in its gut, a gut now twisted and bulging was what it followed. A sense of urgency still helped move the creature as it changed. It was changing, it realized though slowly and the simple realization taking hours to surface.

At one point it had stopped. Once more the brain slowly worked and it took some time before it realized the body at its feet was dead, a hole through its chest. Blood was everywhere, even on the long barbed appendage that used to be something else, but the creature just could not think of what it was. Another bout of body wrenching pain shot through it and it gave up on thinking so heavily. Instead it returned to following that feeling in its gut. It had to be somewhere, it had a purpose, and nothing would stop it. This it knew as it walked on. Screaming had reached its ears but the creature was unaware if they belonged to the other bodies he had passed, or if they belonged to itself.

***

Sophal had been raised by the Queen herself. She was a royal dog through and through and she was also a loyal dog. She fumed at the words Valis had said, about her being the only Princess around. She was a silly child if she thought distance mattered where Sophal's loyalty was concerned.

They had filled her in on the plan to use the serpents tunnel, though she had never heard mention of such a thing before. She had her doubts about the confidence of this plan. Oh she knew she could trust the members of the party but there was still much mystery about the one called Janian. Sophal knew that at least in Carn the practice of the Earth Maidens was forbidden and if one was discovered within their borders they were quickly...relocated. Should they succeed and return quickly to Carn through use of this tunnel she wondered if her loyalty would see her on the other side of friendship with these people.

Sophal waited at the bottom of the path. It had not taken her long to reach the bottom and she had moved quickly while lost in thought. The bond made her aware of more than a simple dog would be aware of and sometimes wished her thoughts could be so simple. She knew how to communicate with a regular dog but she honestly preferred the long conversations she shared with her master. She was almost jealous when the baby had arrived; her master spent so much of her time with the child that often when she spoke, the bond was only met with silence. She had pushed that jealousy aside roughly, she was the Queen's hound, she was a guardian and that extended to the growing family. The man who had shared her bed was not to be trusted and there was something she had always disliked about him. Perhaps that was the reason she had a hard time trusting, Valis. They shared much of the same scent, being as the man was Valis's uncle.

She lay down, off to the side of the path, just under the low hanging branches of a large pine and watched the road a dozen feet ahead. People had passed by; Sophal remained unnoticed as she lay still, watching. Merchants from the east and the west both arrived to head into the city. She could smell the sea air from here and the musty scent of fish drying in the sun.

Her ears picked up the sound of foot prints coming down from the path and she left her cover to stand waiting as her party came into view. The Princess of Petsky led the way followed by the young man who had not slept proper in days. His scent was changed often and she did not like that. The Earth Maiden, who she still withheld judgment on despite their journey so far, was next. Her scent was light as though the wind helped carry it away from her. And finally behind her came the other greyhound in the party, a royal dog, like herself, only much younger and who had a lot to learn in the way of the bond.

"Report?" Valis's question came through the bond. Sophal hesitated still bucking at the chain of command but reported no incidents and no current danger before she allowed it to become a larger issue.

"I'm sorry about earlier," Ce'elevan said as he approached her. They walked off out of the way of the milling humans as they discussed their next move.

"You were right, I am still untrained in the bond and perhaps still just a p..."

"Do not start thinking that you are less than you are. You have come a long way. pup, and we still have a long way ahead of us. I will train you in the bond as best I can in that time. And ...I apologize as well, I should know better than to lose my patience so easily and my temper even faster." Sophal said quickly cutting him off.

Both greyhounds and humans stood in silence for a moment as they looked down the road that would take them to the port city.

"You two have to stay here," Valis said softly, yet with a firm command.

"Why?" Ce'elevan asked almost mimicking the whine of a normal dog in the process.

"Because that is a city full of peasants, pup, if they take us in there we stand out. Two royal greyhounds would draw plenty of attention." Sophal filled the younger dog in earning a surprised look from the Princess.

"Scout along the outskirts of the city. Stay hidden as best you can and wait for me, I'll let you know when we find Jan's tunnel. Alert me to any danger at all and keep yourselves safe." Valis said as she reached down and scratched Ce'elevan behind the ears the familiar press of his head into her hand brought a warm smile to her face. She nodded to Sophal. She stood and with a nod to her friends they left the greyhounds behind, walking east along the well-used road toward the port city of Restwick.

CHAPTER 26

The sun had reached mid-day. Cecil was having a hard time keeping his eyes open during the trip, however, that all changed when the noise and sheer volume of people greeted them just within the city gates.

"There had been hundreds of soldiers when last I was here," Janian said.

There stood a handful of guards at the city's entrance, a few posted as sentries, armour polished and gleaming. They looked more like statues at a royal palace than guards on duty. The others wore less in the way of regalia and more of the simple, more expected guard attire of light plate. Some even had on only black leather, the crest of Carn embroidered proudly in the middle. These men were the ones with swords on hip instead of ornamental lances and performed the general duties of checking wagons and wares for dangerous goods, before allowing them into the city. Cecil had a hard time wondering which ones would be paid more, the actual working guards or the ones dressed as statues.

"Did it have as many people when you were here last?" Valis asked, trying not to let passing people force a gap between her and her friends.

"Oh yes, even though it was freshly taken by Carn at the time, it was still the only major port city. Despite the hundreds of Carn soldiers, business was allowed to continue." Jan explained.

Janian stopped for a moment and Cecil and Valis huddled close as people thronged around them like they were a tree in the middle of a river.

"Do you suppose these people ever stop to eat?" Valis asked as they moved on. She reached out and laced her arm through Cecil's, pulling him close. If her closeness bothered him he didn't show it.

"I'm more worried about what *we* are going to eat; the rations are all but gone. At least the dogs can fend for themselves," was his dower response. The lack of proper rest was still making his mind groggy and the downcast look upon the Princess's face was lost on him.

"Trust in Jan, I'm sure she won't let us starve," Valis mumbled.

Janian led them through street after street. A few of them even had signs standing upon corners to direct them in the proper placement of certain shops or taverns; none of which helped if you had never been there before. Who would care what the place was called? A simple inn that was all Cecil was hoping for at the moment. He had stumbled several times and was now very glad that Valis had held him so close. This was not the city he was used to and he wondered how it could be so much bigger than Petsky's own. That's when the smells hit him.

There were vendors of one type of food or another on nearly every corner they past. He was thankful they had skirted the market itself having only caught a glimpse as they hurried by. Hundreds of stalls and three times as many people from what Cecil had seen and he nearly toppled as the sight made him dizzy. Or perhaps it was just the exhaustion, he was no longer sure.

Cecil wished he could close his eyes; it would not help the noise however. The talking and shouting of the people did little to ease his tension but it was informative. He heard people talk of rumors of war looming between Carn and Petsky. Not within earshot of the guards they occasionally past, it seemed the populace was not truly at ease with their new Carn rulers. There was so much that he knew he was missing as they pressed on and a part of him wanted to just stand in the middle and listen. Though he doubted he could get away with such a thing here, not without someone raising suspicion at the only man not moving. There were rumors about Valis and himself as well, and he wondered if he truly felt her tense up just ever so slightly when he had heard them. "Kidnapped" one group had said "traitor" whispered another. None seemed to guess at the truth.

Cecil wished he was back with the dogs; he would have preferred their company right now to all of this. His mind drifted to thoughts of lying in soft grass staring up at a night sky full of crowded stars. At least the stars would be far, far away from him and they didn't ask any questions.

They moved on, Valis clinging to Cecil as they did their best to keep pace with Janian. The Earth Maiden, her beautiful blue dress plastered to her legs as she moved quickly, steered her friends down an alley that did not fit the same style as the buildings around it. No one seemed to notice or perhaps it was that they did not care that the three of them disappeared from the streets and down the slim alley. Cecil looked back to the entrance as they moved further in and watched the people pass by oblivious. *Their day was uninterrupted, they had things to do, and why would they care?* He thought.

The alley was only little more than Cecil's shoulders were wide and he was all but dragged through it by the young woman using his arm as a leash. His sleep-addled mind returned to the problem of the two of them and thoughts of the kiss she had given him tried to push its way to the forefront of his mind. Cecil shook his head to clear it and nearly fell from the dizziness and blackness that followed, threatening to blot out his world. Valis looked back in concern feeling the odd tug on her arm and he smiled as reassuringly as he could.

Coming out of the alley almost made Cecil want to turn around and go back the way they came. There was just another set of streets but far different than the ones in the city they had seen so far. These were filthy. Shadows were cast everywhere as the buildings were tall but stuck very close together. It looked like another city within the city. Only this one was dark, it smelled, and he was pretty sure he had stepped in something and was too worried to look down and find out.

"Jan," Valis said with concern.

"What are we doing in the slums?"

"Some would say that with a roof over your head, however patched, and food in your belly however spoiled, that this was indeed paradise." Jan said, turning and facing them with a smile on her face. It did not match the look of the others.

"It has been a very long time since I have been in this city, and longer still since I was last in this tavern." Jan lamented as she looked up at the sign above. It swung gently, silently, despite the rust that seemed to be growing over its hinges. "Follow whatever I say, no improvising. And Valis...control any urges you may have to lash out; your title won't save you here."

Valis clenched and with some effort unclenched her jaw.

"Whatever you say, Jan. Not a word from me."

"Stop it, I meant no offense by it. You are rather strong willed, Valis, and it's to be admired...caution is what I should have implied." Jan said sternly bringing another look from Valis reminiscent of one who suddenly bit into a sour grape.

The door to the tavern opened and the party were greeted by a woman nearly as elegant and beautiful as Jan. The only noticeable difference was this lady wore her hair up in a servant's bun and her clothes were patched rags, dismal compared to Jan's blue dress, as dirty and travel worn as it was.

"Even after all these years I can still sense when you stand outside my door. Hello sister," the woman said with a sudden smile and reached out to embrace Jan.

"By the Earth Mother's blessings, it's good to see you again!" Jan excitedly embraced back.

"Well," the woman said as she took in the others, "I trust you need a room for...?" the woman said trying to goad Jan into an answer.

"A room for the night, at least. Is killdory here?" Jan said brushing the question off quickly.

"No... He passed, two years back now." The woman's voice had gone quite as if she had just been reminded after trying so hard to forget. She caught Cecil's movement as he looked up at the swinging sign and followed his gaze. She looked back at Cecil and nodded in acknowledgment that the name on the sign had belonged to the deceased. Cecil was too tired to offer more than a simple nod.

"The blessings of the Earth Mother be forever with him," Jan offered. The look the woman gave in response was cold at first, mixed with the smallest look of betrayal.

"Well now, who are your friends? Sister." she smiled.

"Forgive me, Leana, may I introduce Valis and Cecil, a couple I met along the road and have become fast friends with. This sleeping Prince is Henry, their child. She said uncovering the Prince's face for Leana to coo at. Valis, Cecil, this is Leana, we went to school together."

"You're an Earth Maiden?" Valis blurted out. She could not contain her sudden excitement at meeting another one.

"No, sadly I left the order a very long time ago; it didn't leave much time for matters of the heart you see." Leana smiled politely but the flick of her eyes back at Jan said there was a story not told and Valis would have to accept that for now.

"Now, please come in, come in. Folks are going to wonder why I've been standing in the door way talking to myself," she laughed pleasantly ushering them inside.

With the door closed the empty street returned to its silence, save for the sign that swung gently back and forth, the hinges now squeaking as if glad to be alone so as it may chatter on uninterrupted.

The inside of the tavern was the opposite of the silent street. The entrance was narrow and assorted cloaks, packs and other clothes hung on pegs and more was simply discarded in piles on each side. Valis had a look of disdain on her face but one look from Jan had her quickly composed. At the offer of Leana to take Valis's jacket she panicked, until she discovered the wry smile on the woman's lips and offered a polite one of her own.

214

Beyond that point was the main room; it was large enough to house the thirty or so patrons all of which were too busy with their drink. Or the girls that wore barely anything resembling clothing, who had brought it to them.

Cecil winced as Valis squeezed his arm just that much too tight.

"Please, let me get you some food, I'm sure you must be tired." Leana's eyes lingered on Cecil as she spoke and smiled when Valis clutched him closer.

"I'll have rooms made ready while you dine, one for the lady's and one for the young man" she teased speaking directly to Valis, whose jaw clenched until Janian spoke.

"That will be fine, if you can spare it Leana. It looks like you have a busy night" Jan said as her eyes took in each and every patron, cataloging faces as well as possible threats.

"Most of these folk live in the slums," she sighed. "And most of them won't have the coin promised me upon arrival. Oh don't worry," she said at Jan's concerned look. "My girls are excellent pick pockets, if there's coin on them it soon won't be. You would be surprised how many seem to forget they had any in the first place." With that said Leana smiled warmly at Jan and turned on her heels disappearing into the crowd of noisy patrons.

"Jan, what are we doing here?" Valis felt the need to ask once more as they found a table. Most were occupied but one became available as its sole occupant toppled from his seat to the floor and the three were careful to step around the man passed out with a surprisingly full drink in his hand.

"What about this, Leana? I find it very hard to believe a lady with such...practices can be of any help," Valis said, trying to be as discreet as she could as one of Leana's girls laughed in the lap of a man sitting with others at a table not far from theirs.

Cecil had sat down first and leaned against the wall closing his eyes. He was still awake but the others talked on without him, which for the moment suited him just fine.

Janian waited to speak and before Valis could say anything more, Leana was at the side of the table. It seemed Jan knew this woman well enough as to know when she was most likely to reappear. She arrived with one of her serving girls carrying a tray of watery soup that was little more than a weak broth, but beside it was plenty of thick bread sliced and served with cheese that they had melted on top of. There was wine in Jan's cup and Leana winked as she placed it in front of her friend. For the others, their cups offered nothing more than water and as it met their dried lips and dust filled throats they were thankful for it.

"I'll leave you all to it; I'll send a girl to let you know when the rooms are ready. Jan, don't you go leaving without having a long conversation with me. We have thing to discuss," Leana said politely but with severity.

"When I have these two safely tucked away in their beds I'll be down to have that talk."

This pleased Leana as she nodded and left them in peace. Valis watched her leave and noted the slap on her rear end as she passed a table of drunken fools. Leana laughed and slapped the man's shoulder playfully before moving on. Her eyes raced back to Janian all but demanding an explanation.

"Cecil I know you need your rest but listen as best you can," Janian began.

"Restwick, as you know, is now under Carnian rule. Its location used to sit just outside Petsky boarders and was situated just within Carn's boarders to the west and Vergratto to the south. Now we all know of the long lasting feud, battles and outright war between those two since people roamed those lands. When Carn's King was tired of having to pay the same prices as Vergratto on goods coming in from Restwick, he declared war on this city and the invasion began within the month." Jan sat back and took a sip of her wine, it was bitter and she was sure it was mixed with something but she swallowed anyways thankful for the moment to gather her thoughts.

"Vergratto fought back though not on behalf of the people of Restwick. I remember some of this from my lessons." Valis offered filling in the gap of silence.

"Yes and although Carn was swift to enter Restwick they still had to fight back the pressing forces of Vergratto to maintain their hold here. The small army that Restwick gathered was little more than one hundred trained soldiers and most of them were slaughtered the first day the invasion came."

At the mention of the battle the Prince stirred in his sleep and for a moment the three watched holding their breath in hopes the babe would finally waken. When he fussed no more, Jan sighed and continued.

"The ruling council of Restwick went into hiding, those that escaped sought asylum in Petsky who had sworn to Carn to stay neutral in the matter." Jan stopped and raised an eyebrow at Valis who looked ready to explode. She waited until the young woman took a deep breath and calmed herself.

"I know it's difficult to hear these things but you need to know why we are here." Jan waited until Valis nodded. Cecil had opened his eyes though he still remained silent.

At the time, during the occupation, your father, Alex and I were hired on as mercenaries...as added security for a noble family that refused to leave. This family had accepted the occupation from Carn welcoming their new ruler with open arms. It was hard to stomach but we and those of the house were left largely alone by the soldiers marching daily through the streets. Your father's identity was kept secret, it had always been a game of ours to decide what to call him as we went from place to place" Jan stopped lost in memories and the smile on her lips was warm and genuine.

"One night, while we were on patrol on the estates east side, facing the sea, we failed in our duty. The people of Restwick had not been so easily cowed into accepting the new ruler and an underground resistance had formed. The soldiers who had lived and escaped on that first day of battle went into hiding and slowly started gathering the people. That night they had slipped into the estate and killed the family while they slept. Captured the servants and us mercenaries...we surrendered."

"Oh, Janian I never knew. It must have been awful for you." Valis said covering her mouth with her hand the shock fresh in her eyes.

Jan simply shrugged, "we were paid to do a job and we failed. We found ourselves simply without an employer."

"It's hardly like you needed it considering who you were with," Cecil added.

"It was a different time; your father was hunted, much..." Jan said no more as the serving girl from earlier arrived to take the empty bowls and refill the mugs.

"Much, if not more than you are now, considering it was a time of war. We really had no right being so far from home and worrying our loved ones," Jan said looking at Valis who for some reason could not meet her eyes.

"There are circumstances that force one's hand Jan," Cecil spoke softly.

"So there is. And I am all too aware of this. Everything happens for a reason," she smiled at Valis who did not feel like smiling back.

"How did you get away from this, resistance?" Valis asked leaning forward, resting her chin on her hands.

Jan smiled as for a moment she remembered the same woman as she was a child, hanging on every word whenever Jan would visit.

"We did not. We ended up joining them." She let them think on her words for a while, taking another sip of the bitter wine.

"Your father was as night and day on the issue. On one hand we no longer had a reason to be in Restwick and he hated the idea of being under these peoples control. On the other, once we found out the resistance was smuggling people out, he was one of their biggest supporters."

"Out, out were? Where could they go with Petsky neutral and war on the other sides?" Cecil asked.

"They smuggled them to Petsky without the king's consent. My father nearly brought war to our people," Valis sat back, her face gone white as she realized the severity of the situation.

"Well, yes and no. Carn was far too busy and never really had the troops to wage war on three sides and Petsky's always had the support of the soldiers in the Summer land's, though that's changed as well over time." Jan continued.

"We fought patrols in the night when we had to. There were old sewer networks that someone had discovered and they offered an exit fifteen miles to the north of the city boundaries. There were no Carnian soldiers patrolling that far out."

Jan let them absorb her words before moving on.

"The other side of the resistance was what we all had a problem with. The plan was to attack Carn while their soldiers were spread thin and far from home. And this is why we are here." She waited keeping the others in suspense, she didn't have to of course, but sometimes it was important to try and lighten the mood, especially if the conversation had been fraught with ill mannered news. She smiled, a smirk really as Cecil closed his eyes and leaned back against the wall leaving Valis to sigh in frustration, Jan even thought she caught the sound of a low growl mixed in.

"They called it the serpent's pass. While looking for ways to extradite those seeking a hasty retreat from Restwick, searching the tunnels under the city, a select few came across a tunnel system. A system so ancient that they think it predates the Earth Mother's sacrifice to give us all the spark of life. Built by one of the other gods some would say, though I personally suggested it was not as old as that, merely dated as far back as the time of darker magic. A tunnel created by those who cast magic from the shadows and summoned demons of untold power."

"So the High Druid was right? Even the Earth Mother cannot see into it?" Cecil asked once again very interested. Enough so that for once he looked more awake than he had the last few days.

"The Earth Mother sees all, Cecil" Jan said with a slightly heated voice. The young man made no motion to argue.

"How are we supposed to use something made by dark magic?" Valis said as a glassy expression fell over her face, as she thought deeply.

"The men who discovered it were the first to explore it. The tunnel is large, well over thirty feet tall and just about that in width. They did not encounter anything dangerous or with malicious intent. They did however discover that the time spent inside the tunnel moved in a different way then it did outside the tunnel.

This was discovered of course by where after three hours of travel within the serpent tunnel had brought them to its exit."

"Were does it lead?" Valis asked leaning forward once more, her voice excited.

"The oddest of places, a store room within the lower levels of Carn's own palace." Jan said, not surprised at all to see the look on her friends faces.

"So we can travel straight into the palace within a day thanks to this serpent's pass? Cutting a week of travel?" Cecil asked trying to keep his voice low but letting a hint of his growing fondness for the plan peek through.

"Why didn't the resistance use this to take control of Carn? With their forces spread so thin I can't see it being much of an ordeal," Valis asked.

"I'm not sure. Your father, Alex and I were only taken there once and we were blindfolded at the time. I think they just wanted to show it off." We left to escort refugees through the normal tunnels and see them safely to Petsky. We never came back, until now." Jan said shaking her head with the resurrected memory. "It was so long ago; we were no more than kids really seventeen or nineteen, it's hard to recall."

"Then how are we to use it if you don't even know where it is?" Valis asked.

A groan escaped Cecil's throat and both Jan and Valis looked at him with sudden concern. "Not more sewers! I'll stand guard up top while you look, or better yet bring the dogs in and send them down to look for it!" he pleaded.

"I will talk to Leana and see if she has information on some old contacts that can help us out. Now here comes the girl again I suspect your rooms are ready. Sleep well tonight, with luck we won't be in the city by tomorrow night.

Valis was amazed that Jan was correct; the serving girl was indeed heading their way. How she had done so without looking was only part of Jan's charm she supposed.

"The rooms are ready for you if you will follow me," the skinny girl with a dirty apron around her waist said.

With a nod from Jan they stood and headed for the stairs. The serving girl lingered and smiled at Jan "Mistress Leana wishes to have 'that talk' now, she says. You may find her in the kitchen, just down the hall, doorway on the left." Jan nodded and the girl met the others at the stairs, Cecil being the gentleman that he was let the ladies go first and he cast a quick look back at Jan who was now sitting alone. He had time to see her take another sip of wine before moving up the stairs and out of view.

***

Both eyes had closed shut now and the creature had long since fallen over.

It still moved onward however, slow at first like a worm through moist soil, dragging the back half up then extending the top half out, but its body was still changing and soon it was using the long spider like arms that had itched and burst through its sides. Legs it now had but still no eyes and so the creature had to use the over powering sense it had that still throbbed in its gut.

It had followed this feeling for many long miles and along the way it had encountered more of the other creatures that seemed determined to get in its way. They did not know just how strong the pull was or the desire to get where it was going. They also did not anticipate the sharp needle pointed teeth it had grown when its other rounder teeth had fallen out. It had stopped long enough to dislodge one of the soft creatures from where it had impaled itself upon one of the long spider like legs, but moved on sparing it no second thought. It was getting closer to where it needed to be, it could feel it.

***

Janian stopped in the hall just before heading into the kitchen. She wasn't long, she just had to wait and see if her instincts were true. All night she had noticed they had been watched. Since arriving a man, cloaked and sitting in a darkened corner had watched them. At least she felt he had. It was so poorly lit inside that it was near impossible to see any features. She had however seen the bushy end of a beard sticking out from beneath the hood and that beard had faced their direction. She shouldn't be too worried; however, her instincts on such matters were rarely wrong. She had years of practice thanks to her travels and the adventures her friends had taken her on. Still it was the seediest part of the city and the darker kind of customers were to be expected. She just wished her friend screened her clients a touch better. She sighed when no one followed and so headed into the kitchen.

She found her friend sitting in an old chair leaned back against a counter. Her long auburn hair was tossed over her shoulder and cascaded down her front. Her eyes opened as Jan approached and she offered a wry smile as Jan raised a questioning eyebrow at the black and worn pipe that sat upon the small table between them.

"Killdory's," Leana said closing her eyes and taking a deep breath. The smoke from the pipe sent small plumes of soft grey smoke into the air. It wasn't unpleasant but Jan had never really taken to the smell.

"How did it happen, Leana," Jan asked gently taking a seat in the chair opposite her friend.

Leana's eyes snapped to Janian followed with a harsh look before startling herself and looking down in embarrassment "I'm sorry Jan; it's just been so hard without him. I'm used to having to defend myself more often than not. Even in the slums they have little faith a woman can run a tavern on her own and it's taken a great deal out of me to prove them wrong."

"I meant no offense Leana. He was in fine health when last I saw you both and he was a friend. Please, how did he meet his end? Was he Ill? Or..." Jan could not finish as Leana had suddenly started to cry, she was struggling to stop, hold the tears in but that was only making her anguish fight back all the harder.

Janian stood and pulled her chair with her as she moved to the other side of the table sitting beside Leana. She pulled her friend into her arms in a sisterly embrace. She held her friend and there they sat for some time. Janian sat, allowing Leana to release her pain that she had obviously been neglecting to do, and silently sending thoughts and prayers to the Earth Mother to help lend her friend strength. The sounds of a busy tavern continued on. The sound of a dish breaking the sound of laughter and the silent gloom that permeated the air mixed with the scent of a pipe Janian decided she no longer liked.

Upstairs it was far more quite and down the hall lined with rooms stood a man in a hooded cloak. No one had seen him arrive but some may have seen him leave. He had left through the taverns main entrance but had appeared in the hall with no one below or above the wiser. Save for the three other men he had arrived with, the last of which was just shutting the door that had remained hidden behind the large portrait of a tree. It was an uninspiring tree and so it did its job well in raising no one's interest in that part of the hall nor the painting and the hidden switch behind its frame. The soft click as the third man closed the door was the only sound for the moment and made the first man, the hooded man, with the beard that jutted out from under the hoods concealment, smile.

The hooded man gestured to a particular door and two of his fellows silently creep that way. The remaining man followed the hooded figure to another room two down from the other. He had paid a high price for the info on his targets but the serving girl was as hungry as the rest of them and took little persuasion to tell him what he wanted to know, a few coins lighter did little to damper his spirits. He had waited a long time for revenge and tonight it would be his.

The woman who had arrived may have been gone for a long time and at first as he had sat in his darkened corner and did not, could not believe it was her. But as he watched through the night he did not doubt the woman was Janian Poledouris, the woman who had killed his son.

And so tonight he would take what she valued, a life for a life.

He paused; hand on the knob of the door. He had not always been this way; he had been just, a soldier, a captain, and a good man. But she had taken that all away from him.

CHAPTER 27

The king had watched the carriage that carried his two daughters, the last of his family away. The last of his family save for Valis, his youngest daughter, who occupied his mind now as he marched off down the corridor. Several of the king's knights and a handful of guards followed him out into the courtyard where a larger force had assembled. His mind was set and no man would convince him otherwise, he would ride for Carn himself. Zhamar Damaste the king of Petsky would arrive within three days for an audience with her Grace, the Queen of Carn. Those were the only words he had spoken to the four messengers he had assembled early in the morning. He chose the four swiftest riders he had and to each he gave that simple message. He also sent them to Carn on four different paths each leading to Carn's boarders. When he arrived in person he prayed that he would see them all, or at the very least he hoped one would get through. He didn't need the Queen of Carn thinking he was leading an invasion force to her doorstep.

"How many have returned commander," Zhamar asked the older knight, standing by his side.

"Seventeen knights and twenty soldiers my king" Brannon said with a salute. He had been pulled out of retirement and by the way the man conducted himself you would never know he was gone. If anything Brannon was overjoyed to be back in command.

"Seventeen?" the king mused as he mounted his horse "I didn't realize we had that many knights still at court, commander, well done" he finished with a grin.

"The men are ready to march at your command my king." Brannon smiled after mounting his own horse, an old horse for an old man judging by the way the horse's eyes looked duly on everything and had taken several tries for Brannon to get it moving.

"Why don't you take a younger horse, Brannon? We have plenty of...sturdier mounts."

"My king, Henry and I have seen many battles and many roads, he has never faltered once, and it would be an insult not to take him." He finished, patting the horse's neck and smiled looking back at the king.

"It's a hard three-day ride that I plan on doing in half that time, if we ride hard and walk them at night," the king said cautiously.

This seemed to give the old knight pause. Travel at night is dangerous at the best of times but leading a horse? One wrong step and a leg broken, the horse lost. Brannon nodded solemnly, "I shall have to walk him with great care than, Zham."

The king accepted this and offered a nod, then set his sights on the men around him and hoped he wouldn't need a single one of them. Except for his scouts all his knights and regular soldiers wore their blades tied in peace bonds with a white strip of silk tying the hilt to the sheath.

Zhamar gave one last thought to his family, his son Malik; killed on the very road he now headed out on, his daughters who two of which he had sent away for their own safety and the one who was lost to him for the moment. He wished he had them all with him now and he hoped they all knew he was always with them, even so far apart.

***

Valis stood with eyes raging. Blood dripped from her father's sword and two bodies lay before her. She had arisen to close the room's window from the chilled night air when she caught the faint click of the door opening. She had turned to greet Janian, only it was far from the Earth Maiden that greeted her. Two men entered both with daggers drawn; she saw the large empty sack carried by the one and knew that somehow they must have discovered who she was. A thought streaked by in puzzlement of whether they had been sent from her father or on some sort of bounty, set by mercenaries out to ransom her back.

She gave neither the opportunity to explain and without realizing it she had drawn her sword. How it had arrived so quickly in her hand she would have to puzzle out at a later time. This seemed to have confused her kidnappers as well for they had fallen to the blade quickly as if they had not expected her to be armed or trained to use it. And there she stood with blood dripping from sword to floor as she thought of what to do next.

Janian had arrived a few moments later her face was calm as she looked into the room seeing the bodies on the ground and Valis bent over checking on the baby Prince. They exchanged nods quietly, that everything was ok, and so she moved on to the next room. Here she stopped and her face was no longer calm.

"We don't have time for this!" she shouted in frustration. At that moment Leana came dashing up the stairs and over to her friend

"What is it? You're going to wake all my..." she couldn't finish the sentence as Jan stepped aside to allow her friend to peer into the room.

The room had been upturned everything within smashed to pieces, the window shattered, the bed overturned and what disturbed them the most, at least Janian, was that the room was devoid of occupants.

Valis had come out; sword in one hand the Prince cradled in the other. "What is it?"

"Cecil is gone," Jan stated flatly staring at her old friend who had gone white faced at the carnage within her tavern

"They took Cecil? But left..." Valis caught the look Janian shot at her and she stopped herself in time. She didn't need to announce to the rest of the tavern who they really were.

Still, this thought had reached Janian's mind as well and she stood for a moment trying to figure it out, when her blood suddenly turned cold. The man who had sat in the dark all night observing them, he had to be the key to this sudden and inconvenient puzzle.

"Valis, leave me the child, and go fetch our other friends; I'll meet you outside the back of the tavern."

Her young friend handed her the Prince and took off headlong down the stairs. It was so late and still so quite that the tavern door echoed as it opened and closed.

"Jan, I'm sorry I don't know how..." Leana tried once more.

"Is there another way out of here? A way no one is supposed to know about?" Jan snapped.

Leana looked ashamed as her face went red and for a moment it looked as though she was thinking of keeping the secret to herself. But when she looked back up into her friend's eyes it was not anger she saw, but fear and worry. She knew these emotions well.

"There, behind the painting, a door that leads into the back alleys." Jan was moving before she had even finished and so she followed quickly behind. "Jan I'm sorry, I never meant for something like this to happen."

"Did you know about this? Did you set it up with the bearded man who had been watching us all night?" Jan spun on her friend hissing in anger and frustration.

"No, of course not! That's not what that door is for. I don't know how it was discovered."

Janian nodded stiffly, turned and walked passed her friend and down the stairs.

"Jan where are you going it's the middle of the night? There's no way to track them," Leana whispered harshly as she followed, taking notice of the few heads that peeked through slightly open doors along the way.

She caught up to the Earth Maiden as she arrived at the main entrance and reached out grabbing the woman's wrist and pulling so that Jan faced her. "Please don't go out there; I don't want to lose you to the night as well," Leana pleaded, her eyes welling up.

Jan removed her friend's hand that was clamped around her wrist and took her by the shoulders. "I would do the same for you; I have to go after him." Her expression softened and she pulled her friend into an embrace that somehow they both knew meant goodbye. She smiled reassuringly and when the door closed behind her she could hear Leana's tears start to flow once more. Jan promised herself while looking up into the night sky that she would return one day and take her friend from this place. It was no home for an Earth Maiden.

***

Valis was wide awake now, her blood pumping. She had sent out a call through the bond and it had remained unanswered. She knew her skill with the gift was not the strongest; her brother's link to the greyhound Ce'elevan had been solid from what she was told. Aside from the basic communication and the shared dreams aspect shown her by Sophal, Valis really had no idea how the bond worked or what its full capability was. It frustrated her and at times she wished she had no such gift and then her mind would shift to thoughts of honoring her brother. She would keep learning as much as she could, Malik would be proud of her she was sure of this.

She headed back out into the city streets, she had not intended to go so far, not on her own. But the bond was not working and she hoped it was merely a distance issue. It had never been truly strong in the first place after all, and with a city between her and the dogs it may have rendered her gift useless.

There were still people about, though not nearly as many as the crowds they had traversed through when they had arrived. The night air was laced with a chill carried on the wind that thinned the people out even more. She was making good time without having to dodge her way through hordes of people and she had to admit the city was quite nice. Despite it being night she could see rather well. The streets were well lit from lamp posts on nearly every corner and guards could be seen here and there as she traveled. She felt rather safe even if the guards were from Carn.

She had thoughts about stopping off at a fountain she had just passed that had caught her eye. A fountain in a port city so close to the sea was an easy feat she mused, but she continued on. The worry for the greyhounds taking precedence even over the worry she kept shoving to the back of her mind about the Princess of Carn. She knew she had to be stopped, that kind of dark magic had no place in the world any longer. From what she learned, the druids had seen to that long ago. She had to be stopped before that kind of dark influence had a chance to spread.

She slowed for a moment and stopped long enough to test the bond once more. It was like flicking a lever back and forth and sometimes it was hard to discern if it had been left in one position or the other. She focused, slipping her mind into the half that carried the bond. *"Ce'elevan...Sophal, we need you. Where are you?"* she waited for a response not realizing she was holding her breath and when she finally took a gasp of air there had still been no reply.

She had to move on. She had noticed one guard off to the side of the street had taken notice of her and she scolded herself for leaving Jan behind. She was sure she was going to get a scolding from the women for taking off so far on her own. She knew the Earth Maiden did not mean for her to run to the other end of the city when she told her to fetch the dogs. And now panic was creeping in as a glance back confirmed she was now being followed. She would have growled in frustration if her mind was not entering a panicked state. *"Where are you two?!"* she shouted through the bond that made her head throb to do so.

***

Ce'elevan measured the distance to his opponent and readied for the attack.

His legs wobbled as he tested muscles he would use for his assault and he gave a low growl from the back of his throat. It was the only warning he was going to give his prey. His eyes focused on the moons reflected light off the armored backing his opponent wielded and with deadly precision he leaped. One bite after another, he used his paws to flip his opponent over hoping to score the fatal strike.

"Are you serious?!" came a scolding voice through the bond.

Ce'elevan looked up and almost whimpered as he realized Sophal had caught up to him and would be promptly ruining his fun.

"First I chase you through the woods...again! After a rabbit this time you failed to catch," she began.

"You chased it as well!" he tried to protest.

"I had to chase after you, not the damn rabbit!" she scolded herself for once again using the human word damn; it was un-befitting of a dog no less than a royal greyhound.

"And now, I catch up to you and find you playing around with a damn rock!" she scolded Ce'elevan followed by herself once more.

"I was just playing...we have been patrolling for so long. And we find nothing, which is good, but boring," he defended himself bracing for the sharp retort he knew to expect from Sophal.

But this time none came, she simply turned away from him and started back to the path they had set up for their patrol. *"As you wish pup, have fun. I'll be keeping our friends safe in the mean time if you don't mind."*

And there it was...the being called a pup once more. Ce'elevan hung his head in shame as he loped after her, the fun he was having left behind with the overturned stone.

It wasn't easy, with his old master, Malik the bond had been a blessing, an easy way to communicate with his master and friend. Even with Valis it was little more than a way to speak with ease between dog and human. But with Sophal, she had begun to teach him that the bond was far more than he had ever thought. The first thing that was really irritating him was the fact that the bond worked with other royal greyhounds just as it did with some royal humans, in the way that it bridged their communication through the bond. Instead of just through the natural way dogs communicated. It gave them a voice and he wished he had never learned that fact. With just dog speak and body language he was sure he could have been the dominant one in this relationship, but the voice gave the older dog much more authority and he was still trying to figure out how this was possible.

They had resumed the path chosen for their patrol and Ce'elevan once again felt the boredom soak into his body. It made him irritable and he noticed every ache in his body from the long travel with days where they had very little sleep, and for a greyhound that was a terrible waste of time to be awake for so long.

Sophal however, continued on without so much of a whimper, no limp, no complaining, and that of course did nothing but to further worsen his own mood as he was shamed once more by the older dog. He had learned that putting his pride aside and listening to the words she spoke did improve his understanding of all that was going on and he did feel a growing respect for her even if a side of him wanted nothing more than to resent her even being here.

"I know you're used to there only being the bond with one master and his death is most tragic. And I know that the bond with the new one is weak but you must give that time to grow, it will become much stronger in time you will see. And of course finding out you have a voice when speaking through the bond with another greyhound can be unsettling, I assure you that too will grow easier with time. I will teach you what I can before our time to part arrives."

She had begun to explain these things and he tried his best to listen and understand, he was young still and his attention strayed often. But one of the things she had said, the last part about when our time to part arrives had stuck with him. It irritated his thoughts and he was starting to wonder if it did not have multiple meanings. And then he would shake his head in frustration, learning his voice in the bond with another greyhound was confusing, he much preferred the humans who for the most part still talked to him like a dog. It was simple, and he was used to it.

As they marched along he let his mind drift back to his old master, he really missed, Malik. He liked Valis, she had always been kind to him but the bond was different with her, perhaps Sophal was right and it would grow in time but it was so weak that it was almost frustrating to try and hear unless she was standing a few feet away. The words came sporadically if over long distances like now, he could only make out *"where, Sophal, need"* and a hint of desperation carried on each word.

Ce'elevan stopped as his mind sunk into the realization that he wasn't thinking of the words but hearing them and when he took off at full run past Sophal she growled at him as he past her.

"This better not be another damn rabbit!" then she too heard the words slightly more clearly for the girls control of the bond was indeed weak at such distance and took off after Ce'elevan.

The city walls blurred as they ran toward the gate. They ran with their eyes wide as navigating through people however sparse the streets were at this hour was still tricky work. They also had to open the link to the bond and it was growing better now that they were closing the distance between them and Valis. Several guards made motions as though they were interested in the sight of two greyhounds tearing through the streets but they had also quickly realized how pointless trying to catch the fastest dogs would be and settled back into their posts.

A woman dropped her basket when Ce'elevan had no choice but to dart between her legs and Sophal miscalculated a turn smashing into a stall of vegetables but was on her feet again and at Ce'elevan's side before the merchant could start cursing.

They slowed only for a moment when they tested the bond once more and dashed off in the direction they could feel it from. An alleyway was their target and the greyhound's timing could not have been more perfect. They approached as Valis was walking slowly backwards through the alley. Ce'elevan flanked left and Sophal right and to either side of the alley, branching to the left was the quickly approaching city guard and to the right, another one, the original man whose interest in Valis peaked as she had been quickly walking by. Both stopped as the dogs growled and let loose angry barks, waiting for Valis to pass further behind them before pulling back down the alley themselves. The guards had slowly followed but stood in the intersection and watched them go, the idea of chase fleeing their minds at the looks of the two royal greyhounds.

"Thank you, we have to hurry back to Janian, I'll explain on the way," she said through the bond as she started to jog back the way they had come the first time on the path Jan had taken them.

The guards did not give chase though Sophal expressed her doubt it was the last they would see of them. Their own entrance into the city had gone far from unnoticed and the ones after Valis were sure to report to someone. An investigation would soon be underway. Valis had no argument from the dogs this time, she knew she had been sloppy in fetching them from outside the city but they had little time if they were to pick up Cecil's trail.

As she explained what had happened she had noticed that Ce'elevan had closed off the link and was no longer listening to her, apparently angry that she had lost the man which made her a little cross as Ce'elevan was supposed to be her dog after all. Not that she begrudged them the bond of blood they had shared in battle and the need for vengeance at the death of their master and friend. This line of thought was not helping as she got cross even at that thought, Malik was her brother and thus they as well were bonded in blood and she herself had a strong sense for the need of resolution at his death. She would have to put it aside for now as she and the greyhounds entered the alley to the slums and she braced for the scolding she knew she had coming when they met up with Jan.

Through the alley they sprinted and slowed on the other side, drawing unwanted attention in the slums was just as dangerous as on the city's higher classed streets. The lights were on in the Tavern, perhaps a lantern lit in each window which was far more than when she had left and far more than there should be. Had Jan woken the entire tavern? Questioning each person within? Valis knew her friend was capable of just that and would have to accept that explanation for the time being. They traveled around to the tavern's rear where the horses were stabled and where she was told to meet up with the Earth Maiden after fetching the greyhounds.

Janian stood just outside the stalls, her blue dress showing only a sliver from within the long dark hooded cloak she had borrowed from Leana and she pulled the hood down as the others approached.

"Good, you found them," she stated plainly.

Valis braced herself for the scolding that never came and it would take part of the remaining night for her to relax enough to think she would go un-lectured.

"It was no trouble," she lied. Both greyhounds must have picked up on the tone of her voice as they both lifted their heads to look at her as if they had heard the lie.

"Ask them if they can pick up his scent, we don't have a lot of time. We could lose him in the night and we still have to find were the Serpent's pass is hidden within the city."

"I thought you knew the way? That was the plan!" Valis said a little louder than she had intended.

"I know it's here and I know it's under the city. We were blindfolded the one and only time we were there." Jan said looking away.

"They have the scent," Valis said giving her friend a look of mixed anger and scepticism.

"Then we become hunters in the night," Jan flashed a smile. "Let's go get our friend back."

CHAPTER 28

"Why this one? Why not one of the women? We could have at least had a little fun with." the man who held tightly onto Cecil's right arm spoke with the strain of effort in his voice.

"Are you daft? The others didn't ever come out from the other room, we were lucky we got saddled with this one." The man who held Cecil's left arm said as he worked to keep pace with his companion.

Cecil had heard them both, and for the moment, despite how uncomfortable he was, decided to remain still and silent. This was no easy task as the men who had grabbed him from his room at the tavern were not overly big men, neither was well muscled and so with one on each of his arms they half carried and half dragged his limp body through the city's streets. He cracked an eye from time to time while his two escorts talked and Cecil tried to take in any landmarks he could, hoping to use them to find his way back should he find his freedom.

They were close to the docks now; he knew that from the stronger smell of the sea. As his captures headed down a small path that branched to the left, Cecil had spotted a large ship not far off. He prayed to the Goddess that the ship was not their destination as it would be impossible to reunite with his friends and be any use to them at all in the coming battle. He knew they would be out looking for him, his friends, doing the same for him as he would gladly for them he had no doubts. He just wished they would hurry. His arms and shoulders were burning and he wouldn't have any boots left if they dragged him much farther.

He had managed to sleep for a few hours before his abduction and he was surprised to feel that the ever present feeling of exhaustion was fading. He figured his lapse in energy and the dreams of the void were likely due to it being his own body the shadow assassin had taken up residence in that caused him to recover far longer that, Valis, who had drunk of the same druid's restoration soup.

They continued to drag and carry Cecil until they had headed down a path devoid of people. At the end of the small walkway built into side of the stone wall was a set of bars. Cecil for a moment thought it a crude cell as he watched, the man they had followed removed a key from within the dark folds of his cloak. But as the bars swung open on rusty hinges eaten away from years of salted sea air abuse, it was the man who entered first. With sudden realization, Cecil's eyes went wide with panic as he had no intentions of ever entering another sewer. If there was anything he had learned from his journey so far it was that he hated sewers and he decided this was a good as time as any to end his journey with his current escort.

The moment the man holding his left arm placed a foot inside the small tunnel's opening, Cecil shifted his weight to the right as he planted his own feet firmly on the ground and slammed his shoulder into the man behind him. Both of his captors let loose his arms in surprise and the one with a foot in the tunnel now fell backwards with a startled grunt disappearing within. Cecil had fallen with the man he struck and both tumbled to the ground. Cecil was the first to rise and he kicked with all the power he could find, cracking the jaw of the man before he could follow Cecil to his feet and fell back with a cry of pain.

Cecil swung around to deal with the remaining man who had regained his feet and now stood in the tunnel's entrance with fury in his eyes. He made to take a step forward towards Cecil when a hand fell on his shoulder.

"Enough!" The man in the dark cloak had reappeared and halted his underling, pulling him gently aside and stepping through to stand before him. "Your hostility is not needed I assure you, we meant no harm," a strong voice said.

"No harm? Not needed?" Cecil shook with anger as he spoke. "You drag me from my bed in the dead of night, drag me through the city streets to the docks and then try to take me into a sewer and it's not needed?"

"We have saved you, I'm sorry we could not bring the others but the witch's power..."

"What in the name of the Goddess are you going on about?" Cecil shouted.

The cloaked man whose hood was still drawn forward so only the tuft at the end of his beard was showing, raised his hands for patience and a chance to speak.

"The witch, Janian Poledouris, she has captured you and your friends. She has obviously corrupted the girl but I had hoped there was still a chance to save you. You see I watched last night while you all ate and I could see the tired struggle your body was going through in resisting her powers and I had to act."

Cecil could only stare at the man, who he was now convinced was pretty far separated from his senses.

"We were taking you to the rebels, they have their hideout deep beneath the city streets. You will be safe from her influence there I assure you," the man said calmly gesturing toward the sewer entrance.

"What witch? You make about as much sense as an old man whose mind had left him long ago."

"Janian..."

"I heard you!" Cecil snapped "that's the part I'm having most trouble with. Janian is no witch, she's an Earth Maiden."

"There is no proof that such a creature as the Earth Mother even exists, and in most of the world such talk is forbidden, now we must hurry if..." the man said beginning to turn.

"You truly are out of your mind! There is no chance I'm to follow you in there or anywhere for that matter. If I had a sword you would be dead where you stand!"

"But the witch will be close behind!" the man hissed, turning back.

"Earth Maiden and I have had one strenuous journey so far, I don't trust my own mind not to stop my temper from killing you with your continued insult of my friend," Cecil said lowering his head as he truly fought to keep control.

"Then perhaps I was mistaken, she has already got to you. Did you know that she had controlled another just like you? I knew him well, a level headed boy with his heart on keeping his people safe, on defending his homeland. Then this witch and her friends appear and I watch as she corrupts that young man's heart, twists it turning him against his people."

"Janian would never do such a thing," Cecil replied, warning in his tone.

The cloaked man's shoulders slumped, "I see that there is no saving you. Sadly, I cannot have her corruption reach the others, I'm sorry." The cloaked man pulled aside the fold at his hip and began to draw the long curved blade that hung within.

He stopped short as two deep growls approached from behind Cecil.

Cecil raised an eyebrow as the greyhounds took up defensive postures standing in front of him and looked back up at the cloaked figure.

"If these two are here then my friends are not far behind. I suggest you run back into your hole madman."

"She is a witch, boy! You will see in the end!" the cloaked figure thrust his sword back into place and turned, shoving the other man ahead of him disappearing into the darkness of the tunnel beyond.

By the time Cecil had bent down to rub the necks of the two greyhounds who now panted happily, both Janian and Valis, with the Prince in his backpack had arrived. Valis was the first to rush over wrapping her arms around Cecil.

"Are you alright?" Janian asked as she past him placing a hand on his shoulder which made Cecil smile knowing his trust in the woman was well placed.

"I'm fine; legs are a little sore as they dragged me the entire way here." He said in half jest.

"Was it a man wearing a black cloak... with a tuft of beard sticking out?" Janian asked as she leaned into the tunnel searching within.

"It was. And I'll tell you he had no love for you, kept going on about how the Earth Mother does not exist and kept calling you..."

"A witch," Janian finished for him. "I'm familiar with his term of endearment."

Cecil was sure the man had not meant it in any kind way and he hoped Jan was joking; it was hard to tell with her sometimes.

"I truly am glad to see you two," he said squatting once more to rub the greyhound's heads, neither of them showed any signs of displeasure even the more matriarchal Sophal pressed her head firmly into his hand.

The only one not pleased was Valis as Cecil was not looking he missed the jealous scowl hung on her face.

"Come on you two, Valis please ask the greyhounds to scout ahead, track the man in black if they can. I know it might be tough with all the other... smells." Jan instructed as she entered the sewer tunnel's entrance.

Valis sent the message to the dogs via the bond and without hesitation they darted after the Earth Maiden, Valis following close behind. It was not until they had reached the first branch in the tunnel that Jan had to send her back to fetch Cecil.

CHAPTER 29

Archers stood on the walls, bows up and arrows knocked. Knights stood at the gates with drawn swords. Soldiers were occupying every space within the courtyard of the royal family of Carn's Palace. This is how Zhamar Damaste was greeted upon his arrival. The chancellor, an older man well into his twilight years had come out to greet him.

"Thank you for submitting to the Queen's wishes that your men stay outside the palaces grounds King Zhamar. An unusual request, I admit but then so is the sudden arrival of Petsky's messengers that the King himself has decided to grace us with his presence."

Zham detected no sarcasm or veiled threats in the man's words and his body language was calm and respectful, Zham found himself instantly liking the older man. Egrin, he had said his name was.

"I'm pleased, that for once my men have arrived safely to deliver this message."

"Indeed King Damaste, communication between our lands has seemed...strained as of late, I have the Queens assurances that you are welcome and she is eager for an audience. If we can forgo the usual customs I will show you to her now and then your quarters after," Egrin explained as they walked under heavy escort.

"This will be fine Chancellor I'm eager to talk to the Queen myself."

Egrin offered a polite smile and the two entered the palace. As they crossed through the doors half of their guard departed but they were far from being without security. Guards were still in every hall and every staircase in every room. The rumors of the Carn monarchy enjoying a military lifestyle was present and it hit Zham with the sickening realization that if it truly came to war, Petsky would fall within hours.

For such a no nonsense reputation, Zham noticed, behind soldiers and guards, that the palace was really rather beautiful. Rich tapestries and paintings decorated the halls and warm toned carpets met their feet as they headed toward the Queen's Counsel hall.

Once the attendants had opened the large wooden doors, white in color, from a wood grown only within Carn's boarders. Zham had always found that a pity, and sighed as they were ushered inside. The room was huge, easily three times the size of Zham's council chamber and of course, unlike his own presence, this room was full of the Queen's council members, or advisers he reminded himself, the Queen rules here in everything. Petsky was seen as weak by some nations for letting council members run the more day to day tasks that Zham found tedious.

"By law, King Damaste we are still family, as I have not remarried, I trust that I can be as forthcoming with you as I would a loved one," the Queen of Carn spoke softly but clearly, her words yet still strong even though her body was propped up with over large cushions, her eyes were sunken.

"Then Greetings to you sister, it has been too long since last we spoke in person." Zham bowed low trying not to make it apparent he had seen the sadness in her eyes.

This was a good greeting as the Queen closed her eyes and nodded softly in approval.

"I'm dying, Zhamar, please come closer." she gestured with a thin weak hand.

Zhamar had been rather indifferent about his brother being married off to this woman; he wanted his brother to be happy. But on the day they wed he had seen a very different woman, muscled and fit a warrior in the image of her late father. The woman before him was not that woman, not any longer. For a moment he thought this must be the real her, under the muscles and armour had been this woman, did she hate herself now or was this the real her, this frail and venerable skeleton of a creature before him.

"My sister has told me her side of things, and yet I am no fool, a sister knows when the truth is being withheld between them. She forgets these things, I do not. So speak, and tell me...do you know where my son is?"

***

What is the matter with you? Come on, we are going to be left behind!" Valis said as she burst through the sewer entrance to find Cecil standing in the same spot they had left him. She ran up to grab his arm, pulling him after her.

"I've already been in far too many sewers at your command thank you; I do not intend to ever frequent another." Cecil said, pulling his arm away and held back the wince of pain he felt, his arms being more sore than he had thought from his unbidden tour of the city streets.

"That was to save your life you ungrateful child, now, move!" Valis scolded standing to the side and pointing to the entrance.

Cecil's legs moved as if by their own and when he cursed his friend's name under his breath, he realized that he truly did owe her his life and so much more, and for a moment he worried he would never get to kiss her again. These thoughts fled his mind the moment he stepped within the entrance to the sewer, the smell had chased off any thoughts he had about a romantic relationship with the Princess and he found himself scowling at her in the dark tunnel as he looked back. Valis, pulling the grate shut behind them, made him feel felt as though he had landed right back in the cell this sad side of his adventure had started in.

Cecil waited for Valis to pass, they were already moving she explained, as she at the same moment told Ce'elevan that she had retrieved Cecil and to keep going. Jan must have realized as such and the Earth Maiden and dogs were now much further down the tunnel to the right.

"None of us want to be in here Cecil," Valis said as they moved, trying their best to keep their boots clean.

"Jan seemed eager enough, and please, keep talking, it's easier to stomach this place, knowing I'm not alone," Cecil answered back, sighing heavily as his foot found a larger puddle of what he doubted was water.

"I think she knows more about the man with the beard, yet she has said very little. In all fairness however it's not as if we had a lot of time to get into it. I still don't see why you let those men carry you half across the city." She said as her own foot found something no longer solid to step into.

The smells he was experiencing again for the second time in his life were nothing compared to the glare and look of disapproval he received from Janian as they met back up. He realized that the Earth Maiden had no idea he had been on such an adventure before, or maybe she did as he suspected she had a hand in Valis's plan to free him from prison back in Petsky. In which case it made him want to glare back, yet he still knew better than to douse fire with fire and so he just hung his head staring into the dark trickle of water at his feet.

Valis and Jan discussed the information the greyhounds were reporting back and soon they were moving once more. The tunnels were truly a work of art. They could see the tunnels fairly well now that they had met back up with Jan as she radiated a warm blue light, that, at times seemed almost alive as in the moments when she went left and the aura went right until Jan looked at it and it snapped back into place as her silhouette. He would have asked if the Druids had such abilities if he was not still giving her space and time to cool off. Which, he still felt to be a little unfair considering the circumstances.

The tunnels were a wide range of sizes, some they could have fit an army into and others left barely enough room for them to get through and Cecil being broader of shoulder than the others had caught his clothing on walls more than enough to now own a shirt and jacket torn in several places.

One tunnel saw the end of any doubt in the greyhound's tracking skills as they rounded the corner they caught a brief glimpse of the bearded man slipping through a doorway. This was their first warning to be cautious as they had not come across any rooms with doors down here as of yet. Their second warning should have been that despite the sewer systems size, Janian seemed to be remembering the way and now walked up front with the dogs.

Ce'elevan pawed at the door and when Jan stepped up giving it a push they realised it had been barred from the other side.

"Perhaps there's another way in?" Valis suggested.

"There is but we will never find them, we were lucky the greyhounds could aid us in finding this one."

Jan said while studying the door. She closed her eyes and bowed her head placing both hands flat against the wood of the door. The aura of blue broke away from her hands and enveloped the door basking it in light and within moments the door was decaying at an accelerated pace. It cracked at first, then lost hold on the first hinge, something on the other side, large, a beam perhaps, crashed to the floor. Jan pulled the aurora back to her hands. She gave the decayed door a shove and it fell inwards echoing upon the stone floor within.

Cecil was still not clear on just what the earth maiden's powers were. She could read minds; he was pretty sure of that despite being told otherwise. She could talk to the wind, ask favors of ancient trees, make seeds bloom prematurely, and apparently age doors or perhaps wood itself to the point of rot. No he had made the right choice today, to stay silent on her ire that he felt was directed at him alone. And said nothing now as she indicated they should move forward, the dogs going first.

It was dark. The room must have been so large that not even Jan's blue aura seemed to pierce it; they of course had little time to find out for as they entered the dogs began barking. Valis shouted that it was a trap and the next moment they were blinded by the brightest light Cecil had ever encountered. It was so strong that he clutched his head and dropped to his knees in pain. The next moment he felt the familiar feeling of hands restraining his arms and this time he felt rope spun around his wrists.

He heard angry shouts and someone cry out in pain before orders were being barked. He was lifted; no weak men held him this time and dropped moments later.

"What is the meaning of this? Explain yourself Martivak! Janian, command your dogs to be still!" A voice thundered, strong and commanding, it was not the same as the bearded mans Cecil noted.

"Valis, it's ok, do as he says," Jan instructed and soon the dogs had stopped their growling. Water was splashed in their faces and Cecil flinched so suddenly that they had to repeat the action.

"I'm sorry, the effects of the light will fade soon, nothing special but lamp light mixed with a powder. A trap you well know Janian." The voice spoke again, calmly and addressing Jan as a friend.

Cecil felt the rope around his wrists fall apart and he rubbed his eyes and face, removing the access water. His eyes came into focus slowly but he could see they were surrounded by at least twenty armed men.

"Martivak?" Jan inquired.

"I have him here," the man who was a first name acquaintance of Jan's was a tall figure who wore a set of chain armour, light and well oiled as it made no sound when he moved. His dirty blonde hair was shoulder length, framing a face which sported a short well-maintained beard.

To Cecil's right a man was handing Valis back her sword, head bowed in respect. And to his left Jan was staring intently at the man who they had chased through the streets and sewers of the city. He was removed of hood and it was apparent that the man was older than Jan by at least twenty years, hatred burned in the look he gave back.

"This witch killed my son! I demand that we kill her now before she controls us all!" The man now known as Martivak shouted.

"Reddivan died in the breach on sanders street, Marti...what's this all about?"

Martivak did not respond, instead he leaned forward and spit at Janian as she stood. The blonde haired man, the leader of these men, struck Martivak so hard the man spat out several teeth.

"You disappear with several new recruits for days without reporting in. You tear through the sewers alerting every hidden sentry we have in place on the west side of the network and set off the lanterns in a room full of your brothers! And the worst offense yet, you spit in the face of a woman who has done great deeds to keep our people, our family's safe!" the man roared.

"Trevel, it's true." Jan spoke clearly and all eyes fell on her.

"I know it's true, Jan, I was there!" Trevel shouted before he realized he was yelling at the wrong person.

"I killed his son."

"No you didn't, Jan" Trevel said more calmly.

"He fell in love with me, and I turned him away. If I had accepted his proposal and taken him with me, he would never have been on Sanders Street when the breach happened.

"Trevel lowered his head for a moment and sighed. "Without the sacrifice of those who died that day we would no longer have a resistance. No Jan, you are no more to blame than I for giving the command to hold the position. I chose the men who went to their deaths that day."

Cecil watched Janian closely, for the first time he was seeing a part of the woman's past and he understood now that she was as miserable in this city as the rest of them. It must have been with great difficulty to decide to make this journey. Perhaps she sought some sort of closure, he didn't know, but he saw a women battling with her own demons at the moment and felt useless to help. It would not be today that he returned that favor.

"Take him away, I'll deal with him later" Trevel gestured to Martivak and several of the other resistance members took firm hold of the protesting man and dragged him from the room. Nobody noticed the small satisfied smirk that Cecil flashed him.

"Come, walk with me old friend, the others will be given food and water and shown to a place they can rest while we talk." He held his arm out wide in invitation and Janian accepted this with a nod as she passed. Soon both had left the room. She cast a softer look back at Cecil as if to say all was forgiven although he still did not know for what. The dogs pranced uneasily as they watched her go but stopped as they looked over at Valis who had obviously told them to stop.

After walking through several more corridors Janian and Trevel stopped on a bridge built across a junction where the sewer water mixed with the river water that flowed behind them in a water fall.

"This is the only area down here where the smell isn't so strong, I apologize about that," Travel said leaning against a railing.

"Thank you, this is admittedly rather beautiful," she said, admiring the water as it cascaded and fell far below.

"Why are you here Jan? I was sure you made it clear to us that you, Zham and Alex wouldn't be returning."

"I need access to the serpent's pass," she said looking him in the eyes.

"You're not serious." Trevel said with a leveled tone.

"I wouldn't ask if it wasn't urgent Trevel; we need to reach Carn and it should have been yesterday if you get my meaning."

"I get it Jan, it's just...we don't even use it anymore. The men have all become superstitious fools, claiming they see ghosts and hear talking and foot steps behind them and when they turn of course no one's there. I seriously cannot get them to enter."

"That's fine I'm not asking any of them to come with us," she said with a sly smile.

"You know I could never say no to you," Trevel said after a moment, finally letting loose a laugh that echoed even with the roar of rushing water.

"So you're going to Carn with two royal greyhounds...yes I can tell. And a young man and women and a baby...why in the name of the Earth Mother are you traveling with a baby? Is it yours or the girls?"

"Neither and the less you know the safer you are my old friend," Jan said smiling weakly.

"How goes the resistance? I see you have maintained the ranks; the people are still willing to try taking back their city?" Jan asked nodding back the way they had come.

"We could use you and Zham and even Alex, even though I think they both still owe me money. Zham's a king now maybe you could remind him of that when you see him next," Trevel joked.

"You have my word that I will," Jan said while holding back a laugh.

"The pass? Really?" Trevel said after several moments of silence.

"Yes, the sooner the better" Jan said with all seriousness.

CHAPTER 30

Blindfolded they were led from the large room they had first met the resistance in. Even the dogs had blindfolds on, which Cecil laughed about, only to be met with the cold stares from just about everyone and he quickly went silent. Even with the blindfolds he still heard them discussing who would get the task of carrying the dogs as they couldn't be expected to walk unaided. Cecil cursed when Jan suggested they lead them by makeshift collars ruining his fun. Trevel, he had learned was a commander in the rebellion, said the few soldiers that would talk to them. They were still angry with Valis who had sliced into several of their friends before they could get the sword away from her, back when they were blinded by the man known as Martivak. No one could say for sure how she had got her sword to her hands so quickly in all the confusion.

He thought of her now, he was being led to the Serpent's pass and so had time to let his mind wander. It did not take long to find the topic he was most concerned about in regards to the Princess. It all came down to that kiss she had given him while in the crystal cave, while they were trapped within the void.

Had she always had those feelings for him? Or did they grow from the moment they had started on this journey. He had to admit he had never really been all that nice to her in the past. She had clung to his master. Her brother that often times he had ended up training Valis with the sword more than he ever did with his squire. His was not the place to ask but when Malik and he had become friends he expected things to be different. They were for the most part, only Valis seemed to complicate things. He smiled to himself as he realized that she was still complicating things, only this time it was for him and not her brother. He remembered the words the spirit of

Malik, or at least he believed it had been his spirit, had spoken in the shop when the shadow assassin had fled. "You have work to do. Protect my sister, you are to be her champion." The words echoed in his head for the moment and he wondered how he was ever to accomplish such a task.

Cecil wondered as they traveled, how far *is* this Serpent's pass? He could understand if they were enemies but friends being blindfolded? Wasn't Janian once a part of the resistance herself? These thoughts held no answers and so once more he returned to Valis. It wasn't that he disliked her; she was beautiful as far as women went. She was a little more boyish when it came to matters of the court. He could not remember the last time he had seen her in a dress. She was nothing like her sisters, who were ladies of the court through and through. Yet perhaps it was the fact that she was different than the others that made her stand out in his mind. They fought but what couple didn't. And then he scolded himself for thinking them a couple, he was worldly enough to know that it was the woman who informed the man when they were officially a couple. Perhaps blindfolded and led to a dangerous tunnel was not the best time to think about the condition of a relationship that may or may not even be present.

Without warning they had stopped and the blindfolds were removed. They looked at each other first, making sure they were all present and accounted for. Then they took in the doors that heralded their arrival at the Serpent's pass.

Large doors that reached twenty feet high at least, Cecil figured, stood before them.

Two doors made out of what looked like Jade, a stone usually only seen in small trinkets like necklaces brought in trade ships from far across the sea. To see so much of it here was beyond anything they had ever seen. The doors stood closed with intricate carving throughout.

As they stood looking, the carvings looked as though they almost told a story, but no one not even Janian could make sense of the language it was written in.

"And you have been here once before?" Valis asked Janian with a raised eyebrow.

"Yes, a very long time ago," Janian answered distantly.

"Do you remember how to open it?" Trevel asked with a smirk.

"I do." His friend replied.

"Good, as you can see my men have already run away with their tails between their legs," he said tossing his head to the side.

They all looked except for Janian who was still staring up at the ornate jade doors and sure enough not a single man who had led them here, save Commander Trevel had stayed.

"Cowards," Valis said as she looked at Trevel who only shrugged.

Travel walked up to Janian, placing a hand on her shoulder. "It's not too late; I can at least lead you and your friend's top side.

"No Trevel, thank you. You should go; I don't want you harmed should we encounter something... out of place." She suddenly turned and wrapped the man in her arms, a surprise to her friends and to Trevel as well. "The resistance needs you more now than I do my old friend, may the Goddess hear your voice and feel your soul." When she let him go he nodded stiffly to Valis and Cecil and left the way they had came.

"Ghosts, Jan, the entire resistance won't use this tunnel for fear of ghosts." Cecil said breaking the tension that came on the heels of silence.

"I won't lie to you Cecil, that concerns me as well. Though I cannot see how that's possible," she said as she approached the doors and began to run her hand along one end of an elaborate part of a carving that looked oddly like a giant fish.

"Why's that?" Valis voiced what Cecil was thinking which made him scowl.

"I can't hear the Earth Mother from within the Serpent's pass."

"The Earth Mother is life," Cecil added.

"And so inside we can find only death," Valis finished.

Janian rested her hand on a certain spot, made note of its location and turned to face her friends; even the greyhounds looked up at her expectantly.

"Before I open these doors I want you all to know that even though I can't hear the Earth Mother within, that she is always with us. For when we enter, we are life and so therefore we carry her with us and she will always find a way to be with me. She always has." With that she turned back to the door, found her spot and pushed until they heard something click.

"Valis, hand the Prince to Cecil, I don't know if your sword will retain any magic within the tunnel but it's a good idea to have it at the ready anyways." Janian instructed as the doors opened without a sound, slowly swinging inward.

Cecil had been holding his breath in anticipation. When the doors stood fully open and nothing happened he swallowed air deeply in relief. He adjusted the backpack with the sleeping Prince onto his back and followed the others.

The first thing they noticed was that it was warmer within, this could have been due to leaving the cold sewers but it felt more like the warmth felt from within a baker's kitchen. The smell of fresh baked goods however was absent and the dry smell of dirt and dust filled the air.

They had walked for a few minutes when a sound made them turn around, the doors had closed tightly and securely behind them, not that they were close enough to do anything about it and the fact that they had wanted in anyways not out, at least not at this end.

Several things happened within the first little while they were there. Valis had the sword drawn; only no magic lit the blade, it remained as plain and regular as any other sword. The bond to the dogs had been removed and Janian reported the loss of her gifts as well.

Cecil cursed as they walked on. Jan the Earth Maiden was powerless; Valis wielded only a regular sword and could not communicate through the bond to the greyhounds. And to make matters worse, he cringed as the baby Prince, who had been, through the use of dark magic cast into a deep slumber, had now woken up and began to cry.

CHAPTER 31

There was light within the tunnel. An ominous white mist floated throughout, it could almost be mistaken for dust had it not glowed faintly like a starry night. When they moved through the mist it brightened a little more. Cecil, wondered if he ran through it would the mist light up even brighter? But he had other thoughts to fill his mind with at the moment.

He cradled the baby Prince in his arms as they traveled. Cecil had tried to give the baby to one of the others but the Prince would only settle when he was handed back.

"He likes you, you should feel honored," Jan smiled playfully at the young man.

"He should feel honored, that's my cousin he holds," Valis chimed in walking beside him and smiling down at the baby.

Cecil looked at his friend thinking it odd that now she would show any interest in the babe. She had shown no real bond thus far, perhaps it was because he was awake for the first time since he came into their possession and seemed more real as opposed to the still and silent, enchanted slumber the Prince had been sent into. They had no proof that it was Princess Kerra, the boy's own aunt that had cast the spell. But Cecil did not have to say what he knew was on everyone's mind. They would place the blame with the women who had so far shown the greatest of interest in killing them.

Cecil wondered how someone who was family, someone bonded in blood, could do such a thing, and to a baby no less. He was no fool, as people grew even siblings could end up on separate sides of an issue or an allegiance, brothers fighting on opposite sides of a war was not unthinkable, but this? Cecil looked down at the Prince who even he had to admit was much more of another member of their party now that he could look back at them. The baby's eyes were clear and Jan said she could see nothing physically wrong. She cursed at not having her abilities, wishing she could check further and give the child the Earth Mother's blessings. She said the words anyways and had finished with a heavy sigh.

"Do you think she has always been this way? Princesses Kerra I mean," Cecil asked.

The Serpent's pass so far had yielded no hazards and the tunnel though unusually large, large enough for an army to fit through, was as plain as any other. Aside from the mist, it resembled much of the sewer system they had encountered the rebels in.

"I can't really say," Janian answered, not looking back as she spoke. "I have always stayed clear of Carn as much as possible, and I was never close to the royal family as I am with Petsky and the Damaste's."

"Such a strong military nation, and yet I have heard very little about their past." Valis stated.

"What do they teach you in that court?" Jan asked with a slight laugh to her question.

"I'm more curious about where Princess Kerra learned dark magic," Cecil said with a hint of insistence that said he expected some sort of an answer.

"We can rest for a moment," Jan said stopping and looking around.

"Here?" Valis asked gesturing around them, "in the open?"

"It's as good a place as any, Valis." Cecil said already sitting carefully with the Prince in his arms. The greyhounds had come over to poke their noses at the baby and the Prince cooed at them playfully which made the dogs take a step back in surprise. They still stuck close to Valis despite the bond being beyond their reach.

"The Druids fought the dark mages almost seven hundred years ago." Janian began as she sat, the others instantly focusing on her words.

The dark magic of old was not of this world, the Earth Mother never would have allowed such a taint to fester for it was the opposite of everything she stood for and had sacrificed to give us. Simply put, she was life and *that* magic brings only death. The Druids had stepped forward and offered to form sects of warriors to train in magic that would counter the dark one's own. They were granted this only in the understanding that once the dark magic was cleansed from the lands that they would forget the destructive powers that they themselves had learned." She paused to allow them time to think things through and she smiled when she noticed the alarm in Cecil's eyes.

"But without the knowledge to defeat the dark magic how are we planning to stop Kerra?"

"I'm pleased you asked, such a shame I cannot train you myself. The Druids had asked the Earth Mother this very question and she had to concede that they their point had validity. So the Earth Mother split the power between the Druids and the Earth Maidens, declaring that the brothers and sisters of her children would have to work together should such a time as the darkness ever return."

"But then...should we not have brought a Druid with us then?" Valis asked as she followed along scratching behind Ce'elevan's ear, who, had lain down across her lap.

"Jan I..." Cecil began as the Earth Maiden simply smiled as she locked eyes with the young man at Valis's question.

"We're doomed." Valis stated simply throwing her hands up in the air.

"We must have faith that the Earth Mother will show us the way. It is no accident that you have the gift of blood magic, Cecil. Nor that Valis is here, with a bond between the greyhounds. Nor that should the Prince fall to our protection. Also it is no small matter that you have enlisted the aid of the only Earth Maiden in the kingdom." Jan said as she stood. "Trust in the Earth Mother to provide the way." With that she began the journey forward once more.

***

The creature had grown three times its normal size now. It resembled a large worm more than a snake, its body being bulbous and stout like a caterpillar's. It did however grow scales that linked together so smoothly that perhaps it looked more of a monstrous maggot with snake skin. It was hideous and something deep within new it was an unnatural creature. This was evident in the other creatures that had tried to attack it as it moved to its destination.

They had yelled at it and thrown stones from afar. Others were so bold as to draw swords that deflected off its scaly hide, irritating it but not distracting the creature from its course. It had growled as it found its voice, the creature's head had stopped growing and no more rows of razor sharp teeth had grown; three rows top and bottom seemed to be its set amount. There was something within the creature that wanted out and it struggled to understand why it was here and what it was after. Its mind had become so focused on reaching its destiny that everything else was only agitating it and soon a rage was building along with the frustration.

At one point in its journey it had come across several obstructions that it had unleashed its anger on; it wanted no delays. It needed to move and so when the stone wall had forced it to slow and stop, it roared and snapped its deadly maw. It turned back in frustration, taking only a moment to skewer another creature with one of its long spider like legs and bringing it to its mouth to tear apart when it did not shake loose. A part of the creature's mind rejoiced in the taste of the flesh and the warm liquid that slid down its throat. But the feeling was gone in a moment and this fueled its rage. Turning, the creature began to move as fast as it could manage and slammed its entire body against the stone wall. Stones flew in every direction, no match for the deadly force the creature had become. Unnoticed a small crack had appeared in one of its scales, small for now, being one of the scales on the creature's body to have taken most of the impact of the assault upon the wall.

There was more of the other creatures now, the ones that yelled loudly and swung swords. The part deep within felt a twinge of jealousy as its many eyes took in the blades. With a mighty roar it tore through the hole it had made in the wall and pushed forward renewing its determination to reach its destiny.

The other side of the wall had yielded no easier path but it was close now, it could feel its target getting closer as it traveled. The urgency drove its simple mind to the brink of insanity. More walls and more creatures, many of them had filed around it and the creatures roared in challenge. It had to dispose of these before it could continue. So it began stabbing with pointed legs and gnashing with razor teeth. The blood flowed in greater amounts now and the creatures it attacked began to fill its belly with their meat. It found it liked the feeling.

When no threat was left it began to move again, slower for it now weighed a great deal more but its anger had ebbed slightly. It had even found a hole already within one of the walls in which it now half dragged and half walked its body through. The feeling had grown stronger and as it made its way down a hill it slid into the warm waters of the lake at the bottom. Easily sinking slowly to the bottom where it began to dig, scratching large trenches into the soft bottom of the lake, muddying the water until even it could not see. It dug on with its singular purpose not even aware of what that purpose would be, perhaps an end, some sort of release. With that thought it dug all the harder.

***

Valis had drawn her sword and was swinging it back and forth with a frown upon her face.

"Jan? Do you know the history behind this sword? Father never talked about it, and we were all forbidden to touch it. I wonder if he ever intended to pass it down to Malik."

"I know the story, but perhaps it's best if your father were the one to tell it." Janian said. They had walked about half the time she had been told it would take to cross the Serpent's pass, and by her estimation they should have traveled half way to Carn by now. Only doing so in four hours instead of the two days it would be if they had traveled by normal means. Even on horseback had they the money, would have been much longer than this so far uneventful tunnel.

"And if we don't make it back for him to be able to tell the tale?"

"Valis, I know we have been through much but you must have faith..."

"Faith in the Earth Mother, yes I know Jan. Still, I would like to hear its tale; it will help pass the time." Valis said earning a scowl for interrupting her friend.

"Your father had called it 'rising sun' for this was his signature move, he would hold the sword above his head and as the sword went up he would call forth the flames. It was very effective at distracting which ever opponent he faced that day."

"Father could call the flames at will?" Valis asked surprised holding the blade up before her face.

"Yes. I admit to not understanding the bond it has with those of your family but it had never failed him and lit every time he wished it to. Although now that I think back on it, the sword was, I had assumed just a regular sword. It wasn't until your father was stabbed with it and we took it with us that he later discovered its powers. Perhaps it's bonded to your family's blood now? I truly don't know."

Valis's eyes were wide as Jan spoke, "he was stabbed with it?"

"'Forgive me, I jumped ahead didn't I? It was our third summer of adventuring, we had gotten rather adept at it and we were young and full of confidence. This was an adventure that would shake that faith since the first time I arrived in your home seeking aid.

In the villa of Redwin, the son of the local magistrate had killed his father and declared himself a Duke. We had joined a merchant's caravan working as guards and when we arrived, the Duke's men had striped the wagons declaring it was for their protection."

"That makes little sense, protection from what?" Valis asked.

"That's a problem with madmen, they usually make very little. His men were little more than street thugs but if you have enough of them, convince others that they will be harmed should they question, well then men like that can gain power rather quickly. The villa's usual guard, few as they were, signed up with the Duke instead of having to worry about finding other employment." Jan said evenly as they journeyed on.

"Then they were cowards," Cecil spouted angrily. "They should have stopped this man before he even had a chance to threaten people."

"Lawlessness had quickly begun to spread, shops raided and those who tried to speak out against the Duke had their families killed before their eyes." She paused and when no one interjected, the anger on their faces told of the words they wanted to speak, she continued.

"It did not last long however. Your father, Alex and I had agreed to join the Duke's men."

"How could you!" Valis yelled coldly stopping to wait for an answer.

"We did not do it in a need to join the Duke, you know us better than that. Your father wanted the man dead so the people could return to their peaceful lives; he never was one to put up with bullies. He was also never one to turn from a challenge and that..." she said with a chuckle, "was always getting us into worse trouble."

Valis had picked up her pace and now walked beside the Earth Maiden.

"So how was father stabbed with this sword?" she said looking down at the pommel, resting a hand atop.

"Well, as I was saying, your father wanted him dead, and Alex and I had followed him through the keep the Duke had claimed from his father, late during the night. It was not as hard as it could or should have been seeing as we were posted on duty. The guard outside his chambers was taken care of, I would chat with the man while either Alex or your father would wait and watch for the man's eyes to leave mine and head for...well you know," she shared a smile with Valis who rolled her eyes before scowling back at Cecil as if placing the blame of all men on his shoulders.

"So we opened the door as silently as we could, Alex and I planning to subdue the Duke before Zham could do anything rash and before we could stop him your father had slipped past us and rushed to the side of the duke's bed with a dagger drawn."

"And so what happened?" Cecil asked as Janian had gone silent for a few moments.

"He was stabbed through the side from behind. Don't worry as you know he obviously survived." Jan had to say as Valis suddenly looked very pale even in the odd lighting of the pass.

"I had caught the movement in the shadows of the room and had thrown, with the Earth Mother's blessing a small bust of compressed air and the man's head. The sword meant for your father's stomach, jabbed instead into his side. Alex snapped the man's neck in the next instant, he had proven too much of a threat to try and capture, that and the heat of the moment, well let's just say Alex is still too hard on himself about what happened that night."

"That still doesn't explain how he survived or why the sword lights with blue flames in mine and golden flames in my father's hands." Valis said.

"My you sure share his impatient nature, take the lesson your father had to learn about rushing in to heart Valis, and don't make that same mistake. Yes, your father survived, bless the Mother, but if we had not been there then you would not be here, understand?" Jan said stopping and placing a hand on Valis's shoulder.

"I understand. Does every story you tell have to teach a lesson?" Valis grinned with sarcasm.

"Yes, I'm very wise, now shut up and let me finish the story." Jan said as they resumed walking.

"We snuck back out, leaving the Duke's body in his bead and Alex carried your father through the corridors and out into the street. We sought refuge in an abandoned stable where we tended your father's wound as best we could. While Alex and I sat nearby discussing our next move, Zham, who had been resting peacefully, had awoken and his hand fell on the sword we had left at his side. This had been the first time any of us had been seriously injured in our adventures so far and in our worry we had taken the sword with us." Cecil was giving her a dubious look and Jan met it with a look of mock hurt. "Well it was a nice sword, and adventurers need coin to fund further adventures...anyways, your father touched the sword...the stable went up in flames and that's how we first discovered this...gift of yours," she said quickly shifting the focus back on the sword.

Jan had caught the look of disgust on Valis's face as she looked to the sword at her hip.

"Do not think of it as a dead madman's sword my dear. In your father's hands it served us well, saving many lives, even mine on the rare occasion." She offered a playful wink as Valis looked back up and nodded in agreement.

It was this moment the dogs had stopped and when the others noticed they watched the greyhounds for signs of trouble. Their ears were up and they stood still as statues as they listened to a noise the others could not possibly hear.

"I don't like the look of that," Cecil commented. Giving Valis an expected look as was habit.

"I can't talk to them, the bond doesn't work," she hissed at him.

"Quiet, both of you, watch them, we can get an idea of the situation the normal way." Jan ordered quickly raising a hand to signal their silence.

The greyhound's ears did not fall and they had suddenly begun to bark which startled the others having gone so quite.

"What is it?" Cecil asked knowing full well they could not understand each other.

"Ghosts?" Valis offered.

"Nonsense, if the Earth Mother can't be heard then I highly doubt any spirits could reside within this place." Jan added calmly.

"Magic is kept out. But believe me, spirits can be kept in."

They all whipped around at the sound of the new voice. Valis and Cecil could see nothing but Janian pointed to what she had spied.

"There," she whispered, indicating a slight shimmer of light that floated calmly through the red mist.

The others followed her line of sight and suddenly they were not alone in the Serpent's pass.

"Speak your name friend for we mean you no harm," Janian said with a slight blow of her head in the apparition's direction.

"Not that you could," it whispered in her ear. The others jumped, Janian did not.

"Your name spirit," She continued.

The shimmering light glided through the mist before them and for a moment they could see the form of a man, robed with his hands together hidden in overly large sleeves.

"What's in a name? Power, perhaps? Not ours but in death a name can be used to control. No I believe you shall not have that privilege this day."

"Then we will be on our way and you should go and seek your peaceful rest," Jan stated holding up her hand once more to indicate to the others she would handle this.

"My rest?" the spirit said amused. "If it were so simple Earth Maiden...if it were so simple."

"You have me at a disadvantage spirit, for that is what I shall call you."

"Spirit is fine, call me what you wish. Yes, I know what you are if not who you are. I have killed enough of your kind to recognize one of the Earth Mother's witches."

"Spirit or not you will hold your tongue, should you require a lesson in manners I will be happy to educate you!" the arrival of a spirit had struck Cecil hard, his time in the void had not made such creatures easy to accept and he instantly wanted it gone. He had to back down however as Janian shot him a glare.

Again the spirit shifted in the mist and laughed with a sound that multiplied to sound as though many were in the same area as they.

"I can smell the scent of our jailors within your blood boy. You would have been killed the moment you spawned from your mother's..."

"Enough!" even without her connection to Earth Mother, Jan was still a voice of authority and it quickly silenced the spirit.

"I know who you are now, if not by name spirit than by deeds. So the Druids of old did not destroy you fully. I understand now what the Serpent's pass truly is, a prison for those of dark magic."

"Dark magic, if you only new...but you are correct. This is a prison for those of us with the desire for real power, not that nurse maid's excuse of a gift you call magic." The spirit accepted Jan's taunt and the focus were once again returned to her.

Jan nodded to her friends as she turned her back and began walking. "Let's go, this is nothing more than a distraction, it can't harm us."

"It? You think I'm alone down here!" the spirit roared after them.

They stopped walking as within the mist and all around them spirit after spirit began to form, until a translucent red army of robed men and women stood around them.

"This is a prison for my brothers and sisters, it will not hold us forever and when we are released you will know a suffering the likes that which you have never dreamed," the spirit threatened and began to laugh as they stood and watched, surrounded.

"You were defeated once before, your demon masters slain. Your nothing but a memory, and in time you will be forgotten completely," Jan challenged back.

"But not yet...witch, not in your lifetime."

Jan studied the face of the spirit for several long moments before turning around once more. "Let's go," she said calmly and led the way through the crowd of red robed spirits who parted as they passed.

They came to a bridge that shot out and over a large expanse and the sound of water could be heard far below, "this is a marker, according to the resistance we aren't far now." Jan said to the others, the dogs followed behind and when they had made it across the bridge they had to stop and turn once more.

The greyhounds had not moved past the foot of the bridge once across and now they stood ears up staring towards the tunnel's ceiling, whimpering and dancing back and forth.

The spirits had not crossed over and they as well stood watching, hearing something the others, save the dogs, could not.

"Get back," Jan whispered as she looked up watching the spot the dogs and spirits were fixed on. "Get back! She shouted this time to the dogs, who looked back at her trying to understand her command and finally dashed over to their friends in time to watch the first bits of tunnel drop to land and scatter about on the bridge.

They had retreated further back as larger sections of the ceiling began to crumble, dropping to slam heavily on top of the bridge.

"You know what that is Earth Maiden?" the spirit shouted to across to her "It is our jailer opening our cell with the key of destruction! Our freedom is close at long last!"

One final creak and the tunnel shuttered as one massive chuck of ceiling crashed down. The world would change in that moment. Several things happened at once; the water in the lake above had fallen with the ceiling and burst outward splashing them with such force that it knocked them from their feet. But fortunately most of the water rushed, spilling over the sides of the bridge to join the water below. With the open hole in the Serpent's pass, magic returned. The bond came crashing loudly through Valis's mind, the baby fell into a deep slumber within his pack and Janian could hear the Earth Mother.

The first thing Jan had noticed however was that it was not the normal rhythm she was used to, something was wrong, it was giving off feelings of anger and sadness. She also felt the slightest hint of fear from the Earth Mother's voice.

There was plenty of confusion and fear to go around. As the water ebbed, Jan's breath had caught in her chest. The red mist of the spirits of dark magic users was funneling up and out through the gaping hole along a wide beam of moonlight that shot down from above. This had caused the worry she felt, the fear however was shared by them all. For when the water came it had brought a creature that stood upon the bridge, a creature that had finally reached its destination.

It had stood silent upon its many tall and jagged spider legs, shaking the water from its snake like scaled body. Silent until the dogs who had regained their feet first begin to bark and growl at it. Then with a razor sharp teeth-filled maw, it roared back at them.

Jan was next to stand, her mind sluiced off the problem of the escaping spirits and lowered her eyes to focus on the creature. She stood frozen for a moment, unsure of what to do. "Valis get the dogs back here; don't let them get to close." She ordered knowing that if her gifts were returning then so was the Princess's bond with the greyhounds.

Instantly the dogs turned and bounded back still standing guard before the others but now out of reach of those pointed legs.

The creature did not wait for them to make a move and it lurched forward, its stomached sliding easily along the wet stones of the bridge, propelling it toward them. The long legs keeping it balanced as it went. The massive creature swiped out with its front legs stabbing the ground where the greyhounds had been before they hopped out of the way. One of the legs however, had scored a gash across Valis' arm and she cried out in pain and anger.

Cecil had drawn his borrowed sword compliments of the resistance's armory and brought it down heavily across one of the creature's legs. The force of the blow as it bounced off the leg nearly shook the blade from Cecil's hands. He had to roll out of the way to avoid the angered counter swing of the leg, avoiding it as it stabbed into the ground breaking stone and spraying up dirt.

Jan had closed her eyes and prayed for the Earth Mothers guidance, something was still wrong and her mind flashed to glimpses of something she could not make out.

Valis had drawn her sword after she quickly handed the pack with the sleeping prince to Jan. She was hoping the Earth Maiden would use her powers but she had closed her eyes and so Valis accepted the role of defender once more. The sword, her father's for so long, lit at her command and the light from the blue flames reflected in the many eyes of the creature before her so brightly that it took several steps backwards.

The creature roared angrily; it was where it had to be. It could feel it deep within, but now that it was here it was unsure of why and what it was meant to do. It knew from experience of the past that the creatures that waved swords at it had to be destroyed, it felt the urge to feed and the memory of soft flesh and crunchy bones filled its mind. Several of its eyes, while the others watched the swords, had focused on the one who did not attack. The one that stood with eyes closed and something deep within tugged, was that what it was after? What it had come so far to find?

The light from the sword burning blue had to be dealt with first. But to its shock and painful surprise, when leg and sword met, pain laced through its body. The sword had cut through as if it were made of the soft fur of a lamb not the hardened shell of legs that had not as of yet been damaged.

The creature howled in pain and fury, it still had plenty of legs and it used another few to attack Valis, striking her in the side and knocking the sword from her hand. The Princess had been struck so hard she bounced off the ground as she struck it emitting a painful grunt.

Jan was at a loss; there was nothing she could do from deep within the tunnel. Her powers were returning but she could feel it was slow, the Earth Mother's voice continued to rage and the panic it carried had become to effect Jan as well. She closed her eyes and tried to focus as hard as she ever had but this time, instead of asking for guidance or power she offered calming prayers to the Earth Mother hoping to calm the erratic tide of emotions flooding into her.

Cecil had ducked another leg and struck again in futile effort as once more his blade deflected off. In frustration he had slid forward instead of away from the creature and that's when he saw his opening. It was hard to see and he had nearly missed it, but open, bent back ever so slightly was one of the creature's scales. He sucked in his breath and hoped the dogs could keep it distracted just a little longer and out of the corner of his eye he watched as Sophal was swatted to the ground. He had no time to see if she had got back up or not and took this as his one and only chance. Cecil rolled tucking his sword close to his body and made his way closer, he exhaled his breath and waited for the scale to come into view once more and then thrust his sword with all the strength he could muster under the scale. His sword only went in a few inches and he panicked when the creature realized where he was and had lowered its mouth of death to end the threat from below when Cecil reefed on his sword to the side. A crack rang through the tunnel and the scales flew up striking the creature in the face giving the man just long enough to scramble out from under it and dropped down beside Valis who was holding her head with one hand while groping for the sword at her feet with the other.

Cecil spared a quick look to Jan who was so far unharmed but as well, un-moving and he cursed under his breath before helping Valis to her feet with her arm over his shoulders. Once arisen, Cecil reached down and fetched the sword placing it in her hand and closing her fingers around it. This seemed to give Valis a moment of lucidity and she tightened her grip on the sword's handle. It roared to life with the blue flames and Cecil had to leap back to avoid being scorched.

"Valis! The missing scale!" Cecil shouted and when she met his eyes he pointed to the creature's underbelly. Valis gave him a nod of understanding and she leaped over Ce'elevan as he had slid across the floor, rolling to a stop.

Valis roared as she charged and the creature panicked for only the slightest of moments before jabbing its arms forward hoping to skewer the woman and end the blue flames once again.

It had failed. Valis fainted to the left and brought the sword out in an arc that cleaved through the legs severing the first long digits on four of its legs and the creature wailed in renewed pain. Valis slid to her knees and found the missing scale, the flesh underneath was peach colour mixed with an irritated red that was the result of the scale being pried off. She thrust her father's sword, flames crackling as the blade went upward and she froze with concern as it had felt as though the sword had slid into air. Her arm was covered in a dark bluish toned blood and she pulled her arm down in sudden realization that she had succeeded.

The moment the blade, with its blue fire, slid through the folds of the creature's flesh it had screamed out, not a monster's scream but a man's scream of anguish. And it was then that Jan's powers flooded back. The Earth Mother's voice settled, now only sounding slightly angered. Jan was the only one to hear the human scream, the magic of the sword had seared away a layer of the dark magic that entwined this creature and the face of a man filled her mind's eye. She wanted to fall to her knees as she saw the struggle from within the creature's soul. It was not one, but two, and it suffered greatly, struggling to retain a semblance of humanity it had sought out the only person it knew could help.

Jan thrust her arms out wide and then quickly pulled them to her chest crossing them as she raised her head to the hole in the lake above.

The creature had stilled and tried to shrink back but lacked the legs now to push its bulk backwards across the up-slope of the bridge. Valis had rejoined Cecil and the dogs had limped over to stand guard over Jan at her request while they watched to see what the Earth Maiden had decided to do.

Slowly at first they saw what looked like thick snakes slithering over the gape, but as they moved and slithered further downward they noticed it was thick roots and not snakes at all. Tree roots had lowered down through the hole and moved as Jan moved. Once reaching down to their level she moved the roots into two separate thick strands weaving them together in an intricate pattern and began to wrap around the creature. It resisted at first but in its weakened state it was little match for the reinforced tree roots and soon it looked as weak as a caterpillar in a cocoon of silk. The roots lifted the creature up off the bridge and suspended it in the air, immobilized.

Valis limped forward and re-lit her blade, the creature flinched in its prison but only slightly as it was held tight and firm.

"No!" Jan shouted bringing a look of startled anger from her friend.

"This thing is evil Jan; we should end its life here and now." Valis protested, pointing the sword at the creature.

Jan had taken a few steps toward it before falling to her knees; she could no longer hold back the tears and the others watched as the woman's shoulders heaved with her sorrow.

"I... did not mean to upset you, it's just... this cannot be allowed to live, can it? Do you mean to leave it here to die? What if the ghosts should return and set it free somehow...I really don't see..."

"It's Alex," Jan hushed, but it had been loud enough for Valis to hear and she looked up at the creature with heavy skepticism in her eyes.

"How... are you sure... how?" Valis could only stumble over the words as she said them.

"I have seen his soul, wrapped up with the shadow assassin that fled us, the one you cut with your sword. Through some dark magic, whatever Kerra controls she has merged the two together and grown this creature." She had slowed her tears now and stood beside her friend looking up at the princesses Kerra's creation.

"Can you undo this?" Cecil asked as he joined them.

"No," Jan stated simply. "This is beyond me. And the Earth Mother does not answer my calls as I asked her for a solution; I sense she is most distraught over the dark mage spirits escaping their prison and it's like talking to a wall. She did allow my powers to send for the roots to bind the creature; we were beyond fortunate that trees were not far away."

"So Alex is in there somewhere?" Valis asked.

"Yes, his body has been used as the base for the spell; he has been...shaped, into this." Jan sneered with disgust.

"It must have been painful beyond anything living has ever felt, I'm sorry for your loss, Jan." Cecil said placing a hand on her shoulder; he never thought he would be the one to mirror the gesture.

Valis scowled at him until he looked down to check on the greyhounds.

"He can't be gone; Jan I mean...its Alex. There must be away to reverse this, cut him out of it somehow!" Valis spat urgently.

"I see only one way, and that's to see if the Princess of Carn knows how to undo what she has done to this man." With that said, a chill in her voice, Jan closed her eyes once more.

Above them the moonlight began to grow darker as thick batches of roots spread tightly over the hole sealing it off from the outside world. From above they could hear the sound of thunder and with it rain would soon fill the lake at a much faster pace than was natural, the Earth Mother was seeing to that and Jan felt odd like a scolded child.

Magic retained, the powers that had been working through the Serpent's pass was now gone, broken when the creature cut its way in.

"Are we just leaving him here then?" Valis asked when Jan opened her eyes.

"Yes, unless you want to take him with us," Jan said without humour in her voice and with her powers restored she lit her aura with the soft blue light of the Mother's gift. It brought her little comfort as she began to walk away. She could not bring herself to look back; she had to push herself forward now, for her sake, for Alex. Jan set her Jaw and began to think of ways to get Kerra to talk.

Valis stared up at the creature that was both shadow, man and beast and shook her head sadly before turning to follow after Jan.

Cecil and the dogs slowly made their way after them as well, Sophal favoring one leg and Ce'elevan sounded like it was hard to breath, but they marched on non the less. Each of them had a personal stake now in seeing the sleeping Prince home, for some that reason was now vengeance.

It had taken them three more hours to reach the branch in the tunnel. The resistance had told Jan to take and another hour down a long corridor with walls etched in ruins. With the magic gone from the Serpent's pass they were unsure of just where or how far they were from the Boarders of Carn or if they were indeed anywhere near the royal keep itself. They stayed on course despite this and being tired and beaten was not helping them. They stopped for water only once, the dogs seeming to regain much of their vigor after the short rest. Cecil was sore and bruised but he didn't think anything was broken and Jan who thankfully had taken the baby was unharmed expect her usual motherly way was far less friendly at the moment. Valis had tied a strip of cloth around the gash on her arm where the creature had sliced her, just above the elbow of her right arm and paid it no further mind.

"We are close" Sophal said through the bond to Valis who looked down at the greyhound in surprise, it had been some time since she had heard them, the Serpent's tunnel severing the bond at the start of their journey seemed to have had an odd effect on her grasp of the Bond. Now that it was re-established, gone was the echo she had always experienced when they spoke and it had snapped up into place much quicker with barely a thought when she replied.

"How can you tell?"

"I can feel the bond between my master growing stronger with each step," the greyhound said with excitement.

Valis relayed the message to the others and Jan nodded solemnly.

"We must have traveled the greater length of the tunnel before its magic failed. At least that worked in our favor," it was the most the woman had said for several hours and it for some reason eased the tension the others were feeling.

Valis was curious about the bond now and she tested it with Ce'elevan.

"How are you fairing?"

"I'm fine; I imagine we will all be rather sore in the morning though. Do you think this will end when we reach the castle?" the black greyhound with silver flecks in his fur asked.

"I hope so Ce'elevan, I cannot wait to get home and straighten this all out with father, clear Cecil's name and then take a long hot bath. I think I may even let the servants dress me for once."

"I can sense it you know, the change in the bond between us. It is just as it was with Malik. I believe that we are truly bonded now."

"I know I feel it as well, does this please you? I do not wish to keep you bonded if you no longer wish it, it must be hard I know and…"

"Valis, it is with great honor that we are bonded firmly now, to turn our backs on it would be a slight against Malik. We are bonded in other ways now as well; bonds that we have fought long and with blood spilt to gain. The bond of magic we were granted, the bond of friendship and respect we have earned.

"You have become much wiser through this journey Ce'elevan; I am honored to call you my friend." Valis finished nodding with eyes closed in a show of respect.

"I worry for Janian; this is the first time in all the years I've know her that she has been this upset." Valis said, glad to have a friend she could share her thoughts with and not expose them to others, even Sophal was silent and she wondered if her control of the bond had grown to the point of keeping it private from others with the gift.

"She suffers with her heart and the mind tries to sort that out. It is a painful process to be sure."

Valis did not push the conversation further and she agreed with herself that the greyhound was indeed wiser, then she laughed to herself as she thought her father would find it ridiculous that she was taking wisdom from a dog. He was not a foolish man but he did seem to have little patience for anything to do with magic or even the conversations of such. Which she found slightly amusing considering whose magic sword was at her side. She laid a hand on the handle now as she thought of it and noticed the bandage on her arm had soaked through.

They came finally to a set of stairs and followed them upward for some time, there were plenty of them and they found themselves stopping to catch their breath. Cecil clutched his side with a stitch in it and the dogs panted hard as they fell behind.

"That's a switch" Cecil said pointing back at them "usually they are so far ahead that we lose sight of them."

"Leave them alone they have worked really hard," Valis said scathingly as she passed him.

"I didn't...I was only joking!" Cecil threw his hands up in exasperation only to double over from the pain in his side once more. He thought, as he watched the greyhounds now pass him, that perhaps he had done more damage than first thought and winced when he pressed lightly on his lower ribs. He rolled his eyes and put one foot in front of the other taking each step with a grimace of pain.

"We are here it would seem," Jan spoke softly as they crested the top of the stairs. Down a short hallway was a single door that was etched in the same odd ruins and squiggles that they had come across on the entrance to the Serpent's pass. This door fittingly was etched with a large tail signifying the end.

Valis chose this moment to fall to her knees, clutching the bandaged cut on her arm and the others looked down as they noticed the blood dripping from the now blood red cloth.

CHAPTER 32

Zhamar Damaste, King of Petsky, had slept little. This was partly out of fear for himself but also out of an ever growing fear for his youngest daughter. It had been a long time since she escaped with the accused killer of his son and he had expected to have heard at least a little news. The men he had sent were ordered not to bring her back, only to observe and report. She didn't know this of course and may have seen them before they spied her and fled further away. To other matters he was in the heart of near hostile territory, he had lain awake in the simple fear of Princess Kerra sending assassins to his room while he slept, despite the Queen's assurances that his room was guarded by her own personal knights.

Princess Kerra had made no attempt to greet him. In fact, he had not seen the woman once since his arrival. Something did stick out in his mind however as he was being escorted to his rooms. While they crossed a small courtyard he could have sworn he spied Petsky armour on a knight that had just passed out of sight. Why would one of Carn's men be wearing his country's armour?

This is what ate up most of his thoughts as he paced his room, *where was the Prince? What happened to Jan and Alex!*

He was startled out of his line of thought by a rap upon his room's door.

"Yes?" he tried to hide the terseness from his tone.

"The Queen asks for your presence in her receiving hall King Damaste," the knight on the other side announced.

"At this hour? It was fine if she wanted to exhaust herself to all hours of the night, but had the Queen expected him to as well? Waiting on her summons? She was sick however and he feared this may be that moment, he truly wished they had gotten the baby back in time.

"Of course, at once," He said opening the door and stepping out between the four knight escort.

"Has she news of the Prince?" Zham asked as they began to move.

"She did not say, only that we were to bring you to her in the quickest of haste." The knight replied.

From the end of the hall, opposite the knights, stood a woman in the shadows and after they left the hall, turning the corner out of sight did Princess Kerra, slip the dagger she had drawn back into the small hidden sheath within the fold of her long sleeved night gown. She sent a command through the control she still had over the men from both Petsky though few in numbers and the men she had been adding to her ranks from the guards and knights here in the Palace. They were to meet her outside the receiving hall using the little used side entrance ways. She would end this tonight, end it all.

***

Valis sat propped up against the wall beside the door while Jan untied the bloody bandage. Once off, Cecil had leaned over with a shocked look upon his face.

"What in the mother's name is that?!" he asked, earning a frown from Janian as he had used the mother's name in vain.

Jan studied the wound, it was still freshly open and shown no signs of clotting or slowing and the worried look was not lost on Valis.

"Jan, what's wrong?" Valis spoke, sounding just as worried.

"When the creature who used to be Alex had slashed you with its leg a small splinter had broken off. I have tried to remove it but it only digs further in. Your body is fighting it that's why you haven't stopped bleeding; you have only a few hours before you bleed out if we can't get that stopped... and there's this," she said turning the arm slightly so Valis could see the wound better. "This black splotch is spreading at a worrisome rate and I don't know what it will do should it reach your heart."

"She's been poisoned?" Cecil questioned leaning in once more.

"I'm afraid so, and once again I'm left defenseless as this is dark magic."

"But you said all we needed to combat that was an Earth Maiden and a Druid and we have both here. Though, Cecil's not trained, I..." Valis had begun with a whimper that quickly turned to anger.

"He's untrained and I was counting on the Earth Mother's guidance. She is still not responding to my questions regarding dark magic's" Jan had interrupted, her voice was tired and she looked the same as Cecil had on the journey to the port city.

"Well what do we do?" Cecil asked

"I don't know," Jan answered.

"But you must know, we can't just sit here and do nothing, you must know!"

"I don't know, Cecil!" Jan finally snapped and Cecil kicked the door in anger.

Valis scratched Ce'elevan's head as he placed it in her lap and she nodded resolutely.

"We go on." She said nodding to her arm. Jan took the cue to finish binding it once more.

"What?" Cecil asked with the shake of his head "we can't just leave this to worsen, Valis." he leaned in closer "I'm supposed to keep you safe," he almost whispered.

Valis reached up with her other arm and gently stroked his cheek. Then she pulled back and promptly smacked it hard.

"I know. Foolish boys and their bravado." She stood and smiled at his look of shock as he rubbed his check. Then she quickly rushed forward and kissed his lips with hers, grabbing the back of his head so he couldn't pull away. Not that he had wanted to as confused as he was he returned the kiss with equal affection. "I know, and you are," she said when she broke the seal on their lips letting her eyes meet his.

Cecil stood there dazed and confused while Jan opened the door that led into the Palace. Sophal led the way followed by Valis and Jan. Cecil looked down at Ce'elevan who had stayed by his side.

"Does she ever make any sense to you, even with the bond?" he asked the greyhound.

Ce'elevan only answered with a snuffle of his nose and headed after the others.

"I didn't think so." And Cecil sighed before following as well. He closed the door behind him and then wondered if that was such a wise move. What if they needed an escape? And so he tried to find the handle to the door from the other side and found that he was looking at nothing more than a bare wall with no discernible framework or edges. "Another way, then." He finished and joined the others who had stopped to wait for him.

Sophal had taken the lead as this was her home and knew the quickest ways to go unseen. It was not long into their trek through the palace that Sophal had stopped an opened the bond to Valis.

"I have been filling the Queen in on what has transpired So far, she wishes us to join her in the audience hall, follow me we will not be harmed. The guards are even now being made aware of our arrival."

Valis told the others and it had not taken long until this was proven true. As the group exited one corridor they were met by a knight patrol that had been sent to escort them in.

Valis and Cecil had never seen such a grand Palace and had to admit it was far larger than the one back home, though as grand as castle Petsky was this place was twice the size and Valis had never felt more out of place despite actually being a royal Princess.

They were shown in through two large double doors and inside a chamber with polished stone floors and vaulted ceiling that took one a moment to regain their breath after trying to take it all in.

Valis was the first to notice her father, standing on the stairs of a raised platform that was covered in overly large pillows; a sickly frail woman sat within them and had been bending her father's ear when they arrived.

"Father!" Valis exclaimed with excitement rushing into his outstretched arms.

"Valis, my heart of hearts, you had me worried sick." Zham said with tears in his eyes that quickly fell into his daughter's hair as he kissed her head. Then, he quickly pushed her to arms length but not letting go of her shoulders. "The Queen was telling me of what her greyhound informed her. Valis, I'm so sorry I let you get involved with all this, I swear to never let you out of my sight again." And then he crushed her back into his embrace.

"Father you're embarrassing me. Father I can't breathe," Valis tried to say. "No, father I can't..." she tried once more and the King felt her go slack in his arms. He cast a look first to the Earth Maiden who had rushed over, helping him ease her to the floor while the other stood by and could only watch.

The King had words on his lips when the side door to the chamber burst open and they soon found themselves surrounded by Princess Kerra's small army. The knights and guards already in the room were stripped of their weapons quickly as Kerra entered and the Queen, though sick, had stood to signal her men not to put up a fight.

"Kerra, what is the meaning of this? You dare to..."

"I dare dear sister because I am the stronger one. I dare because I will be Queen this night and I dare because you are powerless to stop me!" Kerra shouted back.

The Queen of Carn stood patiently, studying her sister.

"You!" Jan stood and pointed a finger at the invading sister. "You have cast your lot in with the darkness and now it controls you! You are the only one who can remove the darkness from this young woman's arm; she dies from the poison of the creature you sent after us!"

All eyes fell on Kerra and for a moment she looked surprised by the outcome "I... It's too late for her, she should never have joined you, witch, in trying to destroy my family!" Kerra tried to counter.

"It's too late for that dear sister, your little coupe to overthrow me and the stories I have been told by Sophal have been enough to show me of your guilt," the Queen had said scathingly and Kerra cast a look of utter disgust at the greyhound who had survived her torture and abandonment.

"You would trust the words of a dog over your own..." but Kerra did not get to finish as Valis lying on the floor had shouted out in pain.

Jan spun and dropped to her friend's side taking off the bandage and ignoring the sounds of worry and disgust from the King who was cradling his daughters head in his lap.

"It's spread too far, Zham, she's dying." Jan said as she took in the sight of the woman's arm. She was wrong in how quickly it was spreading and as they made their way here, the dark splotch had spread to most of her arm reaching just about to the top.

"Fix this!" Jan shouted, looking over her shoulder at Kerra.

"You will all burn, my master has promised me this," Kerra spat. And Jan shook her head turning back to Valis.

"Zham, take your sword," Jan said startling the King. "Cecil. Come here, we will have to hold her down." The moment Cecil moved Kerra barked an order to stand where he was and when he ignored her she growled until she realized it was not her growl she was hearing but the greyhounds that had taken up guard of their friends and stood between them and harm's way.

"Zham," Jan said holding the sword out to the King, who looked at her with eyes wide in shock. "She will die you fool if we do not do this, you remember what happened to Zavier when we found his mistress had poisoned him? Now let's not make that same mistake. The King's eyes showed that he did truly remember that adventure, and the friend they had lost that day. Swallowing hard he took his old sword in hand. It lit in golden flames instantly.

He had an idea and with Janian and Cecil holding his daughter down he cut into the flesh that the clearly visible sliver of dark magic was withering around in. He cut and the smell of seared flesh filled the air and Jan and Cecil held onto a screaming Valis.

"Zham, that's not working! Do what needs to be done before we lose her, please!" Jan shouted at him over the vocal pain in the air.

Zham stood and gritted his teeth "forgive me Valis." With one overhead swing the king of Petsky brought the flaming sword down, severing his daughters arm just below the shoulder. The woman bucked against her friends' restraints twice before going still. Jan quickly placed her head against Valis's chest to hear a heart still beating.

Zham turned on Kerra with murder in his eyes.

"King Damaste," the Queen of Carn warned.

With Valis stable, the wound burned closed by the sword, Jan reached out and grabbed Cecil's hand in hers. She pulled a slim dagger and sliced down his palm then let go and did the same to her own. Quickly she dropped the blade and gestured for Cecil to open his torn palm and she held hers above squeezing a stream of her own blood into his palm. "Go for the face, do not miss" she whispered to the young man who after a shocked moment nodded, understanding the plan.

"Do not kill my sister, she will be dealt with according to Carnian laws," the Queen spoke to the King of Petsky, who looked back at her, shocked.

"Did you not see what this daemon controlled fool has forced me to do?" He said through gritted teeth.

The greyhounds had lunged forward drawing Kerra's gaze and when she looked back up it was too late, Cecil had dashed forward with all the speed he could find, right past the King and the blazing blue sword and struck the Princesses Kerra with the flat of his palm. Although he did not stop there, he had his own vengeance filled heart to appease and with his momentum pushed her hard to the ground, slamming her against the polished stone so hard he heard it crack underneath her.

The moment the blood, mixed of Druid filled blood magic and Earth Maiden's gift of the Mother had touched Kerra's face she had felt the connection between her and her master's dark magic begin to drain from her body. The men all around her had slumped to the floor after weeks of being controlled and the Queen had taken that opportunity to order her own men to secure the room. Cecil found himself being pulled off of the Princess and held with his arms behind his back.

"This has gone far enough!" the Queen roared and with the dark magic no longer under Kerra's control the baby Prince had woken up within his pack on Jan's back.

In the commotion and dreadful events that had happened upon their arrival, they had no chance to reunite the Queen with her son and she stood froze at the sound.

Zham had lowered his sword and handed it to Cecil as he was let go with a nod from the Queen and took the baby from the Pack on Jan's back. Cradling his nephew, the King placed the baby in his mother's arms at last.

"No!" Kerra had shouted as she was dragged to her feet. The room was filled with gasps as they took in her face. Every part of flesh that the blood Cecil had attacked her with touched had turned to a scared pulpy mess.

"The child is for my master, so that he may have a strong royal vessel in which to inhabit and rule this world!" her words were slurred as her lips had been hit by the blood as well.

"You have your son and the explanation of how he was kept from you for so long," Jan said approaching the Queen. "I implore you to end her life; she is your sister no longer."

The Queen studied Jan for a few moments before speaking, and she looked down at her son.

"Family is bonded in blood for all time. There is no escape from this even in death," she said to the room but was looking still at her son. "I am dying and I will not have my last command be that of my sister's death." At this she looked up and into her sister's eyes.

"It is not me you have to fear little sister; I could never bring you the harm you tried to place on me." She thought for a moment before sitting down tiredly on her throne of cushions.

"Let those in attendance today bear witness to the mercy of my court. Princess Kerra of Carn...you are hereby banished from these lands, striped of your title and branded a traitor to the kingdom of Carn. Wear your new face proudly sister, you have earned it." And there the Queen of Carn stopped and went back to cooing playfully with her son.

"This will not stop me! I will bring my master back to this world and you will all suffer fates worse than death!" Kerra screamed as she was taken from the room. Her anger could be heard for hours after as she was strapped to a horse and escorted to the boarders of Carn.

"Zham, please come closer." The Queen spoke. She had returned to her pale and failing stature and he worried she would go at any minute. She had called for the Chancellor; the older man he had met before.

"I will not live through the night. I want to thank you for giving me my chance to say goodbye to my son. I know you are angered by my decision to let Kerra go, but her hardships will be many and last the rest of her life from this day forth. She will suffer for what she has done. But I have lost a sister and this saddens me greatly for I loved her truly. Now, when I am gone someone will have to look after my son and my kingdom."

The Chancellor was looking slightly worried and the others were listening intently as well.

"Earth Maiden Janian Poledouris, to you I entrust the safety of my son. For many decades this kingdom has considered your faith to be foolish nonsense, I have seen the error of our ways. Will you keep him safe until such a time as he has grown to the age of rule?"

Janian had regained her composer and once again looked as a matron would, "It would be the greatest of honors. I shall take him to grow and learn under good people, he will grow strong and as wise as his mother," she finished with a bow deep and truly honored.

"Now your daughter Zham, it pains me so very deeply to have watched you do what had to be done to save her life. When she is well again, she will be regent of Carn until the day my son can take his rightful place. I will have no argument from you, she has fought as fiercely I am told as any of my warrior line, and with your sense in her head and words in her ear I have no doubts that Carn will continue to prosper."

She nodded to the Chancellor, who was furiously writing all this down and bowed, "it has been spoken and so now shall be my Queen."

They had been shown to their rooms and tended to by the palace healers, medicine men with no magic. They had received word early the next morning that the Queen had passed in her sleep. Valis, having awoken to discover she now ruled a country had set about with determination to do the job well, despite the lack of an arm that she seemed to have taken rather well. They were not going to be here in the nights to come, when she could feel sorry for herself and cry until sleep found her.

Janian had wasted no time in preparing the Prince to ride with her and now had a proper pack in which to travel in. She was given a fast strong hose, for her journey would be a long one. To the Druids she explained, she would go and there with Cecil's help while he received his own training they would raise the Prince.

Cecil had wanted to say his goodbyes to Valis. He felt ashamed that he had let something so drastic happen to the woman he had sworn to protect. Now that she was made Regent he had little hope of seeing her again while his Druid training took place. He did not seek her out to say his goodbyes and instead found, Ce'elevan.

"You stay and look after her all right? I'm counting on you," he said squatting down to rub the dog's head and neck. He did not understand that the greyhound was bonded to the Princess already and would not have gone with him. He stood, turned and left the dog behind. He had met the Earth Maiden and the baby Prince now fully awake and looking every way he could, at the gates.

"Did you say goodbye?" Jan asked with a smile.

"No, she'll be fine," he stated flatly.

"You still don't know anything about women do you, especially Princesses" Jan teased.

Cecil shrugged his shoulders, he was headed to a new life and he would not have had time for romance anyways, and yet it would be a long time before he went a day without thinking about her. He had wanted to counter with a comment about her love; he knew her plans to discuss with the High Druid ways to heal, Alex. However, he didn't even understand how he would live that long trapped beneath the lake and thought better of it, it was a long ride and he didn't need her angry at him the whole way.

The king would be staying for a while to help his daughter get used to her newly appointed duties and responsibilities. He hovered protectively over her until she had yelled him out of the room one morning while she signed documents. He had finally returned to Petsky a few weeks later. The sword he had left, though neither father nor daughter could bring themselves to look at it and so it was locked in a room in the palace where it could be forgotten about. He did cast one last look back at the Palace as they rode away and he had to admit a part of him was hoping to find Valis watching him go but he did not see any sign of her.

EPILOGUE

The night had brought a heavy storm along with it and by the time Kerra reached the caves she was soaked through. She wore rags now instead of gowns and hid her face from sight. It had taken great care and time to sneak back across the Carn boarder and to the caves she had played in as a young Princess.

She didn't realize just how much she missed being one, when now she had nothing, nothing except the hatred that fueled her heart with rage and kept her empty belly from destroying her mind.

The stone face of the daemon Azamoth was still where she had left it and she pleaded on her knees before it, though it currently made no signs that it heard her.

"Please master, I beg of you, I have failed you I know, but all is not lost!" She pleaded and yet no response from the horrid stone face.

"You wanted an heir and I will bring you one, for even though I was banished I am still bonded by blood to the royal family. *My* son shall be your sacrifice." Kerra had not know that when she had taken Alex the knight of Petsky to her bed so many times that she would bear his child and now she had a second chance, if only her master would hear her.

"I am with child, great Azamoth. And it is yours if you will once again grant me the power to serve you."

She had almost given up and was ready to die here in the cave were it all began when a small black dot hovered before her. And once more she reached out to touch it as the voice of her master echoed off the caves walls.

"Welcome back, my sweet, sweet, Kerra."

THE END

Made in the USA
Charleston, SC
25 November 2016